They came.

A dozen of them.
Lidless eyes wide. Lipless mouths gaped. Skinless
bodies stumbling in a parody of motion. Unseeing.
Moved by someone else, something else. Unbreathing. Behind them, in the shadows, the
skins rustled.

Mahlia screamed, a tiny rabbit sound from
empty lungs, unheard over the sound of shuffling
feet.

Also by Sheri S. Tepper

THE TRUE GAME
THE CHRONICLES OF MAVIN MANYSHAPED
JINIAN FOOTSEER
THE REVENANTS
BLOOD HERITAGE

and published by Corgi Books

THE BONES

Sheri S. Tepper

CORGI BOOKS

THE BONES

A CORGI BOOK   0 552 13262 4

First publication in Great Britain

PRINTING HISTORY

Corgi edition published 1988

Copyright © 1987 Sheri S. Tepper

This book is set in 10/11pt Plantin.

Corgi Books are published by Transworld Publishers Ltd., 61-63 Uxbridge Road, Ealing, London W5 5SA, in Australia by Transworld Publishers (Australia) Pty. Ltd., 15-23 Helles Avenue, Moorebank, NSW 2170, and in New Zealand by Transworld Publishers (N.Z.) Ltd., Cnr. Moselle and Waipareira Avenues, Henderson, Auckland.

Printed and bound in Great Britain by Cox & Wyman Ltd., Reading, Berks.

CHAPTER ONE

'My sagas always seem to start with a change of place,' Mahlia said to the realtor, turning at the end of the drive to look back at the tall, nut-brown house.

'How many sagas have you had?' he asked in an amused tone. He was as lean and nut-brown as the house, of a laconic nature that pleased Mahlia, and he had made no attempt whatsoever to sell her anything. 'I know young people don't like to have their youth pointed out – got a daughter about your age myself – but you look maybe one saga old.'

'Just about that,' she said with a laugh. 'But my childhood saga was in Tahiti. And then I was sent to live with my great-aunt in France, I went to school there, at a convent. A very difficult saga, that. And then I came to Canada for a while, and then to New York as a student. Four sagas, I guess.' She stopped for a moment. There had been another saga, but that was not one she particularly cared to remember. 'I've always thought it would be fun to remodel an old place for myself.'

'Pretty ambitious, for a youngster.' Despite the baby in the pack on her back, she was a youngster, beige-skinned, with hair that flowed like silk down her back and an oval, simple face that did not leap out at you. Her eyes were dark and warm. He approved. Yes, a nice youngster.

'I have time,' she said, and shrugged. Indeed she did have time, entirely too much time. Study would take up part of it, for she was determined to go on with her doctoral work. Marriage and motherhood shouldn't change that. But one could study only so many hours in a day, and Badger was going to be gone for most of six months. She had hardly had time to get used to being married to him before he had gone.

'I want to find us a place,' he had said. 'For you and me and Robby and the baby. I'm tired of New York, tired of apartments. Too many . . . too many difficult memories popping up on odd street corners. I'm always running into people who ask me about Carolyn.' Carolyn, his first wife, had been a main actor in the saga Mahlia did not want to remember; Badger didn't want to remember it either. He had gone on, 'Let's get out of the city. I go to my work, my work doesn't come to me, so why live here?'

Why indeed? Perhaps because, for Mahlia, it was more convenient to the university, but she hadn't argued with him, hadn't demurred when he opened what he called a 'house account' with her name on the checks. 'I've been saving money for a country place for ten years,' he told her. 'Putting some aside out of every job. There's plenty to be rather expansive, if you like.' Expansive. That was Badger's word for using up money at a scandalous rate. 'Whatever. Something like what we've talked about, away from the city. I may get back to admire your choice before the job in Japan. Get something you like. If you like it, I'll like it.'

She looked down the driveway, wondering if she had indeed found something she liked or merely something she was willing to settle for. It hadn't really been that much fun looking at houses, not alone, and she was tired of it. She had an uncomfortable feeling of pressure, which she interpreted as the need to get something done, and she ticked off the house criteria in her mind, wondering whether this one would do. It was away from the city, no doubt about that. Well away!

'The place is in good shape structurally,' the realtor was saying. 'It's post and beam, of course, parts of it more than two hundred years old. Bert and Mary Everett bought it about three years ago, and they had the oldest part insulated and replastered, but then you saw that. Floors have to be redone. Somebody put that ugly vinyl over the old wide boards. I imagine Mary Everett did that. She was a nut about drafts, that woman. Finally had to go back to Florida to get warm. Those floors are pretty awful.'

'I noticed. Also the stairs need to be relocated. I can't imagine why anyone would want them clear at the back of the house that way. The kitchen is terrible — all that plastic and stainless steel. It looks like an airport. And we'll need another bathroom upstairs. Nothing big. Just little stuff.'

'Well, if you consider that little stuff, nothing that's wrong with this place will bother you. What do you think of it?'

They leaned on the gate together, staring at the house they had just explored from cellar to attic. It stared back through half-lidded windows, sending a look of veiled curiosity down its chimney nose. From this angle the house seemed tall and narrow, two stories and an attic reaching up to the peaked roof, the chimneys above that. Three stories high to the ridge, but only two rooms wide. As they walked away from it to the south, however, it seemed to spread out along the brow of the hill, from the dining room and kitchen at the near end through the hall to the parlors and sunroom and then to the connecting studio and garage. There were four bedrooms on the second floor and two baths, and above them a huge, cobwebby attic, empty and echoing. Room up there for a guest suite or quarters for help. 'Seems pretty big,' the realtor acknowledged.

'But not too big,' she admitted, wondering why she did not like the house better. When she considered the requirements, this house met virtually every one. 'Master bedroom upstairs, plus one for Robby and one for Elaine — she's the baby. That still leaves us with one guest room on the second floor if we put a bathroom in where that huge closet is. The studio will make a good office for Badger.'

'Badger being?'

'I'm sorry, I should have explained. Badger is my husband. Badger Ettison. He's a corporate consultant, and he's in India right now. He'll leave there shortly for Japan and is likely to be gone for as long as six months on that

7

trip. I'm supposed to pick out a house, have it remodeled, and be moved into it by the time he gets back.'

'Seems a lot to lay on a young mama with two kids.'

'It keeps me busy. I think that's what he had in mind. Avoiding boredom on my behalf.' Maybe that was it, she mused. And maybe Badger had simply felt guilty about leaving her for so long. 'Whoops . . .'

'Whoops?'

'I forgot to ask. Are there private phone lines out here? Badger needs at least two, one for the computer and one for business. Then we should have one for the house. Three lines.'

'Well, there's a party line in the house now. The former owners never brought in a private line, which, if you know the local phone company, is probably understandable. They're not what you'd call cooperative. But as it happens, you're in luck. The Primack property borders this one on the south – the house is about a quarter of a mile that way. One of the Primack boys works for the phone company, so when the company was running service south to the developments, he got them to run a spur line as far as their house last fall. My understandin' is they brought in more than the Primacks need by two or three lines, which means you can get private phones for the price of a quarter mile of line. Maybe cost you a bit, but there's no right-of-way to worry about, the Primacks being neighbors.'

'Would they be good neighbors?' she asked, facing him directly, demanding an honest answer.

He stalled for a moment, staring at her as though he was taking inventory of the dark brown hair; the slender form; the dark eyes beneath their level brows, where reflected light danced back at him as though to introduce the quick mind behind them. 'I would think so. Primack's the vet. His wife is quite a bug on education, member of the school board, full of theories on proper child-rearing. Mary Lou and James. Not Jim – James. They're lots older than you, of course. Old enough to be your mama, she'd be. He's

8

quiet and she's not. She's pushy and he's reserved. But by and large, I'd say they'd be good neighbors. He's my brother-in-law.'

'Oh, dear.' Mahlia laughed ruefully. 'Then she's your sister.'

'Oldest sister, one of seven. Pain in the ass sometimes. I had a bit of trouble with my boy a few years back. All worked out in the end, but if I'd listened to Mary Lou he'd be going to psychiatrists yet. Still, all in all . . .'

'All in all, they'll make good neighbors. Thank you for your candor, Mr Smarles.'

'Fred,' he said. 'You might as well call me Fred. I'll call you Mahlia. That way we can discuss this whole thing more informal-like. We go on calling each other Mr Um and Mrs Ah, it might add five thousand dollars to the price of this place.'

'As much as that?' She raised her eyebrows. Considering the price being asked for the place, an extra five thousand or so made little difference, but there were other things to spend it on.

He snorted. 'Well, you gonna make me an offer?'

Mahlia turned to take a last look at the house, its windows shattering red sunset on her. 'Probably,' she said. 'Why don't we go back into Millingham and talk about it?'

In his office Fred was all business, seeing that Elaine was settled in her carry-cot with toys around her, seeing that Mahlia had coffee, pulling out the papers on the house and piling them before her. 'Place was built originally in about 1730 by John Byers, burned down about thirty years later, and was rebuilt twenty years after that by Byers's son, William. It was added to some in 1860 when Jerome Casternaught – he was a grandson, I seem to recall – took over the place. So, it's typical for these parts, added onto until you can't tell what was there first. The only original part left is the fireplace and chimney between the kitchen and the dining room. The other fireplaces are newer than that.

'Well, like I said, it's post and beam under that new

9

siding, and the masonry in the fireplace is original. On the old documents it's called Byers' Farm. It's all that's left of the settlement of Byers' Fault. People all moved away from there back in the 1760s, for some reason. Most of 'em came over here to Millingham. The old places all fell in. County filled in a few of the old cellar holes about six or eight years back when they were huntin' some lost kids and one of the searchers damn near killed himself down an old cistern, but there's still plenty of cellars and pits up there, so you need to be careful. If you know a little forestry, you can spot the old town from the growth, but otherwise you can't tell unless you stumble over a foundation. It's to the west, just up the hill from Byers' Farm. Matter of fact, right where the mailbox is at the end of the driveway – that's the old crossroads to Byers' Fault. The driveway used to go on past the house to the town itself, when there was a town. Pretty country up in there. One of these days, some city people will discover it and build it all up again.'

'I can't figure out why they haven't already. According to the chamber of commerce, the county's growing enormously.' She retrieved a rattle that Elaine had just thrown across the room.

'Bedroom community,' he acknowledged. 'Sleepers.' This obscure joke seemed to amuse him, for he chuckled to himself. 'Nothin' around here but Sleepers. As to why, well, they haven't needed to go that far yet. 'Cross the road from the Byers place looks like forest primeval, but you go a quarter of a mile east down Crossroad and you run smack-dab into six new developments along Chyne Road. Mile after mile of Sleepers. And station wagons. And horses, of course. Every kid in the valley has at least one.'

'Good business for your brother-in-law.'

'Oh, Doc Battle was a regular old stock doctor. Cows, sheep, pigs, didn't make him no never mind. James took over from him a few years back, but old James, he seems to prefer dogs and cats.'

'Is there anything else you ought to tell me about the place?'

10

'Well, let's see. There's an old graveyard right at the corner of the property, stones all tumbled down, but that shouldn't bother you none. What else? Ah. If you're not payin' cash, you ought to know about Jessica Casternaught Duplessis because she'll be carrying the paper on the place. Jessie's a direct descendant from old John Byers. Jessie's got five children. She must be seventy-five or so, not that she looks it. Except for that white hair, you'd say she was forty, or younger. There was what folks here used to call "a touch of the tarbrush" in that family, way back in John Byers's time, and they all have that smooth, brown skin that doesn't wrinkle, so they all look a generation younger than they are at least . . .

'Well, Jessie came back to the Byers place in '64. Her oldest three were already off making their own lives, but the two youngest came with her, Lois and John. Early twenties at that time, both of 'em. And the other kids come visiting from time to time. Well, they had a family reunion in 1980, seems like – all of the kids home but John. He was traveling someplace. And they had their usual big dinner and whatnot, and the next day Jessie slams in here and says she's sellin' the place. Seems like they wanted to do some dance at the end of the drive in the middle of the night or play drums in the graveyard or some other fool thing, and somebody from over Chyne Road got all het up and called the police to complain that the Duplessis family was killin' pigs in the middle of the night. Jessie said it was gettin' too settled, too many people around, and she wanted to sell.'

'She sounds like a character.'

'You wouldn't ever say that to her face, let me tell you. Somethin' mighty forbiddin' about Jessica Casternaught Duplessis. You notice I give her all three names. That's because she signs her name that way on everything. If she wrote a note to the milkman, she'd sign it "Jessie Casternaught Duplessis."'

'Well, she and the kids built themselves a new place back on Bent's Mountain, just over the ridge west of Byers' Fault, and I tried to sell the old place with Jessie carryin' the paper. First folks stayed about two years, complainin' the whole time about the services and the stores and everything in general. They took off three years ago last November. Second family was the Everetts. They bought on contract and remodeled the place some. Said it was damp and drafty, so they moved things around. Three years they stayed, and then off they went to Florida – didn't even try to sell, just gave up their equity and left. Course, to my mind, buyin' on contract's the next thing to paying' rent anyhow. So, now, here it is up for sale again. And Jessica Casternaught Duplessis says this is the last time she's goin' to carry it. Next time it'll have to be the bank, and I'll tell you the truth – the bank isn't interested in houses that old out that far.'

'I thought you said the Chyne Road development was within a quarter of a mile?'

'Right. But development isn't moving west, it's going on south. No, the Byers place may be within a hoot and a holler of folks these days, but it's still too far out, so far as the bank's concerned.'

She considered this, remembering the glow of the trees and the mysterious depths of the forest behind the house. She could not say what it was about the place that made her consider it suitable. She had looked at others that were better arranged and that needed less work. Perhaps it was the very fact that it did need work. Time without Badger burdened her, weighed her down, this house would occupy a lot of it.

'Fred,' she said at last, rubbing her forehead where one of her headaches was getting a start, 'I'd like to make you an offer.' The baby had fallen asleep. There was no hurry so far as Mahlia was concerned, so they dickered about details for another hour before she left him with the contract: the house and the 300 acres it sat upon, an offer to be made to Jessica Casternaught Duplessis. 'Mrs Byers' Fault,' Mahlia said punningly, distracted by her pain. The headache had turned into a full-blown monster.

'Just Byers,' Fred Smarles corrected. 'The Fault doesn't

12

go with the family. Way I hear it, it stays with the land.'
Mahlia heard this without paying much attention. Later she
remembered, making a mental note to find out where the
fault lay. This wasn't California. One shouldn't have to
worry about fault lines, earthquakes, or slippages.

She spent the night in Millingham's one decent motel,
tossing restlessly on the unfamiliar mattress, rising
periodically to see to Elaine though the baby slept as
soundlessly as a tree. The headache came and went, came
and went, as though something in her brain were trying to
break out of her skull. The headaches had been getting more
frequent, and she told herself she would see a doctor about
them. Finally, about three in the morning, the pain subsided
and she slept, only to be wakened at sunrise by Elaine,
howling, wet, and hungry.

In the early morning Mahlia put Elaine in the car seat and
went on a tour in the rental car, locating the developments
Fred Smarles had spoken of, finding her way down back
roads, stopping to talk with children and horses. The plane
didn't leave until midafternoon. If her offer was accepted,
she hoped to move in a month or two, after the kitchen had
been redone and the extra bathroom put in upstairs. Other
things could come later, but it was silly to move in if the
plumbing was on again, off again. Badger would probably
be back in time to see it before she moved in – just barely.

For now she simply drove around, coming inevitably back
up the long lane to the house, seeing the sun pouring down
on it, the orchard on the southern slope beginning to burst
into bloom, its scent heavy on the air. Beyond the house
to the west lay a narrow stretch of meadow, then a dark
line of forest running up into the hills. She located the road
and the house on her map, wondering briefly how far back
the Byers land ran. The small, nameless brook shown on
the map glittered out of the forest, through the meadow and
down the north slope to the pond, then out of the pond into
the forest once more.

The pond was the one thing Mahlia really didn't like
about the place. It was dead-looking, a blind eye staring

13

at the sky. Cows had come to drink there, trampling down everything until it was only a slimy puddle with muddy edges. On impulse, first checking to be sure that Elaine was sleeping, Mahlia opened the gate and walked down the drive, apple and cherry trees on her left, on her right a dry stone wall half overgrown with woody, thorny brush that threatened to topple the wall in several places. There was a stile at the midpoint of the drive. She climbed it, catching her skirt on blackberry canes, then wandered down toward the pond through the knee-high grass. Several yards from the edge she stopped, looking ruefully down at her feet. Not the right shoes for this. The earth was littered with cowpats and pocked with slime-filled pits, the bank of the pond mangled by hooves. She stood where she was, not wanting to go any closer. Something about the place was repellent and vaguely sinister. She told herself it was only the mud, the slime, the trampled soil sheened with a faint oily exudate. Abruptly, she regretted the contract, the offer. She had been too tired, too headachy. She had decided too quickly.

Somewhere nearby a cow lowed and was answered by another. From the edge of the forest they ambled purposefully toward her, twenty or so of them, black and white, an inexorable procession. Even at that distance she could see their huge udders swinging and knew they were harmless.

Still. The better part of valor and all that. She beat a prudent retreat over the wall and watched as the animals slogged through the mud at the pond's edge. Obviously not the Everetts' cows, since the Everetts had moved back to Florida. Obviously someone else's cows, licitly or illicitly grazing on the Duplessis-cum-Casternaught-cum-Byers place. She considered the pond, picturing it in her mind without cows, without mud and tracks. There should be willows on the far side and some kind of flowering reed or rush at the water's edge, grassy banks instead of mud. Something pretty to see out of the dining room window instead of the cold, hungry sheet of water. If she did that, she told herself firmly, if she did that it would be all right. Her feeling was only depression from being

14

alone. The place was really almost perfect for them.

Sighing, she turned and walked back down the drive. This would be fun if Badger were here, but he had plunged into work even before he and Mahlia were married, buried himself in it – to escape memories. To escape thought. To escape, Molly had said, the knowledge that he was at least partly responsible for what had happened. Mahlia and Molly had argued about that. It seemed disloyal to think so, but there might be something in it.

Oh, well, it was only temporary. He'd get over it. And the house would seem fun when he returned, when she could tell him about it. Just now – just now it seemed an impossible task.

At the top of the hill she stopped the car and turned to look back at the Byers place once more. The house was hidden behind a grove of trees. Only the pond stared back at her like a cyclopean, lidless eye. Something moved beside it and she blinked, uncertain she was seeing it: a little girl in a high-necked, long-sleeved dress, kneeling in the mud at the pond's edge. Mahlia looked away, and when her eyes came back to the pond the child had vanished, evidently behind a stand of scrubby bushes. Overdressed for the weather, Mahlia thought. Poor kid – she'd catch it when she got home, muddying that dress.

'Willows,' Mahlia said to herself firmly. 'Willows and reeds and something blooming. And get rid of those damned cows.'

*   *   *

When Jessica Casternaught Duplessis accepted Mahlia's offer, getting rid of the cows turned out to be the easiest part of what had to be done. Fred Smarles explained to Horace Racebill, local dairy farmer and neighbor to the north, that Mahlia would prefer not to extend the grazing lease. Horace said he could quite understand that, since she'd probably want it for her own stock, and he withdrew the herd to fresh fields and pastures new. Mahlia moved

15

on to other things, traveling up to Millingham once a week or so, leaving the children in New York to be spoiled rotten by Badger's sister, Vivian.

She decided that plumbers did more destruction and left more mess than any other workmen, that doing so was a measure of craft status in which they took belligerent pride, and that remonstrating with them did no good. She told Fred Smarles this, after which Mr Drysdale became less belligerent. Another of Fred's brothers-in-law, as it turned out.

'How many sisters did you say you have?' she asked in amazement.

'Seven,' he said. 'Six of 'em older'n me. I was the only boy.'

'How many of them are still here in Millingham?'

'All of 'em. I'm brother-in-law to the plumber, the vet, the doctor, two lawyers, the newspaper publisher, and the owner of the lumberyard.'

'What in heaven's name did you say to Ed Drysdale?'

'I told him you wasn't a Sleeper; that you was settling here; that I'd earned a good commission off you, so come off it and do you a good job.'

Ed Drysdale did a good job. Ossie Jeremy, the carpenter from the next town over, also did a good job, though slowly. All in all, it was the third week in June before the mess was cleaned up and the place was ready to move into. Mahlia wandered through the empty house, admiring the look of sunlight on the wide floorboards, the smell of fresh paint. When furnished, the place would have an unquestionable charm. The former owner had been right, though. The house did have a draft, a chill that seemed to originate in the front hall. Well, there would be time enough to locate the source and take care of it.

'Fred, I need someone to help me get set up. Help me unpack, wash windows, you know.'

'I'll give Charlotte Grafton a call. Charlotte may come over herself, in which case don't make the mistake of telling her she's too old. Charlotte's getting a little nearsighted, but she could outwork you or me any day and then chop a cord of wood before supper. She may send one of her daughters or granddaughters. Whichever, any of 'em'll do you a good job.'

Which they did, in tandem or in series. June ended with all the furniture in, the windows washed, the floors polished, the kitchen and new bathroom complete. Robby cried when they left New York but cheered up on the road. Elaine slept in placid, pinky-brown contentment. Elaine spent most of her time sleeping, for which Mahlia was very grateful. And when they arrived, Charlotte Grafton was there to give Mahlia a cup of tea and take Elaine off to her crib and show Robby his room.

'I heard squeals,' Mahlia said wearily when the old woman returned.

'He found that funny little porch off his room, and he's right away making out it's the deck of a ship or something. He's up there talking to some imaginary person.'

'Robby has a good imagination and a whole wardrobe full of imaginary friends.'

'Ayeh. Well, Baby didn't even blink. Just turned over and went on sleeping.'

'Thank heavens.'

'Tired, are you?'

Mahlia nodded. 'We've been staying with Badger's sister, Vivian, since the furniture was shipped. Somehow I didn't sleep very well there.' Part of the reason had been the headaches, but Mahlia didn't mention that. Perhaps the headaches resulted from tension. Or loneliness. Or memories, things better forgotten that she kept being reminded of. Or so she told herself, knowing that none of these reasons explained them at all. 'Robby's been a little apprehensive about the move. He had friends in the apartment house where we lived, and he hasn't been sleeping well either. And then going back and forth so many times.'

'Well it's over now. You can start settling in. Fred said you wanted somebody to help. My granddaughter Georgina will be over twice a week to help out. I figured Mondays and Fridays. That way, if you have weekend people, she

17

can help you get ready for 'em, or get their mess cleaned up right away, early in the week.'

'I don't expect we'll have much company. Badger's sister and her husband maybe. Or the Professor, an old friend of ours. Then I've some women friends who might like to visit from time to time, but not often.' She paused, thinking of her promise to Badger not to call Molly or Martha or Simoney. Somehow that promise seemed even less appropriate now than when she had agreed, months ago.

'They're lovely women,' he had admitted. 'For witches.'

'They saved Robby's life, and mine. Maybe yours, too.'

'I know. And I'm not ungrateful, Mahlia. But I want to forget it, can you understand that?' There was a bitter quirk at the corner of his mouth, one he got sometimes early in the morning, as though he had been dreaming of something horrible. Mahlia was hurt by it, though she never said so. Carolyn was gone. Gone forever. All the horrible things about her were over with, done. And Mahlia was alive and present; so were Robby and Elaine. He should forget, not go on brooding over it. Yet, even though she resented it, she knew it was something he could not control. A kind of curse, perhaps, a haunting. 'Can't you understand my wanting to forget?' he begged her. 'Can't you, Mahlia?'

She could. Who better than she, watching the anguish that often showed in his face when he looked at Robby, remembering how close he came to losing his son. 'I understand,' she had said. 'Really, I do.'

'I'd like to make a break. Not to be reminded. Make new friends . . .' What could she do but assent? As Vivian had always assented when he was a child and had used that same heartbroken tone. Mahlia sometimes thought he would be better off if he faced the past and worked it through rather than burying it, but she didn't want to argue. Not right then, when Badger was under so much tension with these two foreign projects. Not right then when being married and a mother was so new to her. Not right then. Perhaps later. So she agreed. She would suspend her relationship with Molly and Martha and Simoney – at least for now.

She would give him 'normalcy,' as much as she could. Not witchy friends. No witchiness in herself. As a gift to him.

And then with an all-or-nothing, almost vindictive defiance of her past, she had decided to give herself a gift as well. She had learned enough from Molly to believe she could control the frightening premonitory 'visions' that had plagued her since she was a child. Now, since Badger wanted her to be normal, she would force them to stop. Since he wouldn't let her do anything with her strange gift, she would simply stop having it.

And then the headaches had started. She had to admit that that was exactly when the headaches had started, though she had tried to attribute them to a dozen other causes. She made an angry face at herself, hiding it quickly, telling herself it didn't matter, headaches or no headaches. She had agreed, that was the salient point. She had agreed. It was a contract between her and Badger, and she couldn't change it unless Badger was willing.

A comment from Charlotte recalled her to herself. No, she probably wouldn't be having much company if she couldn't call Molly or the others. 'Having company isn't much fun without Badger here,' she said, knowing she was making excuses for him, and for herself.

'How much longer before he gets back?'

'I don't know. He may be able to stop over for a day or two to see the house. After that, it would be the end of September at the earliest. Could be longer.'

'What are you going to do to keep yourself busy, now that the house is pretty well finished?'

'Well, I've got work to do on my doctoral dissertation. It's been hanging fire for months now. And the house is a long way from finished. One of the first things I want to do is put the stairs back where they were originally. But before that, even, something has to be done about that ugly pond. Honestly, Mrs Grafton, I can't stand that mud hole!' It came out as a cry of anguish, almost hysterical, and Mahlia put her hand to her lips, surprised at herself.

'I wish you'd call me Charlotte, child. Everybody around

19

here does. I'm old enough I don't need to stand on dignity. Now, why are you all upset about the cow pond?'

Mahlia calmed herself. 'Now, that's exactly what I mean. Everyone says it's a cow pond. Why does that pond have to be a cow pond!'

Charlotte shook her head, getting up to refill her cup. 'Well, girl, it always has been, but no reason you can't make a goldfish pool out of it if you want to. It's yours.'

'Yes, it is,' Mahlia said firmly. 'And I don't want slime and cowpats in my backyard.' Whenever she went near the pond she felt a cold revulsion that even the cowpats didn't seem to explain.

One of Charlotte's sons-in-law came with a tractor to plow and harrow the edges of the pond, making them reasonably smooth. Three other men, including two of her nephews, came with a huge truck full of rolled turf, sweating as they heaved it out and stretched it almost from the pond's edge back into the meadow. Willows were available at the nearest nursery. Mahlia bought magazines on gardening, scanning the ads, and ordered water plants from a nursery in Ohio. The shallows were planted with pickerelweed, sweet rush, water iris, and several small, creeping bog plants that did nothing for two weeks and then threatened to cover the water surface. The far bank became green with young willow trees and shrubs. The water in the pond began to clear. By the first of August Mahlia could look at it out of the dining room window with some pleasure, though she did not often actually approach it. Whenever she went near it, she felt chilled and headachy, and she was convinced she was allergic to something growing there. Still, it was an improvement.

'There. Isn't that prettier?' she demanded of Charlotte Grafton, admiring it through the steam of her morning coffee.

'So's a chamber pot with roses in it, but that don't necessarily improve its performance. What's it good for?' Charlotte fixed her with a much magnified, myopic eye.

'Charlotte, it's good to look at. It was a real mudhole before,' she protested.

20

'Where are your cows going to drink?'

'I'm not going to have any cows.'

'Pity for that bahn to go to waste.'

'The barn won't go to waste. Robby loves to play in it – him and his imaginary friends. It's full of marvelous junk, and it keeps him out of the house on rainy days.' Privately, Mahlia had been a little worried about the barn, but Charlotte seemed to think the boy was all right out there so she made no fuss about it. As she recalled, children back in Tahiti had often played in some possibly dangerous places without coming to any harm.

Charlotte Grafton shook her head, letting a sly smile creep through. 'Been waitin' to see if you was goin' to put lilies in it. To my mind, if it's not goin' to be good for anythin', you might as well finish it up with lilies.'

Lilies were easier contemplated than planted. Finding them was simple enough. One of Charlotte's nieces had a friend who was an enthusiast, and the enthusiast was happy to supply large, well-grown plants in huge, clay-filled pots, their white roots worming through the drain holes as though ready to attack the world. 'Be sure to plant them in clay,' the woman said, wiping her own earth-stained hand across her brow. 'The roots float unless you anchor them well in clay.'

'I'm going to plant them in the bottom of a pond.'

'Oh, well then, you don't want these,' the enthusiast said, taking back the pots and turning to look for others. 'Those are just little fellahs that don't spread much – for your typical suburban fishpond, don't you know. You want native pond lilies and hybrids, stuff that'll spread out and look natural. Things that will grow four or five feet down. Odorate Gigantea – that's the white native lily. I've got some good pinks, too. Mrs A. F. Bunyan – what kind of name is that for a lily? Mr A. F. Bunyan hybridized it, you just know he did, but it wouldn't have looked right if he'd named it after himself. So did he name it the "Betty Bunyan"? Not on your life. "Mrs A. F. Bunyan!" Now, I ask you! You just take these out of the pots, clay and all, and sink them where you want them. I push them in with my feet,' the enthusiast advised without offering to help do it. 'Put 'em down about eighteen, twenty inches. They'll work their way deeper.'

All of which was preliminary to Mahlia finding herself well dosed with antihistamines and hip-deep in the pond, ready to consign pots, lilies, clay, and pond to the devil in order to be anywhere else that might be clean and dry. Her head felt like a throbbing drum, and for someone who abhorred slime, she was deeply immured in it.

'Charlotte,' she said pleadingly, 'that one rolled off the bank into deep water. I've lost the damn thing.'

'Ayeh,' muttered Mrs Grafton from the dry grassy bank. 'When Billy Jean Brown said they'd work their way deepah, I don't think that's what she had in mind. I'll go get the rake.' She stalked regally away, head crowned with gray braids, every step expressing purpose and conviction as she peered ahead of her in her nearsighted way. Mahlia thought Charlotte got through her days largely by feel, and she shuddered each time Charlotte's old car turned into the drive, certain it was about to splinter the fence posts.

Mahlia squelched out of the clinging clay of the pond edge onto the grassy bank and stood staring at the water where a trail of bubbles rose maddeningly from water surely more than five feet deep. At the bottom of the bubble trail was the heavy clay-filled pot containing the last lily. 'If you'll buy a dozen, I'll give you a better price,' Billy Jean had said. Remembering the size of the pond, Mahlia had assented, thinking of stretches of reflective water between big, pale, sweet-scented lilies, pure and remote.

At the moment they were not big, pale, or sweet-scented. At the moment they were invisible, their rounded pads inches below the surface, the roots trodden into the pond muck by Mahlia's bare feet. Mahlia rubbed her head, tears in the corners of her eyes. Damn this allergy or whatever it is. It made her headaches worse, as though something were damned up inside her head, a seething pressure, wanting out. Charlotte was approaching with the rake.

'I could leave that one in the pot,' Mahlia ruminated aloud.

'Won't grow in theah,' opined Mrs Grafton, handing her the rake. 'Damn plastic's as tight as a cheap girdle.'

Privately Mahlia thought Mrs Grafton had had little truck with girdles, cheap or otherwise, in her seventy years of life. Charlotte was as lean as a rail.

'I don't think this rake will reach,' Mahlia said, trudging back into the water until its chilly embrace reached well over her knees, stretching the rake out to the spot where the last few bubbles rose teasingly. 'No, wait, I can feel it. Round. Heavy. All it wants to do is stay there.'

'Don't try to get it all at once. Roll it a little, then settle your rake behind it, then roll it a little more.'

Moving it even a little was difficult. She could feel the mass of the heavy pot, feel the click of the rake teeth on the plastic, but the rake did not bite. Her forehead throbbed and beat with her pulse. She struggled, bracing the rake under her arm, trying to use it as a lever, and finally succeeded in making the weight move toward her, if only slightly.

'Why don't I just leave it there?' she asked rhetorically. 'I've got eleven already planted.'

'Well begun's half done,' said Mrs Grafton from her comfortable seat on the bank.

'Well begun's exhausting,' Mahlia snarled, unable to concentrate. She released one hand to rub her forehead. 'Where's Robby?'

'Up in th' bahn. Playin' at bein' pirates.'

'In the barn? A pirate should be down here, where it's wet.'

'Buryin' treasure, I sh'd think. Treasure usually gets buried where it's dry.'

Grunting, Mahlia tried again. This time the mass came halfway. 'I worry about him playing in the barn all the time. He could get hurt.' She had resolved not to say this, but it came out anyhow.

'Bahn's perfectly all right. Long's he stays out of the loft, and takin' the ladder down guaranteed that. If he's goin' to be a farm boy, can't be watchin' him every minute. There, it come a good bit, that time.'

23

Mahlia shifted the rake down and heaved once more. The pot rolled upward, stopping in the water at her feet, the long stems twisted around something caught in the growth, the clammy pads tickling her calves.

'Out you come,' she said. It would all have to be untangled before she could plant it. She picked up the soggy, slimy mess, recoiling as she did so from the wave of pure cold that struck upward from her hands. Half carrying, half shoving, she rolled the slimy mass out onto the bank among the empty pots and stooped over it. The red stems were coiled around something half hidden in strands of dark pond weed. She uncoiled weed and lily stems, letting them flop at her feet, then flicked her hands suddenly with an exclamation of revulsion.

'What's the matta?'

She gasped, 'It's just all tangled up with this slimy stick.'

'Oh, my. Somethin' rotten?'

Mahlia swallowed, gagged unaccountably, tried again. 'No, no. It's just all covered with algae and pond weed. There.' She threw the long, slime-covered mass to one side and knelt over the lily, trying to untangle the snaky stems, her vision blurring. She knelt, gasping, shutting her eyes to let the wave of dizziness pass.

The old woman scrambled down the bank with startling agility to lean over the thing Mahlia had thrown aside.

'I saw something shiny on this thing!'

'Probably a piece of wet leaf.' Even through her pain and vertigo, Mahlia felt it was unlikely Charlotte was able to see anything clearly.

'No.' She was wiping at it with a corner of her apron. 'Mahlia, it's gold!'

Mahlia panted for a moment. The dizzy feeling was passing. She sat heavily upon the bank, not caring about the mud. Her vision cleared. The pain diminished and was gone. She turned to look at Charlotte, carefully, as though her head might fall off if she moved too quickly. 'Gold? It wasn't heavy enough for gold.'

'No, not the whole thing. Look here.'

The greenish stick was braceleted in gold. Mahlia stared at it. Stared at it, wondering what it was about it that disturbed her. What she had thought was a single stick was actually two, long slender shapes joined at both ends. She began to shake her head, then suddenly gagged. 'It's a bone. No. Bones. Not a stick. Bones.'

As though this were the most ordinary thing to find in a pond, Charlotte dunked it in the water and wiped at it with her apron, exclaiming over it as she rinsed the clinging muck away. 'Look't that, Mahlia! Now if that don't beat all . . .'

There were two delicate bones, unquestionably a lower arm. Just as unquestionably, it wore a tiny golden bracelet set with blue stones, shining under strands of clinging weed.

Mahlia shuddered uncontrollably. 'Mrs Grafton, don't. Put it down, please.' She turned away, waves of feeling beating at her with such force she could not identify them. Grief? Pity? Sorrow? Horror? 'It's a child, isn't it? Those are tiny, tiny little bones. A child. The bracelet would be a little girl's bracelet. It's some little girl who drowned in here, isn't it?' Her head was pounding with the feeling she sometimes had before 'seeing' something, before having one of her visions. She forced the feeling away, muttering a controlling phrase Molly had taught her, a kind of mantra. She would not see anything, she would not. If she couldn't be a witch, then she wouldn't be anything except normal, normal, normal.

Charlotte Grafton shook her head, making a patting motion with both hands as though to calm her. 'Now, Mahlia, you quit mutterin' like that and settle down. Whatever this is, it's been there for a good many years. It's true the Everetts was here only three years, but they had two kids when they came and two when they left. And the people before that had no children, and before that was Jessica Casternaught Duplessis. She came in 1964, and all five of her kids were grown already. And before that, it stood empty for years and since the early 1900s when Jessica's great-uncle Jerome Casternaught, old John Byers's great-grandson, had the place. And they had no children, never did. His wife, Jeanette, used to tell my mama how sad it made her, but they never had even a scare. So, there's no children missin' from this place. And I was born in 1910, that's seventy-five years, and I never heard of any child lost around the Byers place. So, whatever this is, you can bet on it being old. Older'n me, Mahlia.'

'What . . . what should we do with it?'

'Well, I'll wrap it up in my apron and take it down to my nephew, Paul Goode. Paul's the chief of police. Doubt he'll make head nor tail of it, but that's the proper thing, so that's what we'll do. Police are supposed to handle things like this. Somebody over in Briarford found a skellington more'n two hundred years old and the police still wrote it up. Paul'll prob'ly write this up and forget about it. Two days' hooraw. Two days' hooraw for you, too, so don't get spooky over it. No sense gettin' spooky over things dead and gone, that's what my husband, Willard Grafton, always said. You just think on the place. Those lilies'll be a sight to see in a month or two, and next summer they'll be a treat. Time somebody spent some effort prettyin' up this place. The Duplessis family used to keep it real pretty, but those Everetts sort of let it go.'

Chatting, chatting, she moved Mahlia away from the pond, away from the slender bones lying in the grass, away from the heavy pot with its clay-encased roots.

When Mahlia went down to the pond some hours later, one lonely lily pad floated like a green raft, already occupied by two pond skimmers, and she could see others straining to reach the surface at the ends of their wiry stems. Minnows butted the leaves, harvesting algae from them. The mud was settling. There was a smell of herbage, and Mahlia breathed deeply, relishing it, only then realizing that whatever had caused her violent allergy seemed to have gone. As had the recalcitrant lily she had almost lost, though there were twelve empty pots stacked neatly in the grass.

'I'll bet she just took it out of the pot and heaved it, root and all,' Mahlia said to herself. 'Wish I'd thought of that.'

26

She carefully did not think about the tiny arm bones or the delicate golden bracelet locked tightly about them. How long dead? How long drowned? Who had lived here a hundred years ago? Unthink it. Think about something else. 'Time someone prettied up this place,' she said to herself, suddenly oppressed with a sense of loneliness. 'Get yourself home, Badger. I've done what you wanted, found a place, bought it, furnished it, fixed it up. It's ready for you to make new friends in, ready for you to forget the past in. So come home.'

CHAPTER TWO

Charlotte Grafton did not go immediately to Millingham.
The bones with their bracelet lay on the backseat of her
battered car, between a case of canning jars and a cage for
transporting rabbits. Though she had regarded it with
wonder and without any of the queasiness Mahlia had
shown, the knowledge of what it was began to grow in her,
to build an emerging reality, a presence, a child-person who
had lived and been loved – the bracelet attested to that –
and lost an arm. Lost. In an accident, that implied. Surely
an accident. Could it have been lopped off for any medical
reason? Snake bite? Surely not. Poison of some other kind?
No, no. It had been lost. In one of those accidents of which
rural life knew too many. The sawmill or the combine or the
belt-driven corn sheller. A child drawn into the machinery.
An ax or knife quick wielded, to cut off an arm, to save
a life. Yes. And then the little arm buried somewhere, along
the stream or even at the pond's edge, long and long ago.
Charlotte could envision that.

And yet, it did not lessen the pity one felt, even now, years
and years after it must have happened. A child, probably
much like her own children. A little girl. Charlotte swung
off the paved road onto a shady dirt track that led up and
around the hill. Below the crest of the hill lay an overgrown
graveyard, the stones half hidden in figwort and bindweed,
bright with the blue stars of chicory among doilies of Queen
Anne's lace, lithe saplings growing up between the graves.
She got out of the car, opening the rear door to take out
the apron-wrapped bundle, then wandered down the hill
among the graves, stopping now and then to read a name

28

or date, arriving at last at a low coping of rough ashlar surrounding a neatly tended plot and headstone. The area inside the coping was thickly and uniformly covered with the brilliant red of flowering sedum, which she carefully parted to make a place for her feet as she stepped to the stone and pulled away a few tendrils of weed that clung there.

'Joseph,' she said softly to the stone, 'I've brought something to show you.' She laid the apron at the base of the headstone and stepped back to sit on the coping, dropping onto the stone in the manner of one who has done so repeatedly, year after year, as a bird might settle to its nest or an older woman to her rocker, fully committed to the place. 'I wish you'd look at that, Joseph.'

JOSEPH STANGER, 1905 – 1931
BELOVED SON
REST IN PEACE

She had brought the bones to show him, but as had often happened in recent months, she'd lost track of what she had intended to say to him. The older she got, the easier it was to forget how old she was. Now, sitting there with the sun hot on her shoulders and the sounds of insect and bird returning to their undisturbed state, she forgot she was Charlotte Grafton. She was Charley Stotts again. Twenty again. So in love with Joe Stanger that the world couldn't hold the glory of it. Full of plans – marriage, children. All the wonder of it as new as though it had never happened to anyone else before.

'I don't think you're silly,' she had said to him in that long-ago time. 'Not silly at all.'

'My folks do.' He had laughed, a little self-consciously. 'They never heard of such nonsense.'

'If a man wants to be a poet, why then, he should be a poet, that's all there is to it. They wouldn't say that if you wanted to be a farmer.'

'Oh, they don't say I shouldn't,' he said, stroking his face with one of those long, delicate hands that looked so unlike a farmer's hands. 'They just say I shouldn't starve while I'm at it. And you know, they're right about that, Charley. Nobody makes a living writing poems. Nobody I've ever heard of.'

'So I'll just go on teaching school, that's all.'

'You can't teach school when the babies start coming. School board isn't likely to allow that.'

'Well, maybe we just won't have any for a while.'

'Well, the way I've heard it, sometimes that works and sometimes it doesn't. My sister Steffie claims it doesn't work worth a hoot, and she's due to deliver next month sometime. This makes four for her.' Silence while he thought about it, stroking his face, holding her tight to his chest there on the sun-warmed stone of the old graveyard. It was their place where they met, avoiding the wrath of Charley's father and the possessive interest of Joseph's mother and aunt. 'Ever since Dad died, they figured I'd take over the farm.'

'Let Steffie's husband take it over.'

'He's a lawyer. He couldn't do that.'

'Well, you're a poet and you can't do it either.'

'I could, you know. Poetry all happens inside the head anyhow. Lots of poems could get thought out during plowing. And there's always winter-time . . .' They were silent, thinking of winter, shaken by the similarity of their thoughts of warm, shared beds. 'Oh, Charley, as long as we're together, it doesn't matter. It just doesn't matter . . .'

And they had left it at that. Charley still had a year of school to finish. Joseph hadn't a dime. They were too conventional to become lovers, too sure of the future. They went on meeting, stealing hours to be together, not talking about each other to anyone lest they threaten the fragile marvel that was growing between them. All of life stretched ahead, more intricate and wonderful each time they looked at it. They began to talk of children, of ways they could cope, of marriage sooner than they'd planned. Next year, perhaps, when Charley began teaching. Surely birth control *would* work, if they were careful. Maybe Joseph could find someone to sharecrop the farm – get enough out of it to support the womenfolk while he and Charley lived a life of their own . . .

Everything moving, burgeoning; they grew more and more hopeful. Until Joseph came ashen-faced to Mount Olive one afternoon, trembling, obviously frightened. 'TB. I can't believe it. I told the doctor he had to be kidding! Me? Why me? That's what poor people get in cities, isn't it? Where they don't get enough food or light.'

'Oh, Joseph, Joseph . . .' Never Joe. His name was too dear to shorten it, to trivialize it. 'Joseph, what are you going to do?'

'Colorado,' he said in a bleak, anguished voice. 'He says I have to go to Colorado. There's a hospital there. Oh, I can't leave you, Charley. I can't . . .'

They could not leave one another, not that way. Charley invented a girl friend from school and an invitation to spend a week at her lakeside home. Joseph invented another doctor, a second opinion. Charley borrowed money from her education fund. They spent two illicit weeks in a nearby lakeside town, two weeks dearer than all the years of their lives before, than any of the time after.

And then Joseph got on the train to Colorado and was gone. Charley went back to school, working nights to make up for the borrowed money, writing letters in the late, cold hours, reading his letters over and over.

Poems.

Not that she'd paid much attention to poetry. It was one of the 'nice' things, like music and art and literature. Joseph liked things 'nice.' He liked nice language, clear speech, what Charley's folks would have called a 'hoity-toity sound,' what Charley herself sought to emulate because Joseph liked it. Joseph's poems confused her. She read them aloud to herself in her clearest, least country voice, occasionally reaching through to the subtlety of his intention. She pretended he was there, beside her.

'I see you in the canyonlands,' he wrote, 'the gullied walls your face in age, strong as this stone.'

'But I'm not old,' she cried to herself, wondering what

it was he really saw in her that he could imagine her old. 'I'm not old, I'm young. Oh, Joseph, when are you going to get well and come home?'

'I dreamed the years had left me,' he wrote.

'Never,' she said, wet circles spotting the page as she wept impotently at her inability to comfort him. 'The years will never leave you, Joseph. I'll keep them for you in my apron pocket. You shall have them all.'

'Come where the wild bird flies away,' he wrote, 'and find me in the grass.'

She was trying to answer that one when the hospital called to tell her that he had died.

Charley went to Joseph's mother and aunt. 'Joseph and I planned to marry,' she said. 'He hadn't told you, I know. He did tell them at the hospital, though, and they called me, too.' She showed them Joseph's last letter. They were inclined to be angry, but she had expected that. All they had left was the memory of his love; they did not want to share it.

'Joseph wanted to be buried in the old Mount Olive Cemetery,' she said, dry-eyed and calm. This was what she could do for Joseph now, and it must be done. 'He loved it up there. We used to go up there and talk.'

Joseph's aunt made a nasty suggestion as to what the talking had amounted to. Joseph's mother screamed at her to be quiet, then they screamed at one another in loss and pain. Charley left, but only for a time. Over the next two or three days they worked it out. Joseph's body arrived on the train. There was a funeral at the church. He was buried at Mount Olive, in one of the few remaining plots. Charley took the last of her education fund to buy it and gave up college. It didn't seem important anymore. Two years later, the Mount Olive Cemetery was closed; ten years later it was abandoned. Joseph's mother died. Now Charlotte was almost the only visitor to the old graveyard, and Joseph's grave the only tended one. And through all the years, they talked.

'I'm getting married,' she had told him, eight years after

his death. 'Willard Grafton from over Millingham way. I like him, Joseph. He's a kind man, very honest, and he's not repulsive to me the way most men are. I can't say I love him, not as we do, but I can't see growing old all alone, either. I knew you wouldn't want that.

'This is my little girl,' she had told him. And later, 'This is my son, my second girl, my third girl, my second boy.' Each of them was brought as a baby to Mount Olive to be shown to Joseph. None of them remembered having been there. It didn't matter. It was not for their sakes they had been brought there.

'I'm beginning to sound like a farm woman, Joseph.' She was forty-six, mother of five, grandmother of six, ex-schoolteacher, mainstay of the church, busy with a hundred projects. 'Just like all those people we used to laugh at. I sound rural, a little ignorant, maybe. I drop my *g*'s. I'm becoming a character. I've forgotten my poetry except for yours – I still read yours all the way through every year. I can't carry a tune anymore. You won't know me when you see me again . . .'

It was a certainty she had. She would see him again. She was as sure of it as she was of her own name. How or where was unknown and unimportant. Willard would grow old and die and pass into some other place without waiting for her. He was fond of her and they lived contentedly together, but he would not trouble the universe with waiting or seeking. Joseph – Joseph was still here, waiting, just as she waited. 'You won't know me, love,' she said.

Sometimes when she wakened in the morning, she looked into the mirror without recognizing her own face. The face she sought was a twenty-year-old face, smooth and brown from the sun, with a wealth of maple-wood-colored hair and lips as pink as new-planed cedar. This face was one she didn't know. This face was brown and lined, with eyelids that drooped like tired plants in summer heat. These lips were narrow and pale and wrinkle-rimmed. This hair was almost white, drawn back in a neat knot. This face wasn't her real face. But, a few moments after waking, this face would take over the day, organizing and doing, phoning and setting straight. Nephews and nieces, daughters and sons, grandsons, all to be chivvied into going and doing what was good for them. Sometimes she heard her own voice and did not know whose voice it was.

Now that voice said, 'Bones, Joseph. Some little girl. Nothing in that, you must think, but there's this bracelet around the little wrist, where the little hand was. It's a strange bracelet, Joseph. See there in the gold – rowan and oak leaf designs and what my grandmother called skystones. Protections against evil, she would have said. I wonder if the finger bones are still down there, in the pond. It must have been down there for a long, long time. I'm going to take it into town, to Paul. You remember Paul, my nephew Ben's oldest boy? Police chief. I don't know if I've mentioned that.'

She bent over the apron-wrapped bones, fumbling with the bracelet. 'It has a little latch on it, but I can't get it open. Someone loved her once, Joseph. As I love you.'

When she dropped off the bones at Paul's office, she said nothing about the hour spent in the old cemetery. No one in the family knew she went there. They did not need to know. She had made her own arrangements, a long time ago.

CHAPTER THREE

The days went by and Mahlia fell into the rituals demanded by the new home. Rising, meals, walks, playtimes, bedtimes.

'When's Daddy coming home?' asked Robby, seeing this as a useful change of subject from the one under discussion.

'Not tonight, so there's no point in your trying to put off bedtime, young man.' Mahlia tugged up his pajama bottoms and patted him twice on the rump.

Robby wriggled, a dignified five-year-old wriggle that said he was much too old to have his bottom patted. 'But when's he coming, really?'

'Same answer I gave you last night. He's coming home maybe to see the house, and then again when he finishes the job.'

'From Japan.'

'From Japan. Yes. And he's going to bring you a monstrous big dragon kite, just as he promised, and we're going to go out in the meadow and fly it.'

'It'll be winter.'

'It might be winter. It could be fall, probably.'

'I'll be in school.'

'You won't be in school on weekends. We'll fly it on the weekend.'

'I wish he'd come home now!'

'So do I, Robby.' She hugged him, bruising herself on the pirate sword that he insisted on wearing even in his pajamas. 'You'll puncture yourself on that in your sleep.'

'It isn't sharp,' he said scornfully. 'You wouldn't let me have a sharp one.'

'That's true. Where did you get it?'

'Captain Bone made it for me.'

'Oh?' She elevated one eyebrow, thinking that the lath sword was sufficiently crude that Robby could almost have made it himself. Still, if he preferred to think of it as a gift from an imaginary friend . . . 'Now, you've had your drink, you've had your story. What else can you think of to delay bedtime, hmmm?'

'I want to tell you about Cynthia.'

'All right.'

'Cynthia is my new friend. She used to live around here.'

'Doesn't she live around here anymore?'

'Sort of. Well, anyhow, Cynthia came to look at the pond where the flowers are. Lilies are. And she says they are extremely pretty.'

'Extremely pretty?' She wanted to laugh.

'Extremely pretty and very elegant. She likes it much better than the way it was. She says it was all cold and muddy before. That's what Cynthia says.'

'I see. How old is Cynthia?'

'She's older'n me. Not much, though. And she wears funny clothes.'

Don't they all, she thought. 'Well, I'm glad you have a new friend. And now it's bedtime.'

He was trying very hard to think of something else, but the long and active day had caught up with him. The objection turned into a great gaping yawn, and before he had fully recovered from it she had him tucked in. 'Good night, Badger's boy.'

'Aren't I your boy, too?' he asked sleepily, ritually.

'You're my boy, too. Good night, Mahlia's boy.' She turned out the light, leaving the door into the hallway ajar, wondering vaguely whether Cynthia was a neighbor child or one of Robby's inventions. A gaping yawn of her own stopped the thought and carried her away to bed.

CHAPTER FOUR

She answered the door, the book she had been reading still open in her hand, a pencil behind one ear, expecting a delivery of material she'd use to re-cover the dining room chairs. She found a chunky, medium-sized man in much-washed denim trousers and a checked shirt, peering apologetically through the screen at her out of bright blue eyes in a deeply tanned face.

'Mrs Ettison? I'm Paul Goode.'

'Yes?' she said, with no recognition whatsoever, her mind still deep in the art history of Thailand, her head full of many-armed idols.

'The police chief, ma'am. You know my great-aunt, Charlotte Grafton.' He quirked an eyebrow at her.

She put the book down, shifting mental gears, and pulled open the screen door, inviting him in. 'I'm sorry. I didn't recognize the name for a moment.'

'No reason you should, ma'am.' he shifted uncomfortably from one foot to the other. 'Excuse the clothes, but I'm headed off to do a little fishin' and wanted to take care of this first.'

'It's about the . . . the . . .'

'It's about the gold bracelet, Mrs Ettison. I sent the bones down to the pathology lab at the capital. You know, if they'd been recent at all, we'd have been up to drag that pond. But the fellah there says they're real old. Real old – hundred years, maybe more. Just no point in draggin', even if we thought there was somethin' there, which we don't. Fellah says the arm was cut off. There's marks of a blade on the elbow end. Coulda been a mower blade, or maybe

37

a sawmill accident a long time ago, and the arm buried somewhere up along that little stream in the hills, and sometime or other it washed down here. A limb, cut off that way, they might not put it in a graveyard but just bury it along the stream in the woods. Myself, I think that's likely, but who knows?'

'Charlotte and I wondered about that. I suppose – I suppose no one could possibly know now,' she said. 'Unless there were records kept. Hospital records, perhaps?'

'Could be. If there was any reason, we'd look, but there's no reason. Those bones could have been washed down the brook anytime, ten years ago, eighty years ago. You know, from up Byers' Fault way. Well, I wrote it up, but it's more a curiosity than anything else. But there's that bracelet. When they cut the bones down at the lab, they got that off. Clasp won't open on it. Rusted, I imagine. Bracelet was sort of embedded in the bones, too. Well, there's only two places for that bracelet to be: with the remains, if there was any, or with the person who found it. Treasure trove is what it is. So, I've brought it to you.' He pulled a tissue-wrapped package from his shirt pocket and held it out to her.

Her first instinct was to recoil, to drop the thing. She forced herself to take it, calmly. It felt heavier than it should, and her hand sagged beneath it. Inside the folded tissue the small oval gleamed up at her, a simple, rigid shape, the two halves joined by a tiny hinge and clasp. Around the circlet was engraved a delicate garland of leaf shapes and flowers, and set in the center of each flower was a blue stone. She felt a sudden, very sharp pain between her eyes that made her turn away for an instant. As she put the bracelet on the hall table, the pain departed, leaving a dull vacancy behind. She turned back to the man, who was watching her with a concerned expression.

'Chief Goode, I think this does belong with the remains. Can you arrange that? Or is there something I should do?'

He shifted uncomfortably from foot to foot. 'Well, I guess that's my fault. I didn't tell the lab to save the pieces, you know. I just told 'em to tell me what they could. So, they sent the bracelet back, but the bones're gone. Incinerated, they said, like they do with any specimens they don't need anymore.'

'Then you take it,' she said, picking it up and thrusting it at him.

He put up his hands as if to ward it off. 'Ma'am, I just can't. It's against the law, for one thing, and it'd set a bad example for the men. They all know about it, you know. If you don't want to keep it – and I can sure understand that, I really can – why'n't you donate it to some charity or other? The lab says it's real gold. That little thing weighs over four ounces. It would set you back more than a thousand dollars, just for the gold in it. Make a nice donation.'

'Of course,' she said stupidly. 'Of course it would. That's what I'll do.' And she stood there, holding it, while he nodded himself out, got into his truck, and created a minor dust cloud down the drive. 'That's what I'll do,' she repeated, dropping it into the top drawer of the chest in the hall. 'Some worthy charity. Maybe Mrs Grafton will have an idea.'

Afterwards, she was never sure whether she had actually forgotten the bracelet or forceably put it out of her mind. In either case, she did not mention it to Charlotte Grafton or to anyone else. The tissue-wrapped packet was shoved to the back of the drawer, which, located where it was, collected all the odds and ends that had no place of their own. It was out of sight, out of mind.

To all intents and purposes, it was forgotten.

CHAPTER FIVE

Badger came to Byers' Farm, came and went in thirty-six hours, leaving Mahlia frustrated and hurt. She had to admit to herself that she had been angry before he came – angry a little at him and a lot at herself – and nothing in his visit had served to ameliorate that.

He had stood, red-eyed and rumpled, in the new kitchen as he admired it, admired the pond, the guest suite, her plans for the garden.

'It will suit us, I think.' He did not sound enthusiastic. As though conscious of this, he tried to brighten his tone. 'It suits you, love.'

'I guess it suits me, yes. Except it's a little lonely, Badger.'

'I know, sweet. You've had very little time to make friends with all the work on the place.' He rubbed his eyes; two vertical wrinkles plowed deeply between them. 'Now that things have settled down a little, it won't take you long.' He smiled, still not looking at all like the man she had fallen in love with, looking instead like some harried driven creature she scarcely knew, a creature who very obviously wasn't looking at her.

She had nodded, doubtfully, not wanting to upset him but needing to get her real anxiety out into the open. 'Badger, would it really be so awful if I asked Molly and Simoney for a visit? Just for a visit—'

He had turned on her at once, with obvious hostility. 'I don't need that, Mahlia. I really don't need that. I don't need to think of you here with those . . . women while I'm away. I thought we agreed.'

'I agreed to do what you wanted. I didn't agree with your reasons.'

'Well, if you agreed, for whatever reason, don't start backing and filling now. Don't start attacking me. If I'm going to get through this next job, I need some peace of mind. I don't want to be reminded of that — that time. Or Carolyn. And whether you agree or not, I'm firmly convinced that a diet of the supernatural is not precisely the best nourishment for growing children.'

'Damn it, Badger, I'm having headaches. I know it has something to do with trying to put all that down inside me somewhere and pretend I'm just a *housewife!*' She hadn't meant it to sound like a sneer, but it came out that way.

'There's something wrong with housewives?' His question was ominous in its calm. 'Being a wife and a mother is too onerous or something? Working on your dissertation doesn't give you enough to do?'

'Badger, that's not it. You're not listening.'

'I don't have time to listen right now. I simply don't — have — time. You asked me, and I'm telling you. No. Please do not call Molly or Simoney or Martha. Now's not a good time. When the children are grown a bit, then you can go visit and I'll have no objection!'

His anger was irrational. His unwillingness to talk was irrational. There had been no time to argue it out, and if she had tried there might have been a scene that would have been irreparable. He was exhausted and tense, she said to herself, he shouldn't have come home at all for so brief a time. He fell into bed like a stone, never moving until she woke him to catch his plane. There was no lovemaking, no sweet words. Mahlia accepted this at some level and did not push it, though she felt pure fury at him. Much as she loved him, she could not accept his reasons or his tone or his neglect. He had not been loving.

She tried to set her hurt aside, forget it, but her feelings for him, which had been monolithic and entire, now had an ugly chink. She knew it, even if he did not. When he left, their farewells were almost monosyllabic, and she cried, not entirely becuase he was gone but also because she feared that something she had treasured had gone with him.

41

CHAPTER SIX

'Spoke to my sister, Jeannie, about young Robby,' said Fred, who had dropped by to see whether the carpenter had completed various jobs to Mahlia's satisfaction. 'Since he'll be in kindergarten this fall, he ought to get to know some of the kids hereabouts. He won't feel so lost if he knows some of 'em, so Jeannie says bring him on down to the play-school a few mornings a week.' The summer play-school in Millingham was a venerable institution operating under the dignified patronage of the First Congregational Church and the expert direction of Jeannie Horan, wife of Lanson Horan, the newspaper publisher, and yet another of Fred Smarles's sisters.

'Why, Fred! That's a very considerate thing to do. I would never have thought of it.'

'Well, but then you dont have six older sisters, either, or you might have. First day of school for me, I didn't know what those other kids wearing trousers were. Far as I was concerned, there was only me and girls. Forty-some-odd years ago and I still remember it. Well. Shall I tell her you'll be down?'

'Certainly. Of course. We'll come in to Millingham tomorrow.'

'First Congregational. West side of the square. They start at eight-thirty.'

Robby was less than delighted with the idea. 'Captain Bone was going to hide the treasure today!'

'Captain Bone?' Even as she asked, she knew what the answer would be. 'Robby, who is Captain Bone?'

'He's a friend of mine. And we have to get the treasure hidden to keep it safe.'

'I'm sure the treasure will still be there when you get home. It's only half a day.'

'But you said I didn't have to go to school until fall!'

'This isn't school. This is an opportunity, Robby. If you weren't Mr Smarles's own particular friend, they wouldn't let you in.'

'Why?' He was instantly suspicious.

'Because no one knows you yet. People have to be *known* to get in important places, and Mr Smarles knows you. If we don't show up, Mr Smarles will have gone to all that trouble for nothing.'

'That'd be rude, huh?'

'Very.'

'Well, all right, then. Just for Ol' Fred, though.'

'Just for who?' Mahlia was dumbfounded.

'That's what Captain Bone calls him. Ol' Fred.'

'It doesn't matter what Captain Bone calls him. You call him Mr Smarles.'

Only under threat of extreme penalty would Robby leave his sword at home. He claimed he needed it for protection, that Captain Bone had told him so, and that the Captain was teaching him to use it. Georgina, her wide mouth serious beneath dancing blue eyes, suggested she could use it to protect Elaine while they were away, and Robbie reluctantly loaned it to her for this purpose. Mahlia frowned at this, resolving to do something drastic very soon if the Captain didn't assume a less important place in Robby's life. She privately blessed Fred Smarles for making it possible for Robby to make some real friends.

In the church hall, Mahlia introduced Robby to Jeannie, then seated herself inconspicuously at the back of the room with two books and her dissertation outline. Half an hour later she asked Robby if he would mind if she did some shopping. He replied in a distracted voice that he was fine, thank you. When she returned, shortly before noon, he was once more engaged in violent swordplay, but this time with a real boy and a real girl, all using iris blades as swords and cutting each other up magnificently.

'Hi,' he said. 'This is Cindy. And Bill.'

Cindy appeared to be about eight and very poised. 'How do you do, Mrs Ettison. My friend Julie used to live where you live now. They moved back to Florida. I walk by your place every day.'

So this was the friend Robby had told her about. Mahlia smiled and took the girl's proffered hand while Bill looked at the ceiling, denying all connection with such civilities. When Cindy had occupied center stage long enough, however, he said, 'I've got a horse.'

'Bill says I can come ride it, Mahlia. Is that okay? Can I go ride it?'

'Where do you live, Bill? Is it far from us?'

'Nah. I live with her.' He jerked an elbow in Cindy's direction. 'She's my sister.'

'Why do you call her Mahlia?' Cindy was asking as Mahlia went to thank Jeannie Horan. 'Isn't she your mother?' Amused, Mahlia did not hear Robby's reply.

Cindy and Bill were Robinsons, living on an old farm at the edge of the new development on Chyne Road, only a few hundred yards east of the Byers place, though well hidden from it by a narrow strip of forest. Captain Bone seemed to be eclipsed for a time in favor of Bill's horse and daily play-school.

CHAPTER SEVEN

Badger called. When she'd hung up, Mahlia almost wished he hadn't, though his letters had been infrequent and almost cursory.

'What's the matter?' she'd asked at last, after a distracted, remote conversation that could have been between strangers. 'Badger, you don't sound like yourself.'

'I'm not. These two projects have been the most frustrating, endless jobs I've ever taken on. Every time I think we've made some progress, we're back in the soup again. I can't tell you anything about it, so don't ask.'

'I wouldn't,' she said, offended. 'I never have.'

He was immediately contrite. 'I know you haven't, darling. I'm not fit company for anyone, not even over the phone. I wasn't fit company for you when I was home. I've thought about that a lot, believe me, and I've got some making up to do. Don't hate me, Mahlia. Withhold judgment, won't you? Just till I get home?'

She had forgiven him. Of course.

'How's Byers' Farm?'

She had written him long letters about it, everything about it. 'Better all the time,' she said, making her voice sound energetic and cheerful though she felt anything but cheerful. Her headaches were worse. The doctor's prescription had not worked, and she blamed Badger for that in some obscure way that she knew did not entirely make sense. 'Robby's going to play-school with some of the children he'll be going to school with this fall. The woman who runs it is another of Fred Smarles's sisters, Jeannie Horan. She's Fred's only other sister, very soigné. About thirty-five. More like a model than a schoolmarm – slinky walk, sleek hair, dramatic eyes. She's asked me to help her with the annual picnic.'

He made a halfhearted joke about Fred's sisters, then dropped into a silence that brooded at her through the phone. Mahlia tried frantically to think of something amusing.

'You haven't talked to Molly recently, have you?' he asked finally, apropos of nothing.

'No, Badger,' she said stiffly, all the anger she had tried so hard to bury seething to the surface. 'You made your wishes clear.'

'I just wondered. When I think of you there, alone, I guess you must get lonely. I thought you might be tempted. She's so . . . capable.' This was Badger's best effort at an apology, and she accepted it as such, even as she pursed her lips to keep from snapping at him. Capable! That was one way to refer to Molly Frolius, buxom farm wife, witch.

'I don't think now is the time to discuss it, Badger,' she said, even as she remembered every word he had said. '*No witchiness while the children are little. No supernatural stuff. Just good, solid, ordinary growing up.*' The words popped out. She found herself quoting him, somewhat bitterly.

'Right.' He sounded somewhat reassured, though still doubtful. It struck her suddenly that he was probably as lonely as she.

'You know, Badg, I could come for a visit. Leave the kids with your sister. Fly over for a few days . . .'

'Fly?' He sounded shocked.

'Oh Badger! On a plane!'

'No! Mahlia, don't even offer. Haven't you been listening? I couldn't spend any time with you even if you were here. Not the way this thing is going. And it's only the thought of the children safe with you that gives me the peace of mind to make any progress at all. No, Mahlia. Another month will probably see the end of it. Either that or I'll give up.'

'You, Badger? Give up?' It came out with a bit of a jeer, shocking her. He didn't seem to hear it.

'I sometimes feel like it. But you wouldn't love me if I did, and neither would I.' He laughed shortly, a tired bark.

She relented, feeling her skin heat at the thought of him, suddenly forgiving him for almost everything. 'Do . . . do whatever you need to, Badger. I'll be as patient as possible. And there's plenty to do. I've really got to move the stairs before you get back.'

'Move the stairs? Oh, that's right. You told me.' He didn't sound interested, only polite.

She tried to remind him. 'Remember? They go up way in the back of the house next to your office, and there's a tiny landing only about two feet wide. I'm sure they used to go up out of the front hall. Anyhow, they're impossible where they are. So, that's what I'm going to do next.'

'Do you have enough money?'

'Oh, Badger, of course I do. There's still a third of what you gave me left in the house account, and almost everything's done. Don't worry about it.'

'Oh, I don't worry about you, even if you're really going to move stairs.'

She laughed, almost crying. 'I really am.'

When he hung up, she did cry. Things simply weren't right between them, and she couldn't make them right with him so far away. 'An urgent trip,' he had said. 'Imperative.' Something to do with some Japanese invention or innovation that had become very necessary to US and Japanese defense. So much he had said, but not what the problem was or why they needed a troubleshooter. Not what he was doing every day and half of every night. Not what kept going wrong.

Well. He would either solve it or give up. Whichever. Knowing Badger, he would solve it. And then he would come home, and by the time he came home, those stairs would be moved.

She made calls. Ossie Jeremy, the carpenter, allowed as how he was occupied for the next two months. No one else could even come look at the situation for at least a week. She contented herself with drawing little plans of the house, putting the stairs where she thought they ought to go, prowling the upstairs hallway to stand at the place she knew the stairs had once ended. A spindled rail made a barrier there, and she could look over it down into the front hall. She had never stood here for any length of time before, and now she shivered in a sudden, inexplicable wave of cold.

'Of course the stairs were here,' she said to herself, pulling her sweater around her, looking around to locate the source of the cold. The ceiling was uninterrupted, no vents. The window in the high wall across the hall was tightly closed. Where was the draft coming from? And why was it so cold in midsummer? If it was like this in midwinter, they would need to call in a contractor or architect to find the problem. Just now, though, all she was interested in was the stairs.

'There will probably be a large beam across here,' she told herself resignedly. 'Which will need to be cut and cannot be cut without the roof falling in. Or the main pipes to the upstairs bathrooms will run right through the stairwell. Oh, hell, Mahlia. Let it alone for a week and do something else.'

She knew there would not really be a beam or pipes. The stairs had come up from the front hall to a landing, as stairs usually did. She was standing on the landing. The stairwell was still here, though the stairs weren't. The other stairs hadn't been built that long ago; they only had one or two coats of paint on them. Virtually new.

'Do something else.' She forced herself to follow her own advice.

One of the things else was cleaning out the barn, that vast, cobwebby space with stacks of old things around its edges and its high loft above, full of moldy hay. She spent several days sorting and exclaiming, while Charlotte Grafton suggested the disposition of articles.

'Now, that thing there, that's an antique. You call the agricultural museum up at the college and ask if they want that.'

'What is it, Charlotte?'

'It's a thingy for shelling corn. You put the corn in there and turn the handle there, and the cob comes out here and the shelled corn comes out there. Haven't seen one of those in ages.'

Or, 'Lord, I haven't seen one of those since I was a

pigtailed girl. D'you mind if I take that home and clean it up?' This was some kind of patented butter paddle.

A relative of Charlotte's came with a truck to take much of the clutter away. The ladder was put back temporarily, while they swept out the moldy hay. Finally the place was almost clean and looked virtually empty except for several huge old pieces of furniture and piles of what Charlotte called 'scultch.'

'You got to have scultch, girl. Anybody on a farm knows that. Lots of times you need a piece of two-by-four or some bolts or something. You got to have a scultch pile for things like that.'

And, when the barn was almost empty, she kept her mind off Badger for several days by helping with the annual end-of-summer play-school picnic. She did it resolutely, not really enjoying it, but determined to meet all the other parents, to make new friends if she could not call her own old friends, to cheer on Robby and Bill in the sack race, to eat deviled eggs and baked beans in a spirit of participation. When it was almost over, she lay under a tree at the edge of the meadow while Elaine slept on a blanket, listening to the children singing.

'Tuneful they're not, but they're certainly enthusiastic,' Jeannie Horan remarked, stretching her jeans-clad legs into Mahlia's patch of shade.

'I like children's voices. It doesn't matter if they can keep the tune or not. I never could keep a tune. Whenever my people would sing, back in Tahiti, they would tell me to be quiet.'

'Oh, that's a shame. Such a hurt to the feelings.'

'Well, strangely enough, it didn't hurt mine. If I couldn't sing, I could listen. I always preferred that.'

'Sensible of you. Some children are remarkably sensible. You think they'll be crushed about something and they turn out to be quite accepting.' They sat in companionable silence, the sun scattering bright sequins into their eyes. 'While I'm thinking of it, thank you for your help with this do. You took a considerable load on yourself.'

Mahlia nodded, acknowledging this. 'This is a pretty place for a picnic.' She peered across the meadow, through the railway notch at the distant steeple. 'Very bucolic for a place so close to town. Though the railway tracks spoil the ambience a little.'

'Only two trains a day. One about seven in the morning, then it comes back through about seven at night. We always used to have the Congregationalist picnics up at Bent's Mountain, but after that awful thing that happened there six years ago, no one wanted to go up there anymore.'

'Awful thing?'

'The disappearance. Two families were camping up there, and five children disappeared. Just vanished. Never found.'

'Children . . .' Mahlia choked, suddenly awash in memories of pond muck, algae, bones. 'Little girls?'

'Two of them were, yes. Sisters. Eight and ten years old. Why? She looked curiously into Mahlia's white face and anguished eyes.

'It's just . . .' She stopped, groping, not wanting to become the center of interest, which would be inevitable if she told the whole truth. Lamely she went on, 'It's just that we found a piece of jewelry at our place. Little girl's jewelry. Charlotte Grafton was there and said there hadn't been any children from here who'd been lost – not in her lifetime, she said.' It was only a half-truth, but Mahlia did not want to talk about the bones.

'Well, Charlotte's right, Mahlia. There haven't been any lost children from Millingham as far back as I can remember. Not from here, or Bennet, or Grub's Corners, either. The ones who disappeared were campers, people from out of state. And there's no way anything belonging to those children could have turned up at your place. Bent's Mountain is all the way around the other side of the brook, over the ridge, above Byers' Fault.'

Mahlia assayed a careful smile. 'No, I didn't really connect the jewelry to the children you were talking about. The bracelet was old, antique. Whoever owned it must have lost it a long time ago. Your telling about the disappearance

50

just brought the other thing to mind, that's all. What happened about the five children?'

'Nothing. That's what was so awful about it. They just vanished. The parents, two sets of them, were fishing, oh, maybe a few hundred yards away from the tents. The kids were playing. They'd been told not to wander off. The families had camped there for two or three years, so the children knew the area. The oldest boy was in charge, a very responsible kid from everything his folks said. It's an open, fairly flat area along the stream. Not dangerous; no pits or mine shafts, no cliffs or ravines. Not heavily wooded, so it isn't easy to get lost. There were the two girls and their brother, eleven years old. Then there was the other family, two boys, seven and nine.

'Well, the parents came back to the camp with their catch – they hadn't been away more than an hour – and the kids were gone. They searched for a while. Then they got frightened. One of the men drove down here and Paul Goode called out Millingham Rescue. A day later, Millingham Rescue called for help and we had searchers from all over the state. I remember because Lanson was out with them for over a week. Most of the men around here belong to Search and Rescue – Lans, Fred, and all Fred's and my brothers-in-law, of course. Sometimes even the women go along. My youngest was seven, and I kept thinking about her being lost that way.'

'And they never found any sign of them?'

'Nothing. Not a footprint, not a lost sweater or shoe. We had complete descriptions of the clothes they were wearing. Nothing. The searchers finally decided they'd been kidnapped and called in the federal people. But it was too late to find anything, you know, tire tracks or anything. It's probably pure superstition, but people just don't go up on Bent's Mountain for picnics anymore. Or for anything, come to that. I used to collect mushrooms up there all the time. Haven't been back in six years. Maybe what the searchers all felt about the place was contagious. They were so depressed, so down.'

51

Hearing of children lost, children vanished, Mahlia felt a need to find Robby. 'Watch the baby for me for a minute, will you Jeannie?' And she was up, searching for him among the children. Not there, not there; there. By the fence, talking to a tall, good-looking, slightly sinister, she told herself, slightly sinister stranger. Her legs moved of their own volition, and she hurried toward them.

'Ah,' the man said, looking up toward her, smiling. 'Here's your mother now. Mrs Ettison?' His smile lightened his face, making it warm and welcoming, though there was something about his eyes that caught her up, only for a moment.

'Yes?' Short. Too short. Why be rude to someone just because of something that had happened six years ago? That charming smile had not earned such rudeness. 'Yes,' she said again in a gentler tone. 'I'm Mahlia Ettison.'

'I wanted to say hello! I'm John Duplessis. You're living in my house, the old Duplessis family home. Or rather the Byers home, I should say, or Casternaught. The Duplessises are latecomers in the family tree.' Mahlia struggled with the name for a moment. Duplessis. What had Fred Smarles said? Jessica Duplessis. Jessica Casternaught Duplessis. And her children, of whom this man seemed to be one.

'Are we living in his house, Mahlia?' Robby looked at her doubtfully. 'It's our house, isn't it?'

She laughed, looking into the man's eyes, surprised to hear the warmth in her voice. 'Of course, Robby. When Mr Duplessis said it was his house, he didn't mean he still owned it. He meant it had been built by his family. Yes, it's our house.'

John Duplessis turned his charming smile on to Robby, to which the boy responded in a moment as though hypnotized. When he looked at Mahlia, his strong, bow-curved lips parted over teeth so white they dazzled, she responded as well. It would have been impossible not to. His hair was black with blue lights in it, and it tumbled forward over the forehead in a thick, rich wave reaching almost to his eyebrows. Oh, Lord, Mahlia thought to herself weakly,

Superman. Prince Charming. The voice matched the appearance, rich and warm as morning coffee. 'Don't worry, son. I'm not out to get the old family place back. Jessie sold it because it was getting too crowded with the new developments on Chyne Road, so we certainly wouldn't return to the burgeoning masses. Have you met Jessica?' This was directed at Mahlia.

'Your mother? No. I've heard of her, of course. She seems to be a mainstay of Millingham.'

He laughed with a humorous lilt, his eyes admiring her. 'She'd hate hearing you say that. Jessie's always detested Millingham, always tried to stay as far from it as possible. Oh, not Millingham per se, simply any aggregation of humanity. She is a fixture, though, more by reputation than presence. Come meet her.'

She could not have said no. Not to this man. He took her hand and drew her along the fence towards a huge old car, square-fronted and high-topped. In the backseat a gray-haired woman sat, looking out at the picnic with sardonic amusement.

'Jessica. I'd like to introduce you to Mahlia Ettison. That's her son, Robby, climbing the fence over there.' He pointed to Robby and the woman's eyes flicked toward him like those of a hunting hawk, picking him out of all the children present. Mahlia shivered, then relaxed as the gaze was turned on her. Evidently in this family they didn't call her 'Mother.' Mahlia could see why.

She had eyes like jet, eyes in which a flame danced, laughing and youthful. Jessica Casternaught Duplessis had to be at least seventy-five, Mahlia knew, but she looked barely half that, except for softly curled white hair.

'Mrs Ettison.' A voice like a purr. 'How nice to meet you. Are you enjoying the old house?'

Before she could reply, John had turned her toward others who stood by the car. 'My oldest brother, Bill. My sister Harriet. Jerry and Lois are off in New Orleans on family business. They'll be joining us soon.'

Mahlia smiled, shook hands, exchanged pleasantries.

They all had the family eyes and that expression of slight, remote amusement underlying the charm. Bill was dark-skinned, darker than Mahlia herself. The others were lighter. All had deeply waving hair that tumbled over perfect foreheads, casually tousled. They all had the family charm as well, with stunning smiles and intimate handclasps. She had the feeling she was being inspected, looked at like a specimen. Well, a family naturally would be curious about anyone occupying the old family homestead. She contented herself with a polite smile, a noncommittal 'Very nice to have met you. We're enjoying your old family place.' She was more than merely aware of John Duplessis's hand on her arm. His presence was raising gooseflesh on her skin, a kind of sexy prickling that spurred her into movement. 'I must collect Robby. He's been in the sun long enough.' And she needed to get away from this intent examination.

'May I join you?' That warm smile again from John, that interested voice. He made it sound as though joining her was what he had wanted to do for weeks, for years.

Her immediate inclination was to say no. No, don't join me. Go away. Don't worry my son with your talk. Don't worry me with those marvelous teeth. Don't smile. Don't crinkle your eyes. Go away. But the inclination was no more than that, immediately overruled by some other part of her that responded to his friendly overture like a flower to the sun. She said, 'Of course,' nodding, and led the way, Robby held tightly by one hand. He moved stiffly away from the caressing hand of John Duplessis on his hair with an annoyed shake of his little-boy head.

Jeannie was bouncing Elaine on her lap. As they approached, she glanced up, eyebrows lifting in surprise, mouth pursing a little as though she had tasted something questionable, a tight watchfulness in her face. 'Why, John. Hello.'

A moment's hesitation, perhaps discomfort, before he responded? 'Jeannie. Good to see you.'

'I had no idea you were back. I saw Harriet just the other day, but she didn't mention that you were coming.'

'She probably didn't know. I did write the family that I was coming home, but I think I beat the letter getting here. It was probably on the same plane from Haiti that I took.'

'Haiti? Where's that?' asked Robby, very interested suddenly. 'Mahlia, wasn't Daddy in Haiti?'

'Some time ago, yes. That's where he got the mask he brought you.' She took the baby from Jeannie, made conversation. 'Was it a long trip?'

'Six years you were gone, wasn't it, John? Seven?' There was something acid in Jeannie's voice.

'Seven, actually. I traveled all over the Caribbean and West Africa. Well, nice to have seen you, Jeannie. Mahlia – it is Mahlia – isn't it? – I'd like to drop by sometime, see what you've done to the old place. By all reports, you've improved it immensely.' Another smile, a wave, and he was gone, not without a lingering glance that brought blood to Mahlia's cheeks. It had been not merely admiring, but knowing, as though he read her response to him.

Mahlia murmured, 'Am I mistaken, or did he leave rather suddenly?'

'When he saw me? Yes. He did, rather. I'll tell you about it sometime. Little pitchers.' Jeannie was very pale, almost sick-looking.

'Have big ears,' said Robby. 'That's all right, Mrs Horan. Daddy says it's ap – appro – piate for kids to hear everything because that's how they learn.'

'Well, it's personal, Robby.' She laughed, ruffled his hair, then turned to the meadow full of children and parents once more. 'Much as I dislike the idea, I think the time for the egg race has come. And then the giving of prizes. And then, thank the Lord, home and a bath and a tall glass of something very cold.'

'Could I get you some iced tea?' Robby again, being the perfect gentleman.

'Thanks, sweetie. I had something else in mind.' And she was off.

'Did I say something wrong?'

'No, Rob, my love, you did not. It's just that sometimes

55

people have very personal things they don't want everyone to know. They may tell a special friend, or a sister or mother or something, but they don't want it to be generally discussed.'

'Like a secret.'

'Rather like that, yes.'

'Oh, well, that's okay then. Cynthia and I have secrets, and so does Captain Bone.'

'Of course. And they aren't things you talk about with everyone.'

'Not with Bill. He'd laugh.'

'Right.'

'I'd like to tell you about them, though.'

'And so you shall, whenever you like.' Though not, Mahlia thought to herself, just now. Not just now, love, because my treacherous self has betrayed me. I have smiled at another man, love, and thought of him quite approvingly. Something strange there, though. Jeannie's face when she left them had not been happy. Something between her and John Duplessis – an affair, perhaps? Something seven years old that still rankled? Something that, Mahlia thought sternly, was none of Mahlia's business.

Still, the voices of the afternoon would not be quieted. In the middle of the night she woke, thinking of Byers' Farm and the children who had disappeared. No connection, she told herself. The bone in the pond was more than a hundred years old, the bracelet the same. No connection. It had nothing to do with Byers' Farm and the Duplessis family. But the voice of reason had no effect. She got up, put on her robe, and went down the hallway to the narrow, inconvenient stairs at the back of the house. In the kitchen she paused to put the kettle on before going through into the hall. The top drawer of the chest was damp, stuck tight. She tugged it, jerking it so hard that it came completely out, banging on the floor, scattering its contents.

She sat down with an exclamation of irritation, picking up pencils, rubber bands, receipts, stamps, a long screw that had come out of heaven-knows-what, something broken, an unidentifiable part from something else, a burned-out light bulb – thankfully unbroken. Only when everything was back in the drawer did she remember what she had been looking for. The bracelet. The bracelet, wrapped in a scrap of tissue paper, the little oval packet only about two inches across.

She looked inside the chest, thinking the drawer might have spilled some objects onto the shelf below, then on the floor. She extended her search into the living room, thinking it might have rolled.

Nothing. No bracelet.

After a frustrating time, she gave up the search. There was no bracelet in the drawer. There had been no bracelet in the drawer when she jerked it open. She had no idea when the bracelet had disappeared from the drawer, but she clearly remembered putting it there some weeks before.

Exasperated with herself, with whatever it was that hovered at the edge of her attention, not quite disclosing itself but making a small agitation, she made a cup of tea and took it up to bed. There, after what seemed an endless, nervous time of trying to remember something it seemed she had forgotten, she slept.

CHAPTER EIGHT

'I heard a bang last night,' Robby said in his darkest voice, trying to hide his breakfast egg behind a fragment of toast.

'Eat your egg, Rob. I'll look under the toast, so don't try to hide it.'

'I don't really want it.'

'You never want anything until cookies. No cookies unless you eat the egg.'

'Well, I did hear a bang last night.'

'That was me. I pulled out the drawer in the hall and it fell on the floor. Everything fell out.'

Stillness. Watchful stillness, so wary that it caught Mahlia's attention. Aha. 'I was looking for a little white paper packet that has a tiny gold bracelet in it, Rob. You wouldn't know what happened to it, would you?'

Elaborate unconcern. 'I don't think so. Do you think it might be a treasure?'

'Something like that, yes.'

'Then I'll bet Captain Bone knows where it is. He has all kinds of things like that. He says he's keeping them for when the people want them.'

'What people are those?'

'Oh, you know. People who lose things.'

'Would you tell Captain Bone, please, that I'd like the bracelet back?'

Robby looked troubled at this. 'Is it yours?' he asked at last. 'Really yours?'

She considered this soberly. 'Yes, in a way,' she said finally.

'But it really belongs to someone else?'

'Yes, I suppose it does.'

'I don't think Captain Bone will let me have it. He says buried treasure should stay buried until the people it belongs to need it or come for it. That's the way it should be.'

'I see.' Robby's imaginary companions had always shown personalities and minds of their own. Mahlia and Badger had discussed the matter at some length, deciding at last to let the friends, imaginary or otherwise, live their own lives and vanish when appropriate. 'Otherwise,' Badger had said, 'we might drive them inside. He might end up one of those pathetic creatures with six or seven personalities, all because we hadn't let them alone.' Mahlia wasn't sure this idea was in accord with any accepted psychiatric theory. Nonetheless, she had tolerated Bonnie Roo, the eccentric kangaroo, and Sythvie Platz, a traveler from some other planet, and the Shin-shin twins, who always did the opposite of what they were told. Each had departed in its own time. She had been prepared to tolerate Cynthia — when she thought Cindy was imaginary — and should now be prepared to accept Captain Bone. Should.

'Have I ever met Captain Bone?' she asked.

Robby shook his head. 'No. He doesn't go among people anymore. He says it takes too much out of him.'

'I see,' she said faintly and with some consternation. 'What does he do?'

'He used to be a sea captain in the slave trade, but he gave it up, and became a Christian. That's what he told me.'

'That's what he told you?'

'Yes. I asked him why he didn't go to sea anymore, and he told me he gave up the trade when he became a Christian.'

He had to have heard that somewhere, she told herself. Probably some pseudo-historical something or other on television. 'Well, I would appreciate your asking him if I could have the bracelet back, Robby.'

'I'll ask him,' he said, gulping the last of the egg, the last of the milk, hastily wiping mouth and chin. 'But I don't know if he'll listen. Can I go out now?'

She nodded, sighing. Perhaps this was the time for a

59

confrontation. Who knew? Or perhaps it was the time to leave well enough alone. Again, who knew? Abruptly, she longed for Molly. Molly had such good sense about things like this – at least, she always sounded convincing. She needed Molly. Or Simoney. The need brought swift anger with it and a surge of pain behind her eyebrows.

She shut that thought out as swiftly as it came. She had promised. Her anger subsided, but the pain stayed where it was.

How did one pretend to be like everyone else when one was not? When one had grown up seeing danger where others did not, giving warnings that were resented and unheeded, sometimes knowing the future before it happened without being able to change it – all this attended by suspicion and sometimes fear? Her visions, acceptable enough in Tahiti where some others shared them, weren't the stuff of normal, everyday life in France or Canada or the U.S. Only when she had met Molly Frolius had she learned to accept what she was. It was possible to accept a Mahlia who could sometimes see the future if one could accept a farm wife who was also a witch.

A good witch, Badger would have said patronizingly. A very good witch, Mahlia thought. A weaver of spells, a healer, a hardworking farm wife whose husband has no idea she does anything on those long walks in the woods but pick mushrooms. A kindly woman who had taught Mahlia many very interesting things.

But, Badger would have gone on, *but* it would be better for Robby and Elaine if they had a very normal, unexceptional childhood without traumatic reminders, a childhood with Mahlia fully attentive to their needs.

Because she remembered Badger's first wife, who had been anything but attentive to Robby's needs, Mahlia had acquiesced. Now she felt she had done so with entirely too little argument. 'Well give them a Norman Rockwell childhood,' she had promised in a weak moment. 'Flag, Mom, and apple pie.'

'In the country,' Badger had said. 'We'll have a garden. Maybe a pony. Certainly a dog.'

'And a cat.'

He'd said teasingly that he wasn't sure about the cat. Cats were witchy.

'Cats are just cats,' Mahlia had insisted. 'If we're going to have a pony, that means a barn. Barns mean mice. And mice means cats.'

Badger had agreed to the cat. But Mahlia hadn't really thought yet about getting one.

Certainly one could call Molly just to ask about cats. Or ponies.

'Mahlia,' Robby announced through the screen door. 'Captain Bone says he'd rather wait until he can return the bracelet to its owner.'

Before she could reply, Elaine began to wail from the yellow-painted nursery upstairs. The front-door screen banged — Charlotte's granddaughter Georgina, come to help out. A carpenter's truck turned through the gate into the drive. Perhaps Ossie Jeremy had unexpectedly had a break in his schedule.

'All right, Robby,' she said distractedly. 'We'll talk about it later.'

Oswald Jeremy walked through the hall with her to the stairs, nodded as she spoke, waited until she had finished her lengthy exposition, and then said, 'You want 'em put back where I moved 'em from.'

'You?'

'Me. Mrs Everett was almost hysterical about those stairs. She said there was a cold draft came down those stairs that chilled off the whole living room. Said it smelled like wet, like marsh, maybe. She and I, we went round and round about those stairs.

'Well, I'm not in business to tell people I won't. So, I took 'em down for her, and built new ones. Told her she wouldn't like 'em, and she didn't. The hall back there's too narrow for stairs, and that landin's something silly. And then, when I'd done it, she complained that the place was still drafty.'

'I had noticed the draft,' Mahlia commented, thinking of the winter to come, 'though I didn't think it was that bad. Was it only in cold weather?'

'That Mrs Everett, she called me the Fourth of July the first time.'

'I didn't think it was that cold!'

'Well, it coulda been just her. She was the jumpin'est woman – here, there, everywhere, all the time. Kids just like her. He was hardly ever here, so I don't know about him. Well, you want 'em moved back.'

'I do.' She immediately felt doubtful about this. And yet, the chill she had felt on the old landing hadn't been freezing. Surely they could find the source of it. A space at the edge of the roof, perhaps, where a fascia board had come loose or been gnawed by squirrels. Perhaps an old vent pipe, left open during some previous remodeling. For all its age, the house seemed generally tight and weatherproof. 'I think Fred told me the Everetts insulated the house, too.'

'Oh, they did about ever'thing you could do. Wasn't from lack of tryin'. Place just didn't suit. Me, I think she missed where they lived before they came back here and just couldn't let up until they went back.'

'How about the people before them?'

'Oh, now what was their name? Miggle, Meegle, some-thin' like that. Mandrell, that was it. Don't know a thing about them. No kids, just him and her and her old mother. Kept pretty much to themselves. Lived here less'n two years and went off one day, no word to anybody.'

'People don't seem to have liked the place much,' she faltered. 'Makes me think there must be something wrong with it.'

'Somethin' wrong with them, more like,' he said, not sounding at all sure of that. 'It's a good old house. Can't find anything wrong with it. And you've made it look pretty as can be. That pond is as good as a postcard.'

Mahlia, assuming that this was high praise, pursued the matter no further. Oswald Jeremy and Charlie Steffins set about rebuilding the stairs. 'Left all the old treads and risers out in the bahn,' Ossie commented. 'Stair-rail and all. Broke up the old newel post some gettin' it out, but there's plenty there for a pattern. I'll have another one turned just like it.' And he came and went, whistling between his teeth, sometimes with help, sometimes alone, always with Robby tagging along, fascinated, full of questions: 'What are you doing now?' 'Where does that go?' 'What do you call that thing?'

'Funny little kid you got there,' Ossie commented. 'As full of words as a dictionary.'

Mahlia nodded. 'His father is very . . . verbal.'

'Talks a lot, you mean?'

Mahlia nodded. She guessed she did mean that.

'Not your kid, is he? You his stepmama?'

'Yes. Mr Ettison's first wife died.' Which was true, in a way.

'Baby's yours, though. Looks just like you.'

'Do you think so?' she asked, glowing with pleasure. Elaine was a pretty baby, with Mahlia's black hair and creamy beige skin. 'That's sweet of you to say so.'

The newly turned newel post arrived and was installed. The painter came and went. And the stairs descended into the hallway as they originally had.

'Finished?'

'Unless you want that room uncovered.'

'What room is that, Ossie?' She looked around, confused. There had not been any door involved.

'Well, you go out in the bahn and look in the back, behind that pile of lumber, and you'll find a real old, heavy sideboard. Thing must weigh five hun'red pounds. Marble top, beveled mirror, the whole works. It used to set up there at the top of the stairs. We had to move it when we took the stairs out. Well, behind that sideboard the wall was different. Saw it right away. Somebody'd put wallboard over it. So, I measured it out and there's a room there, all right. Big closet, maybe. I asked Mrs. Everett did she want it uncovered and she said no, she didn't. So I just textured over it to make the wall look better and left it alone.'

'A storeroom, you think?'

'Prob'ly what we'd call a lumber room, yep.'

Mahlia nodded with satisfaction. This, obviously, was the source of the cold. 'Well, I'd like you to restore that, too. I think Mrs Everett must have been a little − odd.'

'Nuttier'n a fruitcake, if you ask me, which you didn't. Glad to do it.'

*   *   *

Badger called again, sounding almost like the man she had married. 'All right, love, the end is in sight. It's not going to be as long as I'd thought. Six weeks, no more, probably no less, and we're through with this mess. I probably won't be able to call you even once during that time because we're going to be . . . well, phones won't be available, put it that way. So, tell me all the news. Are the stairs moved yet?'

She was trying to face the idea of six more weeks alone with no phone calls and do it without weeping over the phone. She tried to cover the loneliness with anticipation. Six weeks. Lonely, yes. Lengthy, yes, but terminable. Finite. An end, a definite end. And Badger sounded almost like himself rather than that angry, hostile person of recent months. Her voice was blurred, but she managed to answer. 'All finished. Ossie and Charlie Steffins packed up their tools and left yesterday. We even got an extra room out of the deal.'

'An extra room?'

She told him, making a serendipitous event of it. 'The door was right there, under the wallboard. All Ossie had to do was put a knob on it and put the trim back on. He says it was probably sealed up before the Duplessises ever left the place. I'm going to clean it out tomorrow. Might be lots of lovely old stuff in it. Probably nobody's been in there for years.'

He said a few things, lovely things. She had been planning to tell him about meeting John Duplessis, but she didn't. Later, she wondered why she had not.

*   *   *

The little room was dark. Ossie had oiled the hinges and the latch, so that the door swung silently out into the hallway, the darkness behind it gaping like an icy mouth. Cold ran out when the door was opened as though from a refrigerator.

'First thing,' said Charlotte Grafton, pulling her shirt closer around her, 'is a bucket with some ammonia water and a rag for that window.' The window had been open when Ossie had first opened the hidden door, the source, so he said, of most of Mrs Everett's drafts. It swung inward, allowing them to wash both sides, opaque with dust and cobwebs. It looked out onto a blind pocket made by the roof ridge over the kitchen and the chimney of the living room, invisible from below.

'Now,' Charlotte said as she wiped the last of the filth away from the window. 'Let's see what we've got here.'

'Don't you want Georgina to do this, Charlotte? You'll get filthy.'

'Which is what the good Lord gave us soap and water for. Look't that.' She was holding something close before her eyes. 'Enough leatherworks there for a tack room.'

There were leather straps with buckles hanging from pegs beside the window, several dozen of them. A dusty cardboard box of children's clothing. Several old mattresses piled in the corner. A bow-backed trunk full of moth-eaten blankets.

'Faugh,' Charlotte cursed. 'Burn these, soon's we can, or take them to the dump. Look at that moth! We'll need to spray your closets, for sure.'

On the shelves were stacks of comic books, an old chamber pot and basin, a packet wrapped in newspaper. Mahlia unrolled it to disclose a cleaver and a set of knives, glittery in the half-light.

'Skinnin' knives,' said Charlotte, peering over her shoulder. 'If you don't want those, Mahlia, my granddaughter's husband would sure like 'em. He gets us a couple deer, maybe an elk, every year.'

Mahlia rerolled the bundle and gave it to the old woman, repressing a shudder at the malevolence of that steely glitter.

'Take them, Charlotte. Take anything you want. I'm going to burn everything, otherwise.'

'Well, these clothes are okay.' She held up a small blue shirt, appliquéd with red gingham ducks. 'Somethin' some visitor's kid left, I s'pose. I'll wash 'em, and they can go to the Salvation Army down in Millingham. We'll take the blankets and mattresses to the dump. I'll take those straps past the ridin' stable. Herm Blair'll prob'ly take 'em off our hands. Good leather – no point in burnin' those. What's that you've got there?'

'I don't know. A carving, I guess. It looks a lot like the mask Badger gave Robby. Same wood, same style.' The thing was a flat slab of dark wood, polished to an oily gloss, with a complicated design incised into it, many lines forming a latticework with curly edges.

'Somethin' some Byers traveler brought home as a souvenir, most likely. They're great ones for travelin' around. You goin' to keep it?'

'Oh, I'll keep it to show Badger. He's interested in this kind of thing.' She rolled it into its flannel wrapping again, setting it outside the door of the little room. 'What else?'

'Not much. Some picnic plates. I don't like that plastic stuff, it gets really dirty-lookin'. Put those with the blankets. I'll have Mike Pettis drop over and carry those to the dump for you.' She bustled out the door, heavily laden with boxes.

Mahlia, left behind, wondered why the Duplessis family had sealed off the little room, deciding it might have been for appearance's sake. The carved sideboard had probably looked much better at the top of the stairs than the door it had replaced. Or perhaps there had always been a draft. Certainly if Mrs Everett hadn't felt drafts all the time, the room would never have been rediscovered. The room was still icy, even though the door was open and the heat from the house should have warmed it. Grimacing, Mahlia went to get a heavier sweater.

She began stripping the shelves of their yellowed newspaper lining. The *Millingham Monitor*, 1930. 'Depression Deepens; Mills Close, Throwing Thousands Out of Work . . .'

Fascinated, she sat down to peruse the faded pages. Local obituaries. Births. Social notes. 'Jessica Casternaught Duplessis entertains visitors from New Orleans at the Byers family home.'

'That's odd,' Mahlia said to herself. 'I thought Fred said she came back here in '64.' Though the article was less factual than gushy, it reported that Jessica, ordinarily resident in New Orleans, had returned to Byers' Fault only to look over the old house and arrange for needed repairs. Ah, well, someone would have had to look out for the place if it had been standing vacant since the early 1900s when Jerome Casternaught left it, or died, or whatever.

She turned the pages idly. 'Tragedy Mars Church Outing.' Two overturned canoes at the Bent's Mountain Reservoir, six children presumed drowned, bodies missing. Again Mahlia's stomach clenched as she remembered the pond, the smell of muck and algae, the green-slimed bones. Nothing to do with the multiple drownings that had taken place more than fifty years ago.

'Children die,' she said sternly to herself. 'In every country, in every generation. A certain number die, and that's all there is to it. Children aren't immune to death; it just seems as if they should be . . .'

Far off, as though from some other country, the doorbell rang. It took her several moments to realize what it was.

The man on the porch was pudgy and sandy-looking, his nose peeling from too much sun, his eyes crinkled behind light gray glasses, which he removed to stare at her. He had a bony, baggy, lived-in look about him, with a scatter of pipe ash down his front and an egg stain on his tie, a look of book-lined studies and untidy desks. Without intending to, Mahlia smiled, remembering such places and times from her own student days, adrift in memory. He had that patient, interested look she had always enjoyed.

'Ms Ettison? Charlotte Grafton suggested I talk with you. My name is Paggott, two *G*'s and two *T*'s, and I'm with the University of Vermont.'

She came to herself with a lurching sensation. 'I'm

sorry, what did you say? I'm afraid I was thinking about something else.'

He introduced himself again, taking a little longer about it this time. 'I've been working on a book about this area, Ms Ettison. Charlotte Grafton has been helping me out. Remarkable woman. Remembers everything anyone ever told her, all the stories her grandparents used to tell. She says this house has the original fireplace John Byers built back in 1730. I wondered if you'd be kind enough to let me take a look at it, take some pictures maybe. I don't suppose there's an inscription?'

'You mean something carved somewhere? "Built by John Byers, 1730?" Not that I've ever seen, Mr . . . uh . . .'

'Paggott. Look, why don't you call Chief Goode and ask him about me? He'll certify that I'm sober and industrious and legitimate. And if this isn't a good time for you, I'll be happy to come back. I'm staying down in Millingham for a few days, so it isn't far . . .'

Silly. She knew he was all right, knew it in that way she sometimes knew things, unequivocally and without doubt. 'What's your name?' she asked. 'Your first name.'

'Claude,' he said, blushing. 'Most people call me Seepy – C.P., you know. I prefer it to Claude, quite frankly.'

She unlatched the door, held it wide. 'Come on in. My name is Mahlia, and I like that better than Mrs Ettison. Do you know anything about old houses? Houses as old as this one? We've just opened up a little old room upstairs, and it's the oddest thing . . .' She wandered off up the stairs, not even looking to see whether he was following her.

He was, tight at her heels up the stairs and through the door of the little room.

'Look at this,' she said. 'The carpenter said it was a lumber room, storage room, but I don't think so. Right next to the chimney like this? It should be warm in the winter, but it's as cold as ice. Can you imagine why?'

'It might have been intended as a child's room,' he suggested. 'Maybe they closed it up when they found it

68

wouldn't stay warm. What's that?' The black carving protruding from its wrapping caught his eye.

'I don't know. It looks very like a mask my husband brought back from a trip to Haiti – the same kind of wood, the same feeling to it.'

'It's not a mask.'

'I know. It just feels like, somehow, African.'

'Around here, anything "African" means the slave trade,' he said, turning the thing over and over in his hands. 'If it is old, it's probably a slaver relic or souvenir. Where have I seen something like this before? Somewhere. It reminds me of things in old Captain Nathaniel Bone's book—'

'Captain Bone! You mean there really is a Captain Bone?'

'Was. Captain Nathaniel Bone. Of course. A slaver captain in the mid-1700s; got religion; became an abolitionist, well before his time. His name might have been "Boehn" originally. He lived in Chester, just down the road from Byers' Fault. He believed Byers was a servant of the devil – John Byers kept on slaving after Bone gave it up. Then, let's see. Bone got the Chester people stirred up about voodoo, and they all got drunk one night and went up and wiped out the Byers' Fault, killed everyone. Except John Byers, of course, and his son, William. The Captain seemed to take great satisfaction in that. Never did repent of it, either.'

'How do you know all this?' She was amazed, mouth open. Charlotte Grafton had mentioned the massacre, and Mahlia had been too dense even to inquire about it. 'About this massacre.'

'Oh, the Captain noted it all down in his journal. He was Charlotte's great-great-great-something, uncle, I think. Whatever the relationship, she ended up with the book. I've got it in the car right now to return to her.' He blinked owlishly at her. 'After making some copies, of course. A couple for me; one for the university library, one for my publisher. He always pretends to think I make this stuff up.'

'Which you would never do,' she remarked distractedly. Captain Bone. 'Is the Captain's name a familiar one around here? Do people in Millingham talk about him a lot?'

'I'd wager that no one but Charlotte knows the man ever existed. Why? You went all white when I mentioned his name.'

'My son,' she confessed. 'We had no sooner moved in here than he began talking about this new friend of his named Captain Bone.'

'Charlotte Grafton, I'd imagine. She probably mentioned the name and your son took it from there. Kids do that sometimes. My sister's six-year-old daughter named her cat Henry the Eighth. She heard the name on TV and liked it.'

'I suppose.' And yet, she thought, the Captain seemed to have such definite opinions. 'Captain Bone wasn't a pirate, by any chance? He didn't search for buried treasure?'

'Pounded the Bible a bit, preached more than a little. Engaged a bit of private vengeance in the massacre, from what I understand. I never heard he was a pirate.'

'Robby thinks so. He talks about Captain Bone and buried treasure.'

'Don't worry about it. My sister works with gifted children, and she says they're the most likely to make up long, involved stories. Now, can I look at the fireplace and chimney?'

'Of course. And you can look anywhere else in the house you like. And in the barn.'

'Can I have these old newspapers?'

'If you want them. Why?' She was mystified by his eagerness.

'Part of the project. I'm covering the history of the area right up to the present. The *Millingham Monitor* went out of business twenty years ago, and I'm not sure anyone has a complete set of file copies.'

'You're welcome to them. I'm going to have Charlotte's granddaughter Georgina vacuum up here, then put up some rods and use it for an off-season closet, so take what you like.'

'You're very helpful. But that's only half of what I came for.'

'Oh?'

He caught the wary tone. 'Oh, nothing burdensome, no,

not at all. I simply want permission to wander up over your hill there and explore in Byers' Fault. My fiancée and I would like to look it over tomorrow, and then next week, if you approve, we'd like to bring some students out for a little early American archaeological dig.'

'You want my permission? To dig?'

'Well, Byers' Fault belongs to you.'

'Does it really!' She was amazed, had never thought about it, had never realized that several hundred acres could cover so much area. If she had thought about it at all, she had assumed her land ended at the foot of the hills, where the meadow stopped. 'I had no idea. Well, of course you can go wherever you like.' She caught him staring at her with an interested, half-amused, but very personal expression. 'You must think I'm very silly not to have known that.'

'Not at all. I was just standing here guessing that you hadn't had the place long. Charlotte didn't tell me that, but I'll bet it's true. Your land runs back a full mile from the road right up to the ridge, and it includes most of Byers' Fault. Your driveway used to extend into Byers' Fault as its main road – the crossroad was right there where your mailbox is. And your land is half a mile wide, too, in case you didn't know. That old graveyard is right at your corner.'

'How did you know?'

'I looked it up. Can't go digging in people's backyards without permission, and we have to know who owns where we want to dig. You'd be surprised how protective some people are. I should think anyone would be interested in the history of wherever they live, but some people don't want us anywhere around.'

She counted on her fingers. 'We've owned this place for about four months, and we've been living here less than six weeks. It seems longer, but that's all it is. And all I've done so far is remodel and clean up the pond and help put on a play-school picnic.'

He gave her that bemused look again, the one that told her he was looking at her as a woman rather than a property owner. Flushing, she went past him onto the stair landing

71

and halfway down the stairs, waiting for him to fold the newspapers into a manageable bundle. She led him through the hall and into the oldest part of the house, the dining room and kitchen. He stared at the fireplace for several minutes, took five or six photographs of it from various angles, then followed her onto the porch, where Robby came running up to be introduced and told what Seepy's intentions were.

'Byers' Fault is right up there,' he said, motioning toward the dark line of forest to the west. 'Just beyond the meadow and a strip of forest, right through the notch where the brook comes through. Those are real pretty woods, though you'll need to watch for poison ivy. All that's left standing of the old village is a few low foundation walls. I scouted it out a few years ago. The village was burned, so we expect to find quite a bit of charcoal, and anything under that should date from the time of the settlement. Might get some cores we could use for tree ring dating, not that it's terribly important. We know pretty well when the place was founded.'

'What are you looking for?' asked Robby, curious as always.

'Oh, buttons, pieces of pottery, glass bottles, coins, nails, gunflints, stuff like that. Digging around in Chester last year we found an old metal box full of letters and deeds – fantastic. One of my students got a major publication out of it.'

'That doesn't sound very interesting. Isn't there any treasure up there?'

'Well, Rob, so far as I'm concerned, buttons and bottles and things like that are treasures, because they tell us the way people lived back then. You know, lots of stuff never got written down, and there are many things we just don't know about how our ancestors lived. So I'd really rather find a bottle than a piece of gold. It tells me more.'

Robby frowned over this intelligence and ran off, presumably to advise Captain Bone of heresy in the ranks. Seepy and Mahlia stood looking at him, both amused. Seepy began to point out the landmarks of Mahlia's property, locating corners for her, the southeast one at the Primack border, the northeast one at the old graveyard. 'That's the old Chester graveyard. Interesting stones there, though they're getting hard to read.'

When he had run out of small talk, she said firmly, 'Well, feel free to climb around up there. If you're going to be taking some students, stop by; Robby and I may go with you. We really ought to find out where our boundaries are.'

He gave her his card, promised to send her his bona fides, seemed reluctant to leave but did so at last, turning to wave from the gate.

And Mahlia, aware of her own reluctance to see him go, mumbled to herself, 'Badger, damn it, you had better not leave me here alone for much longer. My mind is as faithful as the stars, but the rest of me is just plain lonely for company.'

CHAPTER NINE

'Your friend, Captain Bone, was a real sea captain,' Mahlia said at breakfast, unthinkingly.

'I know,' Robby said, making owl eyes at her. 'I told you that.' He stirred his cocoa with great attention, making a whirlpool in the cup. Robby always stirred everything, Mahlia thought, even things better left alone.

Elaine chirruped and threw a spoonful of cereal across the room. Mahlia sighed as she took a cloth to the mess. 'I mean he was a *real* sea captain. He was Charlotte Grafton's great-great-great-something or other.'

'I know,' said Robby in an infuriatingly adult voice. 'He told me. He told me all about Charlotte. She had a very unhappy love affair. Her lover died. His name was Joseph.'

Mahlia froze. There had been a kind of casual compassion in the boy's voice, an emotion too old for him, too understanding.

'Really? When was that?'

'When she was just a girl. They were very much in love, Captain Bone says, and he died of con . . . I forgot the word.'

'Consumption?'

'That's it. He died of that. He's waiting for her, though. They'll be together again.'

She could not keep her face from paling, the skin on her arms from prickling as though from a cold draft. 'That may be a little crowded,' Mahlia said. 'She had a husband later, didn't she? And he died, too?'

'Oh, sure. But her husband didn't wait. He went right on. Captain Bone says it wasn't the same thing at all.'

'Oh.' She turned on him, almost angry. What would

Badger think if he came home to hear Robby talking this way? He would blame her, which certainly wasn't fair. 'What else did Captain Bone say?'

'That's all about Charlotte. He knows some stuff about other people, too, but he says it's none of my business.'

'And Mrs Grafton is your business?'

'No. Except she knows a lot, and Captain Bone says I should pay attention when she talks, and he told me some stuff so's I'd understand how she got so wise.'

Mahlia shut her lips over an emerging cry of protest. This kind of talk could not be entirely out of Robby's imagination, and she questioned whether it was entirely healthy. It certainly wouldn't be acceptable to Badger. Something had to be done to stop it. She would have to do something specific, arrange for some daily companions, perhaps.

'Finish your milk,' she said in irritation. 'You and Elaine and I are going into Millingham to buy some shoes and Elaine some diapers and all of us some groceries.'

'And ice cream for after lunch?'

'I suppose so.'

'Chocolate with nuts,' he demanded in a firm, unyielding voice. Seeing the expression on her face, he decided on a hug as a better sales tool. 'Please.'

She relented. 'If available. Trot now. Go wash your face.'

She watched his retreating little form with worried eyes. Captain Bone was becoming real to her, too, a troublesome presence. What had Seepy Paggott said about him? A Bible-thumping convert; a burner of towns; leader of a band of murdering villagers. 'Suppose,' she told herself, 'suppose it's the ghost of the real Captain Bone.' She did suppose it, trying the idea on for size. If this were the ghost of the man Seepy had described, then one would expect violence and hostility, a fanatic religiosity, perhaps. Not at all the impression one got from Robby.

What did one get from Robby? A picture of a compassionate, willful man, perhaps a little fussy. Someone who put things away to save them for the owners. Who told a child tales – true or false – about someone else, but said it was in order to make the child understand why they acted as they did. A strange personality, surely, but not a murderer or a fanatic.

So? So, it might not be a ghost? Just another imaginary friend, somehow juiced up with things Robby had heard elsewhere? Mahlia shook her head ruefully at her own half-hysteria, trying to convince herself that was what it had been.

'You may try to convince yourself you don't believe in ghosts, Mahlia, but you know better,' she told herself in a fit of honesty. She did know better. There were such things, she had seen them. And ghost or no ghost, Mahlia would have to find out where Robby was actually getting his information. About Charlotte and her long-ago lover, for example. That wasn't altogether appropriate information for a child. Could it be from television, some story he had watched unbeknownst to Mahlia and then translated into his own world? From Cindy Robinson, perhaps? That young lady had a fund of surprisingly adult comments upon the world in general, and her family were longtime community residents who might be expected to know ancient history about the townsfolk. Perhaps they had discussed it in front of the children.

'Ready,' Robby announced from the door. He had his sword with him, but Mahlia pretended not to notice.

At the end of the drive they turned left onto Old Chester Road and rumbled over the wooden bridge that crossed the brook, the same brook that flowed out of the lily pond, augmented at this point by other small flows from the surrounding hills. On their left green pastures and woods-lined streamlets stretched to the foot of the dark forest. On their right that same forest ignored the interruption of meadow and road to make a shadowy wall that breathed wet coolness at them as they drove.

'Rained last night,' Mahlia commented.

'Ayup,' said Robby. Then, seeing the laughter around her mouth, he commented hastily, 'That's what Mrs Grafton says. Ayup. And bahn. And things like that.'

76

'Quite all right, Robby-lad. If you want to sound a proper New Englander, you go right ahead. Your daddy will be monstrously amused.'

They passed the rutted turnoff of the abandoned and overgrown town of Chester, then swung right to the junction with Chyne Road, which had more or less paralleled their route half a mile to the east. A mile farther brought them to the iron bridge over Mill River, into which the many nameless brooks had flowed, and thence onto River Street. On one hand were the dingy bulks of three-storey brick mills, vacant now and ripe for rehabilitation; on the other hand, the strong, noisy flow of water over ruined dams. Their tires rumbled over a rail-road crossing; then there were three tall white steeples, cobbled streets, and the business center of Millingham, such as it was. Two good markets. An ancient, ivy-covered library of such modest size as to be almost unnoticeable. A small branch of a well-known department store. The various accoutrements without which modern man could not survive – appliance shops, TV stores, used car lots, new car lots.

'Millingham,' said Robby, fully satisfied with it. It had ice cream and a toy store. What more could anyone want?

'Millingham looks like a peaceful place to me,' said Mahlia. 'I think it might be polite to leave your sword in the car. Not to show weapons unnecessarily, so to speak.'

'You think that might be rude?' He sounded doubtful of this, but rudeness was something Badger always firmly disallowed.

'Rather, yes. Come on, now. Shoes for you first, and then groceries.' She got out of the car and buckled on Elaine's Snugli, settling the crowing baby on her back with an up-and-down jounce that made Elaine giggle. She took Robby by one slightly unwilling hand and set off across the street, only to be stopped by a voice hailing her. The great, square Duplessis car was stopped in the middle of the street, Jessie Casternaught Duplessis beckoning from the window with a languid hand.

'Mahlia Ettison. Do let me see the baby!' The voice was

a coo, a parody of grandmotherly interest. Something in that voice set Mahlia's teeth on edge, even as she smiled with every evidence of politeness.

'You don't have grandchildren?' she asked, wondering at the quick, almost hostile expression that fled across the woman's face like a shadow.

'No, I haven't been that fortunate. Isn't she sweet. What's her name, Mahlia?'

'Elaine.'

'Elaine. The Lily Maid? And how's the young man today?' Jessica Casternaught Duplessis reached out of the car window to run a hand over Robby's hair and cheek. He stepped back, his dignity much offended, and smoothed his hair with both hands. The woman laughed, turning to someone at her side.

'Lois, isn't he delicious? You haven't met, have you? Mahlia, my daughter Lois. Mrs Ettison, Lois. She bought our old house.' Mahlia took the languid brown hand that was offered and smiled politely at yet another Duplessis face. The same smile; the same hair. 'Speaking of which,' Jessica went on, 'I understand you've transformed the old cow pond into something quite attractive.'

Mahlia nodded. 'Well, I like to think so.'

'Didn't have any trouble?'

'Trouble?'

'With the pond. With . . . ah, drainage?'

'Not at all. It was really just a matter of doing some planting around it.' And in it, she thought to herself. But that was no one's business, really. What was the woman after?

'Well, lovely to have seen you. Nice to see you again, Robby. We will see you again soon.' She leaned forward, tapped on the glass before her, and was driven away. Lois had not spoken, had barely acknowledged the introduction.

'I don't like her,' said Robby.

'Now, Rob.'

'Well, I don't. I am not delicious. Girls are delicious.'

'You mean sugar and spice and everything nice?'

'That's right. That's what Charlotte says. And she says I'm made out of puppy dogs' tails. And snails. And something else.'

'Snips,' said Mahlia.

'I don't know what that is.'

'Neither do I,' Mahlia said, staring after the great square Rolls as it turned the corner. Strange woman. Strange family.

Both shoes and groceries had been accounted for when they encountered Claude Paggott outside Millingham's one decent motel. 'Mrs Ettison! Mahlia! Hey, great to run into you. I've got some information for you. Wait a minute. There's someone I want you to meet.' He turned, beckoning, and was joined in a moment by a lean girl in blue jeans and a sweat shirt that said, 'Archaeologists dig it.'

'Marcia Talent, my fiancée. This is Mahlia Ettison, and her son.' He was bubbling, waving his hands.

'My son, Robby,' Mahlia finished for him, smiling at his obvious enthusiasm.

'Marcy's my assistant this season. We thought we'd go out to Byers' Fault today and take a preliminary look.'

'I'm looking forward to it,' the girl said in a cold, patronizing voice. She had swept Mahlia with one swift, dismissing look from pale, predatory eyes, and now twisted thin, blood-red lips in almost a parody of politeness. 'It's good of you to give us permission to dig, and it's nice to meet you. I'm sorry, I have to run. Seepy, would you excuse me? I promised Natalie I'd call her this morning before ten, and it's pushing ten right now.'

He waved her off, turning to Mahlia and Robby again with a wide grin, seemingly unaware of Marcia's rude and unsociable haste. Over his shoulder Mahlia saw a familiar form turn the corner and come toward them, and her heart did a quick extra pump. Well, well, the whole family was in town. John Duplessis.

Seepy bubbled on. 'That thing you found at your place, that carving – I found out what it was. I called an anthropologist friend who spent some time in the Caribbean. From my description, he says the design on the wood is probably a *vèvè*. Two of them, really, one on each side of that piece of mahogany.'

'Lovely,' said Mahlia, 'if I knew what that was.'

'Oh, what could I call them? Let's see. A kind of summoning formula or signature, I guess, used to call up certain African gods – *loa*, they're called. It probably dates to the time of the slave trade and might have been made by a slave, or maybe by one of old John Byers' wives. My bet is it's several hundred years old. I'll return it to you later, if you don't mind. I want to show it to Lars Sigurdson. He's the one I—'

His enthusiastic outpouring was interrupted by John Duplessis, who greeted Mahlia as though she had been quite alone. 'Well, hello, Mahlia Ettison. We met at the picnic, remember? John Duplessis.' He had come up beside them as Seepy talked, and turned to the archaeologist now with one of those ultra-charming smiles. 'We haven't met.'

'Seepy Paggott,' he said, pumping the hand that was offered to him. 'Down from the university to do a little digging in the area.'

'Digging?'

'Byers' Fault. Oh, maybe do a little more at the old Chester site, too.' He grinned. 'We've already found some interesting things in Mahlia's house – interesting, that is, from a historical perspective.'

'Have you really?' An interested quirk of the eyebrows, a hooded glance at Mahlia. Deep inside her something responded to that glance, a shiver, almost like anticipation.

'Oh, yes. Mahlia discovered a secret room,' Seepy bubbled, 'full of artifacts.'

'What would those have been?' John asked. Something in his tone made her uncomfortably aware that the secret room, if it could be called that, had been in his own home and that he might have a very legitimate interest in its contents.

'Trash,' she said firmly, 'except to someone like Mr Paggott, who likes old newspapers and things. I'm afraid it's out of my field. Oh, by the way, I met your mother again a few minutes ago. And your sister Lois.'

'Well, yes, the whole family's gathering for one of Jessie's dos. Next week sometime.' He turned back toward Seepy, as though to continue the conversation.

Elaine stirred in her carrier, made a fretful noise. Mahlia came to herself at the sound, pulled herself sharply into the present. 'Seepy, it's great to have seen you. Good luck with your explorations. John, sorry to have to run, but this baby needs changing and I have two more stops to make. See you again soon.' She waved herself off, smiling, feeling as though she were running from something, though she had no idea why.

'Why are we in such a hurry?' complained Robby, who had been listening to Seepy with open mouth and complete attention.

'Elaine's wet. And I have to stop two more places.'

'She's always wet. Was I always wet when I was her age?'

'Probably. Most babies are.'

As they got into the car, she saw Seepy still beaming at John Duplessis, talking a mile a minute, arms gesturing, hands pointing; the other man nodded, not looking very interested. As they drove away, she saw Seepy return to the motel, John staring after him. As they drove by, he looked up, saw her, waved and smiled, eyes alight, and she was all at once aware of how she looked. The shirt she was wearing was wrinkled from the straps, damp from Elaine's hands and mouth. Her hair was untidy. Self-consciously she smoothed it and waved back, careful not to seem too eager. He was simply too good-looking. If Jeannie Horan was any evidence, he had women falling all over him, and Mahlia didn't want him thinking she was one of them.

Deciding not to think of John Duplessis or anyone else, she went on with her errands and drove home, Robby singing tunelessly yo-ho-hos beside her, some kind of sea chanty he had undoubtedly learned from Captain Bone.

CHAPTER TEN

Little more than an hour after Mahlia left him on the street
in Millingham, Seepy Paggott found himself pushing his
way between two towering fir trees to look across the glade
among the thicket-grown hillocks of Byers' Fault. He hoped
Marcy would wait for him while he made this totally
unplanned expedition, but the unexpected opportunity to
meet someone who had actually found artifacts in the area
had been irresistible. Even the warning to come alone did
not seem out of line. Seepy had dealt with self-styled recluses
and mountain men before. Some of them were as nervous
as deer, taking flight from any but the most innocent
encounters. Seepy prided himself on looking innocent when
the occasion warranted – dealing with landowners and
developers and farm widows, suspicious as old dogs. He put
on his most butter-wouldn't-melt expression and peered
between the trees. If the informant who had driven him here
was right, the hermit's campsite should be somewhere at
the center of the old town, among the overgrown hillocks
that were all that was left of the homes that had once
sheltered old John Byers's offspring.

'Mr Carfor?' he called. 'Mr Carfor, can I talk to you,
please?'

No response. He moved into the clearing, searching the
area for any sign of habitation. Nothing. Absolute silence;
still air; no birds singing. He looked down, listening intently
for any sound. Nothing. 'Mr Carfor, I've been told you
might help me. I'd be willing to pay for your help. I'm a
history teacher from the university.' History teacher was
close enough to the truth. Likely the fellow wouldn't know

the word 'archaeologist,' and there was no point in confusing him. 'I've come to do some digging here in Byers' Fault. Trying to find things the people who lived here may have left – bottles, crocks or china, things like that?' One had to be careful not to hint at buried treasure. Nothing shut up an informant faster than thinking they might be sitting on a treasure trove.

There was no response except a faint rustling in the trees as though dried leaves rubbed together. He walked forward, stopping suddenly as the rustling sound was repeated, then noticed that he had walked across some kind of design drawn upon the ground. Lines drawn in flour or meal – a very purposeful drawing. The ground had been smoothed flat, all leaves brushed away.

Well, so the man who camped here was not only a recluse but a ritualist of some kind. He stared at the remaining lines. Pollen? Something yellowish, at any rate. Pollen was used by the southwestern Indians, but Carfor didn't suggest any Hopi or Navajo implications. He couldn't tell what the picture had been meant to be. A kind of ornamental cross? Probably a kind of hex sign, something meant to keep away devils – like police and park rangers and other interfering types.

'Mr Carfor?'

Silence. The rustling again, closer. Seepy made a bet with himself that the hermit was right out there in the woods, drawing closer, peering between the branches. If he just stayed where he was, perhaps the man would get used to his being there and say something. Seepy took out his pipe, went through the long process of filling it and lighting it, then stood quiet, head wreathed in smoke.

There was a child standing across the clearing in the shade of the trees. A naked child. Seepy took the pipe from his mouth and waved away the smoke, and the vision disappeared; the figure must have been an illusion created by the smoke and the shadow. He ran his hand over the back of his neck where the hair stood on end, prickling, then shrugged uneasily. The place was too quiet. Birds should be calling. Even if the hermit was out there in the woods, the birds should have gone on with their usual chatter, their ordinary hot-afternoon territorial comments. When he had been here the previous year, the sapsuckers had been full of loud, nesting-site noise, screaming, 'What, what, what?' and making continual di-di-di dit-dit-dit drumtaps on the trees.

Too quiet. And too empty. Mr Carfor wasn't home now, if, indeed, he had ever been. Best get back to Millingham to make apologies to Marcy.

And suddenly he saw the hermit, standing back among the trees, a dark figure with a white shirt-front and a battered top hat, among the children – the naked children who seemed to be running toward Seepy like misty smoke. Disbelieving, he took off his glasses to rub his eyes. He felt the glasses snatched from his hand as if in play and blindly reached out to grab them from the child's hand. He had time only to feel with terror the dry, papery skin that pressed around him before his eyes were within reach of the tiny, terribly sharp fingernails . . .

CHAPTER ELEVEN

When the phone rang in midafternoon, Mahlia knew it was John Duplessis even before she answered it.

'You ran away so fast I didn't have a chance to ask you if you'd go to the University Shakespeare Festival performance with me on Saturday. They're sometimes surprisingly good, sometimes amazingly bad, but don't you feel it's a civic duty to support their efforts?'

'No,' her head said. 'No, I'd rather not leave the children.'

'Where is it?' her mouth asked, unheeding of the warnings. 'At the university?'

'Heavens, no,' he said, laughing. 'Even my dedication to civic duty doesn't extend to a two-hour drive – four, round-trip. Not that I wouldn't love your company. No, it's at the community hall here in Millingham. Each year they prepare one play for tour – minimum costumes, minimum lighting – and trot it around to the benighted heathen. Do say you'll go.'

'I'll have to see about a sitter,' she temporized, aghast at herself. Had the man hypnotized her, for God's sake?

'Of course you do. I'd forgotten for the moment that you had the wee ones at home. I'll call you back tomorrow – Wednesday. During the afternoon?'

'All right,' she was saying. 'That sounds like fun.' While all the time part of her was sternly lecturing, 'No, this is a mistake, Mahlia. Not the right thing to do.'

'Oh, by the way,' he went on, disarmingly. 'My sisters, Lois and Harriet, will be coming along. And maybe my brother Bill, though he ordinarily scorns the arts. Jessica, too, if we can get her out of the house. I know you wouldn't want a tête-à-tête with your husband away. Small-town gossip and all.'

Then he was gone and the phone hummed in her ear. Very faintly someone said on the line, 'I told him he should have gone to Louisiana for that . . .' Then only silence, and she became aware that she was holding the phone, hardly breathing.

'What's the matter?' asked Robby, brows knotted into an expression of intent concern. 'You look all funny.'

'Nothing, really.' She carefully replaced the phone, feeling as she did so that she was laying down an explosive of some kind, willing it not to go off. 'I just agreed to go with the Duplessis family to a play Saturday night, and I'm wondering if I should leave you and Elaine with Georgina at night. I never have, you know.'

'Well, you can't sit around here forever,' he replied. 'That's what Captain Bone says. Only you should be very careful who you 'sociate with. I'm pretty sure he doesn't like Mr Duplessis at all.'

Outside the window a blackbird swooped from left to right to sway upon a twig, chirring at its mate in the grasses along the stream. A little wind tossed the branch, seeming to toss the bird into motion, and he fled away along the wind trail, calling to his mate as he passed. Mahlia stood very still in the center of the moment, wanting not to ask, asking anyhow.

'Did he say why?'

'Nope. He won't tell me anything about him at all. I just don't think he does.'

Guardian of the household, Mahlia told herself. Even at age five, he will guard me for his father, and he doesn't think I should be going out with men. 'Could I go out with Seepy?' she asked, expecting a similar opinion from Captain Bone.

'I like Seepy,' Robby said unexpectedly. 'That'd be fun. I'm hungry. Can I have some more ice cream?'

'If you'll promise to have a short nap right after.'

Robby stirred his ice cream until it was paste, then carved mountains in it, making it last. Mahlia gave up waiting for him to finish and tried to call Georgina while he sat there, accusing her with his eyes. No answer. She was probably out doing day work for someone, or baby-sitting, or helping Charlotte Grafton in the enormous Grafton vegetable garden at her daughter's place.

While Robby napped, a car turned into the drive, and she went eagerly to the door, hoping for a special delivery letter from Badger. It was only Ossie Jeremy, his hands full of paint buckets and small tools.

'I had some time this afternoon, so I thought I'd put up those clothes rods you wanted and paint the room. Only take an hour or two, and Georgina said it was all cleaned out.'

'Yes. She came by yesterday with a man in an old, rackety truck, and when they left it was empty as a used eggshell.'

'Well, this is some good white paint I had left over. If you're paintin' a closet, no sense piddlin' around over this color or that color. Make it white and no nonsense. You keep that raccoony boy of yours out of there until I'm finished. He stirs my paint when I'm not lookin' and drips it all over. I'll lock the room when I'm through and put the key up on the mantel here.'

And with that he went toiling upstairs, where she could hear his patient monologue going on and on and on.

And another car came, a strange car, first passing the gate, then stopping to turn laboriously on the roadway and drive in, waveringly, as though doubtful. When Mahlia went to the door she found the girl she had met in town that morning fidgeting on the doorstep, tapping her foot in obvious self-important impatience.

'Marcy Talent, Ms Ettison, remember me? Seepy introduced us this morning? Right. Well, anyhow, have you seen him? I was supposed to meet him in the coffee shop at eleven-thirty and then we were coming out here, but he didn't show up.' She was staring at Mahlia as she spoke, a challenging look, as though accusing her of making off with Seepy Paggott.

Mahlia stiffened, but managed to keep her voice pleasant. 'I left him talking with someone when we went to our car,

Marcy. Then he was heading back into the motel when I drove by. That would have been about ten-thirty or so.'

'Oh, I saw him then. I was making a call from the lobby and I saw him go by. He was supposed to meet me in the coffee shop an hour later. Like I say, he didn't show. All his things were already in the car, and the keys were in it. I've told him repeatedly to lock the car, but he's foolishly naive about people. I've got your what-you-call-it, that design carved on the piece of mahogany. Seepy called Lars Sigurdson last night – he's in the anthropology department – to find out what it was, and when Lars called back I took the call.'

'I still don't understand what it is.'

'Well, it's really not my field. Something African, is what Professor Sigurdson said. A kind of symbolic rendering of the name of the *loa*, that's the god. I shouldn't have said African, really. The derivation is African, but he was really talking more about Haiti and other places in the Caribbean. Sigurdson did a lot of work there back in the seventies. Of course, he hasn't done anything since, but Seepy finds the man admirable, Lord knows why.'

'It's not just some kind of tourist souvenir?'

'Probably not that, but I doubt it has any value,' she said, half sneering. 'I think Seepy said it was probably quite old, but then he hasn't had it tested yet. It's in the trunk of Seepy's car. I'll give it back to you now, if you like. Seepy wanted to take it back and have Lars look at it.' Her attitude implied that only a fool would pass up any such opportunity, no matter that Marcy considered the man incompetent.

Mahlia was suddenly weary of her and simply didn't care. 'Keep it for now. I haven't seen Seepy. It's strange that he didn't meet you, but I'm sure there's some explanation. Did you leave a message for him at the motel?'

'Yes. I told him I'd be here, and then if he didn't show up, I'd leave his car at the police station and take the bus back. I already checked with Stephen Ware, at the police department. I knew him before. We did some digging at Chester last year, and Steve Ware got us the permits.'

'Well, I'll certainly give him the message if he turns up here.' Even though she wanted to be rid of the woman, Mahlia could not deny her sense of appropriate hospitality. 'Would you like some tea? Or coffee?'

'Not really. I drank about ten cups of coffee waiting for Seepy. And if I'm going to get back, I'll have to catch the four o'clock bus. No, I'd better run for it. Just give him the message, if you please. I can't imagine what he was thinking of.' And she was gone, making another of those laborious turns and then weaving down the driveway and out onto Old Chester Road where she turned right, then left toward the developments along Chyne Road, and disappeared eastward. Mahlia rubbed her forehead. She hadn't had a headache for two or three days, but one had started when the girl had asked for Seepy.

'Where did Seepy go?' It was Robby, sleepy-eyed, clutching his sword for comfort as though it were a stuffed animal.

'She doesn't know, honey. He seems to have wandered off somewhere.'

Suddenly, for no discernible reason, Robby began to cry. Great, gemlike tears flowed from his eyes. 'Seepy. Poor Seepy,' he said, then in a tone of childlike complaint, 'I'm thirsty.'

She gave him a drink and took two aspirins, put Robby back to bed, tucked him in tightly, and then sat there as he slept, his face rosy and warm beneath the moist ringlets of hair. The headache deepened, and she lay down beside him, hoping a nap would cure it.

When Robby woke, he was full of plans for quelling some pirate insurrection and did not seem to remember his earlier unhappiness. Mahlia thought he had probably had a bad dream, as she herself had had. The nap hadn't helped.

Ossie Jeremy had finished his work and departed, locking the door carefully behind him and leaving the key on the mantel as he had said he would do. Mahlia took the key and unlocked the door, stared at the pristine area that reeked of very wet paint, then hastily closed and locked it again. It was only a big closet. A big, very old closet.

There was to be yet one more visitor that day. Evening brought the tootle of a car horn as Jeannie Horan swung expertly into the drive and stopped at the front door with a great splash of gravel. 'Hey, Mahlia, I've come to give you a present.' She backed from the car with a basket in her hand. 'A gift, for housewarming. I picked up two cases of this, and it's so good I have to share it.'

'Housewarming? Look at all those bottles! Jeannie!'

'Well, yes, why not? You wouldn't want to have a real housewarming until Badger gets back, would you? But you're entitled to one, right? So, what better than a new friend toasting a new house with some sort-of-old wine? Look at this.' She lifted a bottle from the basket and smoothed her hand over the label. 'Château Hortevie, 1978, St Julien. Lovely. I thought you and I could have a little with crackers and pâté, which I also happen to have in the car, while Robby fights off the dragons and before I have to go home and cook for the family. How about that?'

Mahlia shrugged. What about that, indeed? One could hardly object, and truthfully, she felt no desire to. 'Jeannie, this was a very nice thought. Thanks so much.'

'I can't stay long. Long enough for one glass.' She draped a sinuous arm around Mahlia's shoulder and hugged her. 'Besides, I wanted to say thanks for all your help with the kids.'

'My pleasure.'

'Your pleasure, my ass. You did the whole thing with a kind of grim deliberation. I know make-work when I see it. What were you doing, staying busy?'

Mahlia reddened, turned away to fetch wine glasses and a corkscrew, returned with her composure restored. 'Jeannie, I was keeping busy. Even with Robby and the baby, the time drags. I'll be glad to have Badger home.'

'Well, share a bottle of this with him when he comes. And take care until he gets here, lady. There are varmints in these hills.' She took a slice of pâté, seemed about to say something else, then shook her head and made some inconsequential remark about the weather. They chatted, saying nothing much, while the sun fell behind the broken line of forest.

Jeannie was staring westward at the line of forest. 'You know, I don't think I ever realized before how close you are to Byers' Fault. It must be just a little way inside the woods.'

'It is. In fact, just yesterday I gave some people from Vermont, from the university there, permission to dig up there.' She described Seepy and Marcia Talent, not bothering to hide either her liking for the former or her dislike for the latter.

'Funny. I wonder what happened to him? Another thing: if you're that close to Byers' Fault, I'll bet you can see the Duplessis house from right here. Look, see that ridge running up behind the first one? There's a road just down behind there. The Duplessis house is almost at the top of that ridge. If you got up early in the morning, I'm sure you'd see the sun reflected off their windows. I'll bet John Duplessis can look right into your bedroom window with his telescope.'

'Telescope?' Mahlia faltered.

'Oh, he's an astronomy nut. At least, so he told me once.' Jeannie threw a sideways glance at Mahlia, was met with a curious, half-apprehensive look. 'He told me he had a telescope. I suppose he still has it. Not that it matters – just keep your window shades pulled, sweetie. And, Mahlia – I'd be careful of him.' She flushed. 'Just a word to the wise, that's all. He's a real charmer, almost a damned hypnotist, so be careful. Lord, look at the time. I've got to run.'

She was out of her chair and into her car before Mahlia could comment. Wheels spun, gravel flew, the car swept down the drive and away toward Millingham. Robby came running from the barn.

'Can I have some wine?'

'If you like. With water.'

He sipped, made a face, sipped once or twice more to prove he liked it, then grabbed a handful of crackers and ran off once more.

'Supper in half an hour,' she called after him, but did not move to go prepare it. The shadows lengthened. Her head was throbbing, a rhythmic pulsing. She couldn't fight it, and the pain was wearing her down. Far off in the woods came a sound, half muffled, as though someone had been choked in mid-cry. 'Owl,' she told herself, half believing it until she heard the shots, three of them, spaced out in the deliberate sequence of a signal.

She waited. Above the line of hills the sun bulged, a bloody ball, sinking beneath the dark, broken line of distant trees. Finally there was only a thin, red line, a knife edge of brilliance.

And it was then that she saw the stocky form of Paul Goode emerge from the distant line of trees and trudge toward her house, a black, troll-like approach, head down.

When he looked up at her from the foot of the porch steps, his face was a half shadowed, half-pallid reflection from her windows. 'Mrs Ettison, sorry to bother you, but I have to use your phone.' She took him inside, not questioning, afraid she already knew. All the visions she had refused to see for weeks, for months, crowded at the edge of her mind. She rejected them, holding herself rigid, still refusing to see them, even as the pain grew more and more intense and her vision blurred.

She barely heard him as he called for the coroner and the ambulance, and Robby came to stand beside her, tears rolling down his cheeks as he repeated what he had said earlier, over and over again.

'Poor Seepy. Poor, poor Seepy.' And at his words the dam broke, the pain erupted, and the vision came upon her, unstoppable as a tide.

CHAPTER TWELVE

Outside in the troubled dark the north wind was rising. Mahlia lay on her bed where Paul Goode had put her, carrying her up the stairs as effortlessly as if she had been Robby's size. Robby was snuggled beside her, half covered with a blanket, wide-eyed, as still as a small frightened animal. When the blackness had cleared, she had reached for the bedroom extension and called Molly. There had been nothing else to do. It didn't matter what promises had been made, what foolish decisions had been made. What Badger wanted was irrelevant. The swirling black and red and gray of her vision had contained a threat, to herself, to Robby. It had flooded over her in a terrifying, unstoppable torrent. There was no way she could pretend to meet it alone.

Molly had promised to be there before morning. Oh, yes, thank God, Molly. And maybe Martha and Simoney, if they could get away on such short notice, though Molly had said something to indicate that Martha might not be willing to come at all. Martha was angry, Molly said. Molly herself was angry, but not too angry to listen. Mahlia, waiting, felt a peculiar combination of relief and guilt. Relief that they were coming; guilt at having called them when she had promised Badger she wouldn't; guilt at having made the promise in the first place; relief at having broken it. What could she have done otherwise? Packed up the children, put them in the car and simply left? Gone back to New York, to Vivian's doorstep: 'Vivian, terribly sorry, but the place in the country is haunted. There's something up there killing people. I had this vision, see, and I think it's after me.' How to convey this sense of personal threat, the horror, the blind fear the vision had brought? How to convey the hideous vagueness of it? How to convey that one could have a vision without actually seeing anything at all? Horror, she could say, and what did that mean? 'Little pale shadows, Vivian, which were quite horrible.'

Or perhaps she could have said, 'Vivian, I'm terribly sorry to impose, but it was simply too lonely for me there with Badger gone.'

Yes. She could have done something like that. Every instinct encouraged it. But she hadn't.

Outside on the drive the ambulance was pulling away. Men were gathered there. Some of them started purposefully for the house. Cradling Robby against her shoulder, she went downstairs to the door.

'Are you feeling better?' Paul Goode asked her from the door. In his experience women didn't faint all that often, but Mahlia had fainted while he was calling the coroner, and he was worried about her, even though she looked better after her brief lie-down. 'I checked on the baby – she's sound asleep. If you hadn't come around, I was going to call Aunt Charlotte. Wouldn't you like to put the little fellow to bed?'

It was almost ten o'clock, and Robby had had nothing to eat except the crackers he had snitched early in the evening. 'I think we both need something to eat, and he probably doesn't want to be alone,' she said, cuddling him in her lap. She had looked into the nursery on her way by to see Elaine sleeping a deep, dreamless sleep, rosy and warm. On Mahlia's lap, Robby cowered like some hapless little creature, shivering from time to time. Dimly, she thought she might know what ailed him, but there was nothing she could do about it but understand how he felt. She couldn't question him now, not with these men about, moving from the forest to the road, in and out of the house, as they used the phone and conferred in whispering groups.

'This is Ralph Winter, Mrs Ettison. Ralph is our coroner. He'd like to ask you a few questions, if you don't mind.'

'I can't tell you very much.'

'I just want to confirm what you told Chief Goode, Mrs Ettison. He tells me you saw Mr Paggott in Millingham this morning, talked with him.'

'That's right. I met Mr Paggott yesterday for the first time when he came here with an introduction from Charlotte Grafton. He wanted to see the fireplace, and he wanted permission to dig in Byers' Fault. I let him in; he took pictures of the fireplace; I gave him some old newspapers we'd found around the place; I told him he could dig up in Byers' Fault if he liked.'

'Then, this morning, we met him outside the motel.'

'We?'

'The children and I. Robby and the baby and I. He was very excited about the dig. He introduced us to the girl he's going to marry, Marcia Talent. An acquaintance of mine, John Duplessis, came up, and I introduced him to Mr Paggott. Then the baby began to fret and we left. I saw them talking, Mr Paggott and John Duplessis, and then as we drove off I saw Mr Paggott going into the motel.'

'Paul Goode says you and your litle boy called him something else. Not "Mr Paggott".'

'Seepy,' Mahlia replied wearily. 'His initials. He didn't like to be called Claude. He asked us to call him that.'

'It wasn't because you'd known him before?'

'No. He just told us to call him that.'

'Also, on the phone, Marcy Talent mentioned something you had given him, something besides the newspapers.'

'Oh, that thing. A kind of carving. I've forgotten now what he called it.'

'Seepy said it was a *vèvè*,' said Robby from the circle of her arms.

Mahlia nodded, too weary to be astonished at the correctness of his memory. 'That's right. She said it was in his car with the rest of his things.'

'It's in the police station,' said Paul. 'I don't like leaving stuff in cars, not even locked. I had Marcy leave all his stuff in the station. It's locked in that back cell, Ralph, the one we never use.'

95

'Was it your impression that this thing was valuable, Mrs Ettison? Valuable enough that someone would assault Mr Paggott to get it?'

'Valuable?' She couldn't think what they meant. It was only a piece of wood. Though possibly an antique, she didn't believe it had any real value. 'I don't know. I doubt it. He seemed to regard it as interesting but not – not a treasure of any kind.'

Paul Goode shook his head, wandered over to the dark window to stand staring out at the night. 'That's what the Talent girl said, Doc. No intrinsic value.'

You said "assault"?' Mahlia wondered aloud, then fell silent as she saw Paul's eyes upon Robby.

'We have to consider all possibilities,' he said soothingly, motioning to the other man. They moved away toward the hall and spoke almost in whispers for a time before Paul returned. 'We're going to get back to town, Mahlia. Since we really don't know what happened, I'm going to have Joe Demmis park outside tonight. Joe's a good, reliable man, the best one I've got, as a matter of fact. Steve Ware can't get his mind off the women long enough to do the job right. But Joe, Joe's solid. You can trust him to stay put and look out for you the way he's told. If there is some tramp camped up in the woods, he won't come down this way with a police car in the drive. Then, come light, we'll have a search party go all through there and get a better idea of what's going on, who might have been in the area.'

She set Robby in the chair, left him for a moment to ask Paul quietly, 'Are you saying he was murdered?'

'We don't know yet what actually killed him, Mahlia, but it wasn't an accident. Look, would you like me to ask Aunt Charlotte if she'd come over and spend the night? Or Cousin Georgina?'

'No.' She shook her head. 'No, Paul, thanks. I never asked you how you happened to find him.'

'It was Marcy Talent, kicking up a fuss, which she does better that just about anyone I know. She was real angry when she came back from here. She stopped at the station to leave the car. I got to know her some last summer – pain in the ass. Her family has more money than good sense, and she never lets you forget it. About the money that is; she doesn't even know about the good sense. Treats people like dirt and then fusses when they don't help her when she needs it. Don't know why, but she and Steve Ware hit it off pretty good – no, that's not true. I do know why. It's because Steve's family used to be pretty well off. Steve went to a bunch of the right schools, even though he got kicked out of all of 'em. I guess in her mind that's all that matters. Anyhow, she got him all riled up and he told me.

'Well, Seepy Paggott had a bunch of college kids – including Marcy – diggin' up there at Chester last year, and I got to know him pretty well. When she came in today and Seepy hadn't showed up, it didn't seem like him. He was a real fussy kind of guy. If he said eight o'clock, he showed up at eight. If he said five past, it was five past. So, when she said Byers' Fault was where they planned on going today, I just took a chance. Steve Ware and Joe and I found him after about an hour of looking.'

'How did he die?' Her vision had been full of violent swirling, gray and red, pale forms and bloody splotches, and a cresting pain that had broken like a wave and left her weak and gasping, but she had seen nothing specific. Nothing at all.

'It isn't important how. Just wasn't an accident, that's all. Take my word for it. Sure you don't want me to call Aunt Charlotte?'

She shook her head, turned back to pick Robby up; his head lolled wearily on her shoulder. She heard them leaving and shutting the door solidly behind them.

'Would you like to sleep in my bed?' she asked him.

He nodded, eyes as wide as lanterns.

'Did you see something that bothered you, Mahlia's boy? Hmm? Is that why you said, "Poor Seepy"?'

'I think I dreamed it.'

'Maybe. Do you remember what you dreamed?'

'Just there was Seepy and the little pigs, is all. And

97

the cemetery man who keeps the pigs. And Seepy was scared.'

Ah. So he had had a bad dream. Or seen some vague reflection of the vision Mahlia herself had seen, though that seemed unlikely. There was no reason for Robby to share her curse. If he had been her own son, she might have expected it. It was, after all, a kind of familial thing. Her own aunt had had it, and there were rumors of a great-aunt or some other relative known for the same uncomfortable ability. But Robby? Could it be mere propinquity, simply being near her? Or some touch of the otherworldly he had picked up from being near Molly, Martha, and Simoney during that terrible time with Carolyn? She shivered, wanting Molly to arrive, wanting someone to talk to, someone to advise her. But there was no one here, no one at all.

She moved about the house, checking the doors, the windows. All were locked, latched, fastened tight. The house felt enclosed, airless. In the driveway a flame showed scarlet for a moment: Joe Demmis, lighting his pipe. She could see the tiny glow as he drew breath, the hint of shadowy face behind it. She knew Joe by sight. It was comforting to have him there. She thought briefly of calling Charlotte as Paul had suggested. No. Why disturb her? She could do nothing but offer a shoulder to cry on, an ear to listen. What Mahlia really needed was sleep.

She went to the kitchen, gave Robby a cookie and a glass of milk, and drank one herself. Then up the stairs, seeing the shadows of tree branches move restlessly on the upstairs wall. A wind had come up outside, out of a clear sky. She stopped in Robby's room for a clean pair of pajamas, went to check on Elaine, then entered her own corner room – hers and Badger's room, she corrected herself. There was something she ought to be doing. Something. The omission nagged at her, but her mind felt limp, beaten. The pain was gone, but in the wake of the pain was only flotsam.

'I shouldn't have done it,' she admitted to herself, 'never

should have agreed to what Badger wanted. Never.' It had damaged her somehow, shutting it up, keeping the visions away. Now she would have to try to repair whatever the damage was.

'Damn you, Badger,' she said to herself, too weary to think anything at all. 'Damn you.'

CHAPTER THIRTEEN

Mahlia slept for only a few minutes, then woke, as though someone had called her name. She rose, tying a bathrobe around herself. The bedroom had casement windows in the corner, one opening south, one west, unscreened. She leaned from the southern window to peer at the driveway. A car there, with someone sitting inside; the flame of a lit match. As she drew back into the room, a glare of mirrored light caught her attention. Something off to the west, brightly lighted, doubly reflected. She turned to the west window to locate the source, high above the ebony folds of Byers' Fault: a tall house with many staring windows, lighted as though for a fete. 'The Duplessis house,' she murmured to herself, wonderingly. She had never noticed it before, and yet tonight it glowed there like a flickering beacon. As it vanished behind wind-blown boughs, she realized it was ordinarily hidden behind trees at the crest of the ridge. It sparkled in and out of view until the wind fell, then vanished completely in the calm. If the trees that hid it were deciduous, in the winter it would be as obvious as a lighthouse. In the winter John Duplessis could, indeed, look into her bedroom window with his telescope.

She closed the window hastily, drawing the curtains to cover it, sealing them as though for a blackout, then laughed at her outraged modesty. 'Don't be silly. If I can't see them, they can't see me. Ridiculous.' Still, until the curtains were overlapped and secure, she did not leave the window.

Then she lay down beside the sleeping child, listening to his soft breathing, hoping to be lulled by it, quieted by it enough to fall asleep again herself.

It was no good. She couldn't sleep. She got up, put on the robe once more, and went down the stairs. There was still a glimmer of embers in the fireplace. She added a log, and stood staring into the flames, preternaturally alert and yet unable to focus on any particular thought.

'What I would like to know,' demanded a voice from the doorway, 'is what you thought you were doing.'

She screamed, spun to see a bulky, gray-haired woman standing in the hall doorway. Molly. She tried to meet Molly's eyes and could not. Her own dropped.

'There was not a single protection set on this house,' Molly said accusingly, an ancient carpet bag dangling from one hand, plumply stuffed.

'Molly, I'm sorry.' She cursed herself. Of course she should have set protections on the house, long ago.

'Yes, I suppose you are. Not that being sorry means very much. Did this person who died mean anything to you?'

'Not in a personal way, but he was a nice man. Yes, I suppose in that sense he meant something to me.'

'Anything leading up to it? Any strange little things?'

Her eyes dropped again. 'Well, not directly. But sort of. I found something strange in my pond. And there have been children disappearing from time to time.'

'From time to time,' Molly mimicked harshly. 'A little something strange in your pond and children vanishing from time to time, but you didn't bother to do anything about this?'

'I promised Badger—'

'Promised him to go deaf, did you? Promised him to go blind? Give up your ears and your eyes, did you?'

'He wanted everything to be normal, Molly. For the children. He didn't want to remember that other time. He thought he could forget it better if I didn't—'

'If you didn't use the gifts God gave you, is that it? If you pretended to be some suburban college-girl-turned-wifey, is that it? Some women's club type? Play cards at the club in the afternoon, learn to play golf – or tennis. Wasn't that his first wife's game? Among other things.'

'No! No, he wouldn't have wanted—'

'Damn right he wouldn't have wanted, not if he'd known what he was wanting! Easier for you not to bother to explain, though. Always easier to make promises: Yes, dear; no, dear; I won't, dear. Did he make any in return?' The big woman turned away, making a gesture of negation, as though wiping Mahlia from some fouled slate to make it clean. 'Did he promise to give up his career and stay home to protect you?'

She cried out, unable to help it. 'Molly, that's not fair!'

Molly turned toward her again, shaking her head. 'No, it's not, child. Not fair at all. But then, was he fair? From our point of view, you've repudiated us. Don't you see? Martha and Simoney and me — we took some trouble over you and Badger and Robby. And then you let us be set aside as though we were nothing.'

'That wasn't what he meant.'

'We don't much care what he meant. What we're really interested in is what *you* meant.'

'I guess . . . I guess I didn't mean anything. I didn't even think.'

The gray-haired woman's face softened, but only a little. She took off the heavy sweater she was wearing, plunked down the battered suitcase. 'That's what I thought. Martha advised me not even to bother coming. Simoney — well, Simoney had a soft spot for Badger. She says she can see what you were up against — I think she meant that salaciously, by the way. Think, hell; she did mean it salaciously. I wish that girl could find a man who appeals to her. Well, I'm willing to give you something for being pregnant at the time. Thinking kind of slows down then, as I recall, goes into low gear, so to speak. Point is, I have to be very clear with you, Mahlia. If you want our help, you don't pick it up and put it down when it suits you — or when it suits Badger, either. You commit yourself to providing help as well as getting it, which means you don't run off into the wilderness all alone and try to forget you're a witch.' She stared about herself as though in the depths of a forest, lips curling at the antique farm implements Mahlia had used as accents in the room. 'My God, this place looks decorated!' It was the same tone in which she might have said, 'Cockroaches!'

Mahlia shook her head miserably. 'I never really intended to forget I'm a witch, Molly. Badger didn't ask me to do that. It was only while the children were little.'

'Great way for them to grow bigger, take their protection away. Lord love you, girl, you think there isn't an open channel right into Robby's head? From what you told me, there is. And into the baby's, come to that?'

'How? How could there be?'

'You ever watch how water runs, Mahlia? Say there's a rivulet going down a hill. Say somebody builds a little dam down at the bottom of the hill where that rivulet runs. The water up at the top of the hill doesn't say, "Well, there's a dam down there. I'll run down some other way." No, ma'am. The water comes the same old way it always has, and it builds up behind the dam, higher and higher, until it spills over. And when it spills over it pours onto anything that happens to be around. So when you built your little dams in your head, lady, you just let the power build up to run over onto Robby, and onto Elaine, and onto anybody else round close. The influences, the powers, they just keep running the same old way. You've probably worked real hard at damming up yours. Refused to have any visions, just pretended it wasn't possible? Gave you one hell of a headache, I'll bet. Well, Robby been havin' visitations, by any chance? Havin' bad dreams? Seein' things?'

Mutely, miserably, she nodded. 'But then, it's hard to tell. He has such a vivid imagination.'

'Well, that's what I might have expected. Now, if the bad dreams come to *you*, presumably you'd have had the sense to call us sooner.'

'Molly, are you going to help me or are you just going to scold me? I feel bad enough. I don't know what Badger's going to say.'

'If he says anything when I'm through with him, he's invincibly stupid. Now, girl, let's hear it.'

103

Mahlia told it in the best order she could, starting with her discovery of the bones and bracelet, continuing with Byers' Fault, and ending with Seepy Paggott. 'Before we'd heard anything, Robby started saying, "Poor, poor Seepy." I don't know whether it was just a bad dream or not. Then the vision hit me, and right after that I called you.'

Molly grunted, thinking. 'Where's this thing you gave the Paggott man? This design on wood?'

'I imagine it's still with his things, down at the jail. Paul Goode locked Seepy's things into a cell. You think that's what whoever killed him was looking for?'

'I don't know. What I do know is you need some protection around here, gates set on your windows and doors. Where do you think the bracelet is?'

'Wherever Robby put it. Him and his imaginary friend.'

'I'm not at all sure he's imaginary, Mahlia. Put that right out of your head as an absolute answer. He might be real. Here and now. Impalpable, maybe, but not imaginary.'

'He doesn't seem like – like the historic person, I guess. The zealot, the pillager.'

'Things change. People change. Spirits change. The only thing you can be sure of is that things change.'

'I didn't think of that.'

'You didn't think, girl. I guess we've established that.'

'I guess we have.' She was too weary to argue, too resentful to take pleasure in Molly's presence. Surely normal women could make promises to their husbands without this pulling and tearing.

'No,' said Molly, reading her mind. 'If you were a singer and your husband asked you to give it up for him, it would be the same. If you were an actress, or an artist, or a doctor – it doesn't matter. Only if you were nothing would it make no difference, because that's what they make us when they ask us to give up what we are.'

'He didn't know he was doing that.'

'I know. Which is why I'm here. Now, enough of this. I've spoken my piece and that's the end of that. I'm not going to go on chewing old meat over and over. Now we have to decide what to do to help. First off is to protect this place and the children. Then some sleep for you, girl. Simoney will be here tomorrow, or the next day. Martha may think better of it by then, too, though I wouldn't count on it. Still, three heads are better than one, and tomorrow we'd better start using them.' She started towards the stairs. 'Told that fellah out in the drive I was your aunt. Brought Robby some cookies, too. Come on, girl, don't stand there with your mouth open. We've got windows and doors to close.'

Mahlia went with her as she made the circuit of the doors and windows in the house, laying protections over them. Then Molly took herself into the guest room with a firm 'Good night.'

Mahlia lay down beside Robby and fell into an exhausted sleep.

She dreamed of walking in the dark, through long, strange corridors, seeking a particular door. There were other doors to either side, but the one she sought eluded her. Outside the place where she was, wherever it was, the night was alive with storm. Lightning flashes lit her way, showed her where the hallway turned, where it went up the stairs, the strange, turning stairs. Someone was waiting at the top of the stairs. Someone she dreaded seeing. Could not bear to see . . .

A deafening crash brought her bolt upright in bed to hear Robby beside her screaming, 'It got in, it got in, it got in!'

There was a furious hammering on the front door. She stumbled from the bed to the south window, almost falling. Joe Demmis looked up as she leaned out, her hair flying wildly in the risen wind. 'We're all right. What was it?'

'Something inside the house. Stay where you are. Lock your door!'

He stood back from the door and kicked at it, once, twice. Mahlia heard it splinter open as she ran to the bedroom door and turned the latch. She put her ear to the door, hearing nothing inside the house. Outside the drive was a crackle and a howl as Joe belatedly thought to use his radio. Then silence. A creak from the stairs. Ossie hadn't been able to stop the fourth stair from the top from creaking.

'It's me, Ms Ettison.' Joe's voice, from inside the house now. 'Stay where you are.'

'My aunt's in the guest room, Joe.'

Then Molly's voice. 'What in heaven's name is going on here?'

Footsteps. Something moving. A click as someone turned on lights. More footsteps.

'Nobody up here. You ladies just stay in there until Paul gets here, will you?' Retreating footsteps, doors opening and closing. Down the hall in the nursery the baby began to cry, and Mahlia heard the man curse.

'Ms Ettison? I'm going to bring the baby, okay? Just take her in there with you, if you don't mind.' The sound of approaching feet and a tap on the door. She shivered, reaching for the latch, wondering if she should open it.

'It's okay,' said Robby. 'He's got Elaine. It's all right, Mahlia.'

Joe handed her Elaine and relatched the door. Sensible man, he had brought spare diapers along with the baby. Now she heard him moving around below, opening closet doors, shutting them again. A siren sounded out on Old Chester Road and she joined Robby at the window to see Paul Goode's car skid into the drive. Then there were two voices downstairs, and before long a firm knock on the door.

'Mahlia? You can unlock now. Whoever it was is gone.' She opened the door, moved out into the hall as he went past her to examine her closets, the adjoining bath. 'Can't be too careful,' he said, smiling at her, a strained, unconvincing smile. 'Come on, young Mr Ettison,' he said to Robby, lifting him from the bed. 'Let's go downstairs.'

At the head of the stairs, Molly joined them as they stared incredulously into the little room Ossie had painted the previous afternoon. The door lay on the landing, its panels burst out, its hinges torn from their mortises and bent by some incredible force.

'The storm?' Mahlia asked. 'Were we hit by lightning?'

Paul drew her to the door, pointed out into the calm of the night. 'No storm, Mahlia. This was something else.'

'I thought – maybe I dreamed thunder.'

'Joe says he heard the kid yelling, "It got in." Would you know what that was about?'

'Nightmare,' Molly said firmly, taking Robby and carrying him down the stairs. 'He was having a nightmare. Yesterday was pretty upsetting.' Her eyes stayed fixed on the head of the stairs. 'What did it?'

'Something in that room wanted out,' he said.

'Something wanted in,' breathed Robby, 'It got in, it did.'

Mahlia shrugged, trying to keep from screaming. 'Robby was in bed with me. It was a dream.'

'Dream or not,' said Joe, 'It could have been something getting out.'

'How?' Paul demanded. 'You could break it like that pushing from inside, but how would you pull it out? The doorknob wouldn't take that kind of pull.'

'Why?' It was the only question that really mattered to Mahlia. 'Why would anyone want in there?'

'Was that where you found the thing you gave to Paggott?'

She nodded in suddenly perceptive terror, a host of threatening visions thronging into her mind. She shuddered, thrusting them away from her with a psychic blow. Molly was watching her from the foot of the stairs. 'Yes,' Mahlia answered. 'That's where it was.'

'Was there anything else in there?'

'The newspapers I told you about. Odds and ends. Charlotte took some of it away, and Georgina came with the junkman and cleared out the rest. Ossie Jeremy came yesterday to put the clothes rods in and paint it. He locked the door to keep Robby out of the fresh paint.'

'Nothing valuable in there? Nothing that would bring about this kind of attempted burglary?'

'What?' she screamed at him, unable to control it any longer. 'Ask Charlotte! She saw everything there was.' She gulped, barely able to keep from weeping.

'Okay, okay, simmer down. Sorry. We're just trying to find a motive, is all. Can't figure out any of this, except it appears this and Paggott are somehow connected. His car was broken into as well, out behind the station. The trunk was forced open and one of the windows was shattered. I hadn't left anything in it but some books.'

'Have you been through his things?' she asked, forcing herself into a pretense of calm. 'Isn't that the place to start? If you think somebody is after something he had or I had, why don't you look through his things? And call Georgina. Ask her where the junkman took the stuff. Call Charlotte. She took some of it.' She heard her voice rising in hysteria and fought to calm it again. 'Meantime, I'm afraid to stay here.' Molly had set protections on the doors and windows. Whatever had come in had come *through* them. Mahlia shivered, holding herself steady with an enormous effort.

'Joe's going to stay right here in the house, where I should have had him in the first place. Listen, Mahlia, whoever it was knows now that there's nothing in that room. Tomorrow I'll ask Lanson Horan to publish a story in the paper about all this. I'll tell him the stuff was cleared out, tell him part of it's in the jailhouse and the rest is at the junkyard. If whoever is botherin' you reads the paper, that'll make 'em leave you alone, at least. Meantime, I ought to find out about that thing you gave Paggott.'

'Ask Marcy Talent. Seepy called someone at the university about it. Marcy knows who it was. Some anthropologist, a Scandinavian name.'

'All right. Now, you ladies and the kids go on back to your rooms and settle down. You want me to call Dr Scott? Mike Scott's a good guy – married to Fred Smarles's sister Ruth. Give you something to calm you down, maybe.'

'I'm all right, Paul. Really.' Molly came back up the stairs to put a strong arm around her. 'We'll be all right.' She went down the hallway to her room, Molly following.

When the door shut behind them, Molly said, 'I put protections on this house.' It was said flatly, an assertion, something of anger in it.

'I know.'

'I don't know what kind of creature could have come

through those protections, Mahlia! Not anything I know of. But damn sure not something merely human!'

Mahlia nodded, gritting her teeth to keep from chattering. 'Paul Goode subscribes to a madman theory.'

'I think not. Would you like me to stay in here with you?'

'Yes. It's a king-size bed. There's room for all of us.'

Mahlia spent the rest of the night huddled on her pillow, reaching out from time to time to touch one or the other of the children, both of whom slept soundly and evidently peacefully, though Robby twitched occasionally as though he were running in his sleep. Molly's breathing was deep, quiet, uninterrupted by an occasional little snore. Mahlia kept hearing things. A nonexistent someone on the stairs. A dry, rustling sound, like leaves. When she rose at dawn, she had dark, shadowed circles under her eyes and a pain in her ears from having gritted her teeth so tightly to keep from screaming. Molly made a large lump under the covers, obviously still deeply asleep.

Joe already had coffee made when she came downstairs. Charlotte arrived within minutes of sunrise. Stephen Ware came to take Joe's place, and Charlotte fed him breakfast on the porch where he lounged indolently, seemingly indifferent to what had happened. A photographer came from the newspaper to take pictures of the shattered door, though not of Mahlia or the children. 'The boss says only the door,' she remarked, cocking the camera at a new angle. 'He told me he didn't want to let you in for any oddball interest. Nice man, Lanson Horan. Guess you know his wife?' There was a certain wistfulness in the young woman's face, and Mahlia guessed at an infatuation.

'She's lovely,' Mahlia answered, and remembering Jeannie's voice when she spoke of her husband, she added, 'and very, very fond of her husband.'

'Yeah. So I've heard.' The photographer clattered off down the stairs, and Mahlia heard a voice summoning her to the kitchen.

'You eat these eggs and bacon,' Charlotte instructed Mahlia, waving a spatula at her, 'and at least one piece of toast. Robby's out on the front porch. Baby's in her play-pen. Paul's sending young John Depew to replace that Ware boy — in my opinion, Stephen Ware never was good for much. John will keep an eye on things, and I'll have him watch both the children. You haven't slept a wink, have you? I shouldn't wonder. Lord, what's the world coming to?'

'Paul thinks someone was looking for something that was in that room.'

'Not likely, I'd say. Some moth-eaten blankets? Some mattresses? Georgina sent those off to the dump.'

'Was that all?' It was Molly, speaking from the kitchen door. 'You must be Charlotte Grafton. Mahlia's said so many nice things about you. Was there anything in the little room besides blankets and mattresses?'

'Well . . .' Charlotte broke another egg into the pan and took mental inventory. 'There were some straps with buckles.'

'You took the straps to the riding stable?' Molly asked.

'That's right. Some kids' clothes, and I took them to the Salvation Army in Millingham.'

Mahlia said, 'I gave the newpapers and the carving to Mr Paggott. What else was there?'

'The knives — just ordinary old skinnin' knives. Nice enough, but nothin' unusual.'

'Comic books,' said Mahlia, a little wildly. 'Old comic books. Don't people collect comic books? Aren't some of them very valuable?'

'Mahlia, you sit and eat. The very idea. Comic books! Who in his right mind would break into a house right under the noses of the police for comic books? I ask you. How did he get in, anyhow?'

'He broke the door,' suggested Molly in a mild voice.

'No, that was inside. I mean, how did he get into the house in the first place?' Then, informed by the blank expression on Mahlia's face that she had no idea, 'You mean that silly nephew of mine didn't find out how he got in?'

Mahlia got up from the table, leaving her toast, and they made a tour of the house. All of the windows were unbroken and still locked. The side door was locked. The back and front doors were now unlocked, but Mahlia remembered having locked them in Molly's company the night before. They went reluctantly into the little, freshly painted room to find the tiny window ajar.

'Ossie left it open to let the paint smell air out,' said Mahlia. 'It isn't big enough for any person to come through.'

'Whoever it was sent a monkey through to unlock the door from inside,' suggested Charlotte. 'I saw that in a movie once.'

'And, having unlocked the door from the inside, whoever it was then saw fit to break it down as well?' said Molly doubtfully. 'Perhaps the person was in the house the whole time.'

'Down cellah?'

'Likely, yes. But there's no one down cellar now, because I've looked.' Molly was thoughtful for a time, then asked. 'Charlotte, did Paul tell you how Seepy Paggott died? He wouldn't tell Mahlia.'

Charlotte turned away, lips thinned, obviously preferring to say as little as possible. 'He just said somebody took a knife to him, what they call it – mutilated him. Prob'ly to get him to tell somethin' or other. Poor Claude. Diggin' away up there at Chester for bits of old china, buttons, buckles. Any old junk at all and he was just tickled over it. But there's folks don't understand that. They think anybody diggin' must be diggin' for something wonderful. Gold, I shouldn't wonder, or jewels. So, somebody took a knife to him to get him to tell where the treasure was hid. Had a bad heart, Claude did. Told me all about it last year. Him and me spent a lot of time together, talkin' over those old times, what life must've been like for those people. No matter what they did to him, it was his heart that killed him. Just up and quit. Good thing, prob'ly.'

Molly let the matter drop, and Mahlia, remembering Robby's words the afternoon before, did not ask any more questions.

Molly spent the morning roaming around the house and

111

grounds, stopping every few steps to mutter under her breath and cock her head as though listening. She came in at noon, shaking her head in irritation, and told Mahlia that the only places she could get any sense of presences at all were near the pond and in the little room upstairs. 'Which we already knew. When Simoney gets here, we'll try something a bit more ambitious . . .' Her voice trailed away and she stood, eyes fixed on some unseeable horizon.

When John Duplessis telephoned they were in the kitchen, fixing lunch for the children. At first Mahlia was unable to remember what he was calling about. When it all came together in her mind she said, 'John, we've had a bit of an upset here. I really can't think about social things right now. No, I don't want to talk about it, but I understand the afternoon paper will have a story. Perhaps another time.' He was sweetly sympathetic, so much so that she was sorry to have broken their date, wanting to recant and tell him she'd go, even while telling herself that she could not possibly think of leaving the children while her house was being invaded and her family threatened.

'I won't keep you,' he said soothingly. 'I'll call back later.'

She didn't want to let him go, but managed to say something polite, hardly aware of what it was, and hung up the phone, trying to put him out of her mind.

Charlotte, however, had overheard the call. 'John Duplessis? You know he's a great-great-something or other, nephew I guess, of old John Byers, him that built this house in the first place?' She settled at the kitchen table, fixing Mahlia and Molly with an intent gaze, owllike through her thick glasses, obviously intent on distraction. 'Now, that's an interestin' story. I've got a book written by a man who knew him, you know that? Captain Nathaniel Bone. He was my great-great-great-grandfather. Two greats? Or three? I get confused about it.'

Molly brought her far-away gaze back to those around the table and began to pay attention.

'Well, anyhow, Captain Bone, he knew John Byers. Knew

him to talk to and drink with because they were both slavers and used to meet up here and there in port. John Byers, he got him a black wife from somewhere over there in Africa, a princess, according to Captain Bone, and her three sisters came with her, too. I don't know if they were slaves or what, might have been, but Captain Bone called the three of 'em Byers's concubines and the other one his wife, so he might have married her somewhere or other. Some heathen rite, I suppose. No Christian minister would have married a white man to a heathen black woman, not back then.

'Well, the way the Captain tells it, John Byers begat a flock of kids by all four of those women, and they grew up and went off and found wives and husbands of their own, maybe some of 'em married each other for all I know. And they settled up there in the hollow above this place. It got quite a reputation over the years, people disappearing near it, things like that, which is about what you'd expect of such heathen if you stopped to think about it. Anyhow, the people in Chester, which is where Captain Bone lived, they said the place was Byers's fault for having those four black wives. Ever'body's always askin' if it's like that San Andreas Fault, and here it is somethin' else entirely. Just people sayin' the town was Byers's fault.'

Molly nodded in fascination and poured coffee for them. Charlotte wiped her face with a corner of her apron, took a mouthful of hot coffee, and went on.

'Well, the people there in Chester had bad luck. Kids kept disappearin' and dyin'. Animals wandered off. People got sick, sometimes, and nobody could tell why. Graveyard filled up. You look at those stones, sometime, you'll see what I mean. Meantime, up in Byers' Fault ever'body was havin' babies right and left and nobody sick ever. Well, likely it was the water, the way I see it. Likely the well in Chester was contaminated, God knows that'll cause sickness year after year, but nobody thought about it in those days. Well, one night they found one of those black women of John Byers's out on the road, all beaten and bloody. Captain Bone was a converted Christian and he said they should take her

113

in and nurse her, which they did, but she died before mornin' anyhow. Before she died, though, she was mumblin' about John Byers being a devil who was takin' the life out of the people of Chester to give it to his descendants. "They're drinkin' up your blood," is what she said, along with some other stuff that told the Captain they were devil worshipers.'

'Ah, ummm,' said Molly thoughtfully. 'Would *you* say they were devil worshipers?'

The carving she had given to Claude Paggott came to Mahlia's mind. 'Really devil worshipers, Charlotte? Or maybe just their own gods, African gods?'

'It wouldn't have mattered to Captain Bone. Both the same, so far as he'd have thought. Well, soon after that there was a child went missin' and the people got all riled and Captain Bone preached to 'em, and ever'body got wild with his preachin' and probably with rum, too, if I know how revivals go, and they went up in the night and set fire to the town of Byers' Fault and killed ever'body there. Every child, every woman and man. All except John Byers and his oldest son, William. And that was the Byers' Fault Massacre. It happened in 1760, more'n two hundred years ago. That's why young Paggott was goin' to dig up there – lookin' for bits and pieces about the history.'

'Why didn't they kill John and William?' Molly asked, finishing her coffee.

'Couldn't find 'em, according to the book. Oh, they found the black women, the three of 'em that were left. They were there in Byers House, with their throats cut, and John and William Byers were gone. That's what Captain Bone wrote about it. William would have been about thirty, then. Well, about twenty years after that, here came William back. He said his daddy was dead. I guess he must have been, because Captain Bone wrote that he saw the ghost of John Byers riding a horse up near Byers' Fault that same year. That was seventeen and eighty, and that was the year William rebuilt this house around the old chimney that was still standin'. That's why Claude Paggott wanted to see it. Not real old, according to those pyramids or old places in China, but pretty old for the USA.'

'What happened to Captain Bone?' Mahlia asked.

'Oh, he lived on in Chester for a while. Chester was just a hard-luck place, though. After a while the people all either died or left there. The Captain came to Millingham and settled. He died here in 1791, a hundred and one years old, he was, too.

'After he died, his granddaughter wrote in his journal. I've got it. Her married name was Amelia Stotts – that's my family, Stotts. She went on tellin' about the Byers family right up to the Civil War times when she died.'

'I take it William got married?'

'Brought himself home a young wife in 1800, and him in his seventies then. She had a girl baby, Harriet. Only the one. Then when Harriet was about twenty, she was married off to this fellah from New Orleans, and that's where the Casternaught family came into it. He was a Casternaught. William Byers went off to New Orleans, and I guess he died down there. Then in 1830, Harriet came back to visit with her two children – Jerome and Eloise, they were – and two men cousins. Amelia wrote about them coming to Millingham and opening up the old house. That was the same year those children got lost in the mine over near Grubb's Corners and never were found. Five of 'em, poor things. Amelia wrote about that, too.

'Well, Harriet and the children stayed after that. Eloise went off and got married to another New Orleans man, and her daughter was Jessalee Casternaught Duplessis. That would've been about 1855, I guess. Before the war, it was, because the whole family left about then, and it wasn't until 1860 that Jerome came back and opened up the house again.'

'And your great-grandmother kept track of all these comings and goings?'

'She said Captain Bone had told her to do it, so she did. Oh, he didn't like John Byers. So far as Captain Bone was concerned, John Byers was the devil incarnate.'

'But the history ends in 1862.'

Charlotte flushed. 'No. Because then my grandma started keeping track. Kind of a tradition it was by then. Jerome never had any children. He had a wife, strange little woman according to Grandma, but she never kindled. Not even a scare. Grandma used to make dresses for her, and she'd cry about it and cry about it, but never a child. Well, according to her, Jessalee Casternaught Duplessis married her cousin somebody Duplessis, and she had a boy, and then he grew up and married and had a girl about 1910. And that girl was Jessica Casternaught Duplessis. Jerome moved away and died about that time.'

'And this place stood empty until Jessica came back to it in 1964?' Molly asked.

'Except for a visit in 1930, that's true.'

'Oh, I remember!' Mahlia exclaimed. 'It was in those papers upstairs! About Jessica coming for a visit with some of her relatives.' She shook her head. 'In this country, that's quite a record of habitation. One family for more than two and a half centuries.' She worried at it, noting Molly's absorbed look. 'Did Jessica marry a cousin as well? Or somebody else with the same last name? If she was born Jessica Casternaught Duplessis, then she must have, if her children are named Duplessis.'

Charlotte gave her a sideways look. 'Some have wondered if she ever married at all. Opinion is Jessica Casternaught Duplessis does as she pleases, when she pleases. But that's not the strangest thing about that family.'

'What is the strangest thing, Charlotte?' Molly had been oddly intent during this narrative, nose twitching from time to time as though she smelled something.

'The strangest thing is how they always die somewhere else. My husband, Willard, used to say that to me. Willard had no imagination at all – take him to one of these new movies, these *Star Wars* kinds of things, he'd think you were crazy. But he used to shake his head over the Duplessises. "Born somewheres else, married somewheres else, die somewheres else," he'd say. "Not like they belonged here at all." Well, you got to remember Willard was in the

116

tombstone business along with his brother, Robert Henry Grafton, and he was sure to notice there was no Byers or Casternaught or Duplessis stones up at the cemetery.' She got up briskly, dumping her cup and saucer in the dishpan and reaching for the soap. 'And the other funny thing is most of 'em still look like cross-breeds, what you call 'em, mulattos. You'd think if they'd been marrying white people for two hundred years they'd have gotten lighter as time went on. But they're just as dark as Captain Bone wrote that William and all his descendants were. Except for John, of course. He's the only light one, as though he'd had another daddy than the other Duplessises entirely.'

'Fred Smarles mentioned that. He said people used to call it "a touch of the tarbrush".' Mahlia smiled at the phrase, so expressive of Victorian discrimination.

'Well, that was true in bigoted times. Lord, I hope we're not bigoted like that anymore. My grandson, Willard the Third, he has an Asian wife – we used to say Oriental, you know, but that's not nice anymore. Pretty little thing, and the children are like pictures. Handsome! My, yes. And smart, too. I do think the Asian people just have more brains than the rest of us. Like Jews. But there was a time when it would have just been the worst thing you could do, marry someone like that.'

Molly laughed, snorting into her cup, and Charlotte gave her a sharp glance. 'Well, now. Mahlia, you look like you could use a nap, and you, too, Molly. If I set right here and do a little crochet – this is an afghan for that newest great-grandchild of mine; pretty, isn't it? – would you feel like a sleep? I'll look after the little ones. And I tell you what. You come over to my place tomorrow and I'll lend you old Captain Bone's journal.'

Mahlia nodded, suddenly overcome by fatigue. The blood that had coursed madly through her brain all night now seemed occupied with her stomach. Molly wandered off, saying nothing but not headed toward her bedroom. Not wanting to be alone, Mahlia lay down on the couch and Charlotte covered her with a quilt. When she woke it was late afternoon, and Charlotte was shaking her by one shoulder.

'Mahlia? Jeannie Horan's here. She wants to know if you'd like to bring the children over to have barbecue at their house?'

Over Charlotte's shoulder Jeannie smiled encouragement. 'Lanson ran a great story, Mahlia, lunatic-at-large kind of thing. Made me shiver just reading it. Why don't you pack up the kids and come on over? Robby can help me barbecue hamburgers and Lanson can tell you all his war stories.'

'Come on, Mahlia.' Robby tugged at her. 'Let's go. I want to do a barbecue.' He seemed fully recovered from the night, no shadows around his eyes. If he had had visions, they had indeed been in dreams, and like dreams were now forgotten. 'Come on.'

'I will. Thanks, Jeannie. I was sort of dreading this evening. I have a house guest. Can she come along?'

'Bring whoever's around. Paul Goode says he's going to have a man out here for several nights, so you'll be all right, but an evening out should help the grues. Me, I think whoever did it is long gone. Probably two states away by now.'

Mahlia insisted on driving her own car to the Horans'. From the end of the drive, she looked back at the house over Molly's bulky shoulder, seeing the brooding stare of the windows down the chimney nose as she had seen it the first time, wondering whether she would be another of the brief tenants of the place. The Mandrells had stayed two years; the Everetts had stayed three. Had they, too, had doors smashed? Unlikely. Fred Smarles would have known about it, and Fred wouldn't have kept such matters to himself.

When they arrived at the Horans', she asked. 'Jeannie, did you ever hear of anything like this happening before out at my place?'

'At Byers' Farm? Never. Jessica liked to keep to herself. As long as she was there, we never heard or saw anything about the place except once, back in '80, when the Duplessises were having some kind of family feast and the neighbors complained about the noise. Which is why

118

Jessie moved, I guess you've heard. She's not one to bear complaint. The Mandrells were creepy. I called on them, once; they were like something out of a Charles Addams cartoon. The Everetts were just people. She was a little whiny, always going on about the drafty house. But no, to answer your question, never any rumor of disturbance. I'm afraid it's your own phenomenon.'

If so, it was a short-lived phenomenon. When they returned home after dinner, the door had been repaired and repainted and Ossie Jeremy was packing up his tools. Steve Ware was lounging beside the front gate, looking bored. Robby wandered uneasily through the house like a puppy, sniffing, gradually becoming his own ebullient self.

'Quiet as a tomb, so far,' said Steve, leering at her from beneath heavy eyelids, giving her what he thought of as his sexy smile. 'Ol' Goodie says one of us'll stick around for a couple of nights, though, just to be sure. I'll give you odds whoever was hanging around here is long gone.'

This seemed to be the consensus of opinion. Mahlia herself could feel no sense of menace. The little room with its new door was simply a closet, though she propped the door open and left it that way. If anyone wanted to look in, she would make it as convenient as possible.

She went through the house. All seemed in order, but she had the feeling things had been moved. Nothing missing. Nothing really disturbed, and yet drawers had been looked into. Even her underwear had been shifted, searched through. The police, she decided at last, going through the house while she was away. Just to see if there was anything there that might explain the break-in. She would ask Paul about it, next time she saw him. This thought was derailed when she entered the living room to see a lovely arrangement of late summer flowers, August lilies and early pink mums. The card lay beside them. 'Terribly sorry to hear you were involved in unpleasantness. Please give us an early opportunity to show you that Millingham has its good qualities. Fondly, John. And Harriet, Lois, and Jessica Casternaught Duplessis.' She stared at it, warmed and delighted. How

119

thoughtful of him – not only to have sent the flowers, but to include the female members of the family on the card, for she was sure Stephen Ware had read it, just as she was sure he had been through the house. Ah, well, in his place she would be curious, too, and what was there to find? Badger didn't even keep his confidential papers at home, so what harm could it do?

She lifted one of the lilies, taking a deep breath of its fragrance, wishing for a moment that it had been Badger who had sent the flowers, angry at him for abandoning her, leaving her to be wooed in this fashion by someone else. She had no doubt the gift was more than mere thoughtfulness, more than mere neighborliness. No, left to herself, Jessica Casternaught Deplessis would not have sent flowers. John. Only John. She could imagine his face, intent on her own, dark brows drawn down in concern . . . Enough of that.

Molly was looking at her strangely, so she thrust the lily back into the arrangement and headed towards the stairs and bed.

'An admirer?' Molly wanted to know.

'Someone I met,' she admitted. 'And a very thoughtful man. But I don't think I should call him an admirer.'

'If you can set your love life aside for the moment, I'd like some help here,' Molly said, indicating certain things she had laid out on the table.

Mahlia flushed. This time they were going to set serious protections on the house, and she had not even thought of it herself. She reached within herself, trying to remember things she had spent almost a year trying to forget, hearing Molly coach her with a sense of impatient annoyance at herself.

When they were finished, she went wearily up to her room in a mood of total inadequacy, not seeing the speculative, worried look in Molly's frowning eyes.

CHAPTER FOURTEEN

Morning came. Molly announced her intentions of talking to some local people about old times. She looked pale and drawn, not her usual robust self.

'Are you okay, Molly?'

'Obviously not,' the woman snapped. 'I've been wandering around this place for one day and two nights and found absolutely nothing worth mentioning. Oh, a whispering answer when I do some resonance spells out by the pond, but whatever it is doesn't want to come out and talk. I've got a few ideas, mostly from what Charlotte Grafton said, but nothing concrete. Captain Bone — if there is a Captain Bone — is in hiding, and likely it will take Simoney to winkle him out.'

'No idea what broke into the house?'

'None. And no way to find out without bringing it back — which would be a damned silly thing to do, considering what it did to my protections. As soon as Simoney gets here, we'll go up in the woods where — well, where it happened, and see what we can find out there.'

Robby came in and tugged at Mahlia's shirt, demanding milk, and she flushed guiltily. The refrigerator contained only a nearly empty bottle and an empty egg box, a Mother Hubbard bareness that boded ill for Robby's incessant appetite.

'Come along, Rob. Let's pack up old Elaine and go into town for milk. We need a bit of everything, come to that.' She found herself glad of the excuse to move, to do something. There were too many things unresolved to sit around. Better to have something to do.

She found other excuses to linger in town. Clothes to be taken to the cleaners. A stop at the electric company to pay a bill. A stop at the local hamburger haven for her and Robby while Elaine tried her two teeth on a french fry and bits of bun. A stop at the local nursery to ask about the trees she had ordered for the end of the drive. Finally, a stop at Charlotte's, with a gift of candy and thanks for her help. Robby was immediately diverted by the mama cat sunning herself beside the drive under a tumble of kittens. He settled beside them. Happy to have him occupied, Mahlia jounced Elaine into the Snugli and opened the creaking gate.

Charlotte was perched on an old, black-painted rocking chair, fanning herself, face flushed and eyes glassy. 'Oh, Mahlia, is that you? Oh, but I'm glad to see you!' She staggered to her feet. 'I've had such a scare . . .'

'A scare? Charlotte, what's happened?'

'Oh, I shouldn't say a scare. It was one of those what-d'-you-callems, when you think you've seen something before? I used to know that word. It's got some French name to it.'

'Déjà vu, Charlotte?'

'That's it! Déjà vu. Lord, but that's never happened to me before. Always thought it was a lot of hogwash, you know, people thinking they'd lived before and things like that. Darned if it doesn't seem like that, though.'

'You went someplace new and had the feeling you'd been in the same place before, was that it?'

'Someplace new? Lord, girl, no. Downtown Millingham is where I was. In the park, there, sitting on the bench, waiting for the driver's license office to open in the courthouse. That bench behind the lilacs there, half hid. Well – tell the truth, now, Charlotte – I didn't want to talk to anybody. Me'n the license office are having this little dispute over my eyesight, and I was some hot about it. That's why I went in so early – I see better early in the morning, and that's the truth.' Her voice faded away and she nodded to herself, fanning vigorously. 'Damn fool doesn't think I ought to drive. Hell, I could drive these roads stone-blind.'

'So what happened, Charlotte?'

'Nobody around. That's the funny part of it – Thursday morning and nobody around. Park all empty except for one dog and a few pigeons. Car going by now and then over on Main, but nobody around in the park or the courthouse. They came down the alley, the six of 'em.'

'Who?'

'The Duplessises. Old Jessie and her brood, all six. I'd heard John was back, from you, I guess, but I hadn't seen him till then. They went up the steps there and tried the door. I coulda told 'em it was locked yet. Thursdays they don't open until ten. Tom Bunker, he's the janitor there, and he never in his life opened a door one minute early or closed it one minute late. Tom's too lazy to clean up any more litterin' than the law allows.'

There was a long pause. Mahlia hesitated to prompt the old woman again, but after a lengthy silence she said, 'So, Charlotte? What happened?'

'Well, they turned around there on the steps, Jessie with John on one side of her and Bill on the other. Harriet was off to one side, farther down the steps, and Jerry and Lois off to the other, still on the sidewalk. And I saw 'em standing like that and let out a yelp. They saw me, then, and took off down the alley without so much as a hello. Funny.'

'I'm sorry, dear, but I don't understand what was funny.'

'Why, it was seein' 'em like that. Took me back. The other time, I was fifteen. Mama brought me into town to buy me a birthday dress. I was a late baby, you know. Mama was over forty when she had me. We're all late breeders, us Stotts. Grandma was over forty when Mama was born. Lord, my great-great-grandma was born in 1760, the year of the massacre.'

'You were fifteen?' Mahlia prompted.

'And we'd come into town early, just like this morning. And we were sittin' on that same bench in the park, just like this morning, waitin' for the stores to open. And the Duplessises come down that same alley and went up those same steps and turned, just that way, six of 'em. That was nineteen and thirty, that was. Six of 'em. Alike as peas.'

'You mean a family resemblance?'

'I mean alike as peas, girl, that's what I said. There was these six Duplessis cousins up from New Orleans, Jessica and five others, two women, three men. And they stood just that way, Jessica with a man on each side of her, one of 'em white and one of 'em dark, and one dark woman down on the left – looked like Harriet like one bean looks like another bean. And down on the sidewalk a man and a woman, just like Jerry and Lois. Skirts are down now, you know. Long, like in the thirties. It wasn't just resemblance. I mean, they were like! Jessie was about twenty then, and she'd be seventy now, but I coulda swore this morning she was the same, not aged a year. And John. Well, John was the same John. That's all there is to it.'

The rest of the story had only confused Mahlia, but this final statement was one she could make a reasonable statement about. 'Well, it couldn't have been,' she said in a calming voice. 'John's only in his early forties. He wasn't even born in 1930.'

Charlotte's face went still and watchful, like that of an old dog who has heard a threatening noise, weary but alert. 'He's a handsome man, John. Wouldn't surprise me if he'd set his cap for you.'

'I've met him – you know how it is in a small town. He's single, and I seemed to be. He asked me out, but it was with the whole family.'

'And I heard you turn him down.'

'It seemed best, under the circumstances.'

'I wouldn't get involved. No, I wouldn't. That John Duplessis, he seems just like to put a spell on some women.' There was another silence, a bit uncomfortable this time. 'I told you about Captain Bone's journal, but did I ever tell you about my writin'?'

'Your writing?' Mahlia was grateful for the change of subject. 'No, you never did.'

'My grandma used to tell me stories, Oh, Lord, her grandma used to tell her stories, too, and she remembered 'em. She

124

had stories goin' back to when Byers' Fault was nothing but forest and Indians. Anyhow, when I was just young, expecting my first I was, my sister said I ought to write Grandma's stories down for the family. None of the rest of 'em had the time to listen to her, poor old thing, and so I had all of 'em told to me time and again. Well, so, I wasn't doing too well with that first baby and the doctor said sit quiet. Me! Sit quiet, he said. So, I wrote Grandma's stories down. Then time went on and I heard other people tell stories, too, and I wrote them down. All there in the back of the Captain's journal. I had a good hand back then. Gone all to pot, now, with this arthur-itis, but you can read the stories all right.

'Anyhow, I said I'd lend you Captain Bone's journal, and so you'll take my writin' along, too.' The old woman heaved herself out of the chair and started inside. The phone rang as she went. Mahlia could hear her through the open porch window as she answered it. The caller's voice sounded as a faint interrogative buzz.

'Hello.'

'_____?'

'Yes, it's me.'

'_____?'

'Oh, yes, Jessica. Well, I did, didn't I? Didn't mean to startle you all when I hollered. Just rememberin' when I was younger, that's all.'

'_____.'

'Just kind of surprised at lookin' up to see you there. Forgot where I was for a minute.'

'_____?'

'With me? No. There's nobody with me.'

'_____.'

'Well, that's kind, but you don't have to . . .'

'_____!'

'Well, all right then. But you really shouldn't. All right then. Bye.'

A moment's scraping of drawers and shuffling of papers preceded her return with a stained, scuffed volume cradled against her chest.

'Here. There's the Captain's book and Great-Grandma's and Grandma's and mine. You can bring it back when you've read it all. Mebbe you could even make another copy. Seepy said he'd made some copies, but I don't know where they are now. I've worried sometimes about it being burned if the house caught fire. Nobody knows those stories now.'

Mahlia took the book in silence. Charlotte's fingers stroked the worn cover as she relinquished it. 'Thanks, Charlotte. I'll enjoy reading the whole thing.'

'Made me think of it, seeing those Duplessises there. Like ghosts. The Captain said somethin' like that to my great-grandma, about Duplessis ghosts. No, it would have been Byers ghosts. Humph. Guess I startled some this morning. Jessica heard me yelp, so she said. Thought mebbe I'd had a stroke or somethin'. Told me if I was alone she'd come along and bring me some tomatoes from her place up on the ridge. Nice of her. Can't grow tomatoes down here worth spit – too shady. Didn't tell her you were here.'

'Well, I won't be in half a minute.'

'None of her business who I have for company. Jessica's a real old gossip. Always wants to know everything about everyone, wants to know about their kids, their husbands. If she knew you'd been here, I'd have to talk about you and Robby for a half hour or more.' She grinned, a little shamefaced. 'Way I see it, your business is your business, not Jessica Casternaught Duplessis's. Well. You take that book along. I think I'll have a little lie-down . . .'

Mahlia felt the urge to take the woman's arm, hug her, guide her inside the house to the couch, maybe cover her with the bright afghan visible through the window. It was an urge she sternly quelled. Charlotte wouldn't thank her for it. Erect as an oak, she stood now with her shoulders back, obviously shaken by some emotional storm but just as obviously unswayed. Mahlia could not understand the emotion, the storm, the shattering feeling so evident on Charlotte's face that had not been made at all plain by her words. A resemblance like that could be disturbing, Mahlia imagined, though she discounted nine-tenths of what Charlotte had said. Early morning or no, Charlotte's eyes simply weren't good, and any slight similarity could have been interpreted as something more.

Still, Mahlia found herself shivering as she went out through the picket gate, hearing it shriek a rusty complaint behind her. She collected Robby, who demanded to have two of the kittens as soon as they were old enough, and had to be forcibly separated from them. When she got into her car she felt a wave of formless anxiety, a sense of threat, as though there were something she ought to do. What? She checked the gas gauge, finding that it read almost full. She felt her grocery bags; the milk was still cool and the frozen foods seemingly still frozen. Something gnawed at her, but it didn't seem to be a material, present worry. Still fretting, she drove home feeling like an athlete after some unsuccessful competition, physically exhausted and emotionally drained. She could not understand her own feelings, but they were too like feelings she could remember from the past to let her dismiss them.

'I'd rather not have any visions about this,' she told herself weakly. 'Couldn't I just let Molly and Simoney handle it? I don't want to . . .'

The words didn't help. She could feel a huge, ominous threat looming invisibly in the midafternoon sky, and gathering at the edges of the road. A voice seemed to speak words that she did not want to hear.

'Let's hurry home, Mahlia,' said Robby. 'I'm really hungry. That hamburger was inad . . . inad-equal.'

'Inadequate, Rob. Right. It sure was.' Ashamed, she tried to stop worrying about her visions, or lack of them, and drove them home.

CHAPTER FIFTEEN

Charlotte, left behind on her porch, continued to rock for a time, soothing herself into quiet. There were a few dishes left beside the kitchen sink, and she went in to finish washing them, comforting herself with the warm water, laying her glasses beside the sink and closing her eyes. Sometimes it was easier not to try to see. Lots of things could be done without seeing, or almost without. Afghans, for instance. Leaving the glasses in the kitchen, she took her crocheting back onto the porch with her, finishing up one multicolored square and starting another with quick, decisive pulls of the hook, her fingers managing it all by themselves while she thought of other things.

Joseph, mostly. Ever since the day she had taken the child's bones to his grave, he had seemed very close to her. Two or three times in the past few weeks she had thought she heard his voice or smelled that particular odor that no one else had ever had. A kind of mixed herbal and people smell that had always clung to Joseph's body, distilled from what he ate and drank, a kind of sweetness. Men, in Charlotte's opinion, smelled pretty much the way horses did, pleasant when they were clean and unpleasant when they were dirty. But the scent she always thought of as Joseph's was something other than that, something gently pervasive and heavy with recollection.

And she smelled it today, blowing through the yard on an early evening breeze, as though he stood somewhere just out of sight, watching her. She laid the yarn down, leaned her head back, just rocked, not remembering anything in particular, just drifting in that scent.

A faint rustling in the trees made her open her eyes, but there was nothing there. Old mama cat, probably, playing with the kittens, hiding in the rhubarb, running through the raspberries. Have to be finding homes for those kittens soon. Mahlia would take at least one, maybe two – the pretty little white-faced calico and the ginger tom. Let the female have one litter and then take her down to Doc Primack to be fixed. Mahlia would be sensible about it. Not like some Charlotte could think of, who would let the mama cats go to all that trouble and then drown the kittens.

The rustling again. Like taffeta. Like dried leaves. Not a catlike sound at all. Charlotte sat up, staring at mist-edged shapes, only half seen. Damn, but that driver's license man had a point. She sure couldn't see the way she used to except up real close, and the prescription for her glasses had been changed this spring, so she couldn't blame it on that. Something light-colored there in the shade. Deer? Could be deer. They did come down here from time to time, following the stream, getting themselves killed on the highway, paralyzed by car headlights.

She sat back, keeping her eyes on the light-colored blob. If it came closer, she could tell what it was. If it didn't, she'd assume it was a deer and let it be.

That rustling again. Nothing wrong with her ears. A kind of quiet rubbing and a little voice in it. 'Mama,' was that it? Some little child. A tiny wind blew into her face, carrying the Joseph smell. It was as though she could hear his voice: 'Don't, Charley. Just sit still.'

Don't what? Don't go to some little child, lost along the road? Probably some fool woman stopped to pick berries, then got back in the car and drove off, never seeing that the little one wasn't along. Charlotte rose, stepping down the porch steps with the ease of one who could have done it blind. 'It's all right, Joseph,' she said. 'Just some lost child.'

She went down the drive toward the road, but the light-colored shape faded back among the trees. Charlotte sighed. Poor baby, afraid of strangers. 'It's all right, child,' she called. 'It's all right. I can help you find your mama.'

CHAPTER SIXTEEN

Molly was waiting for them when they arrived home, the willowy form of Simoney close beside her. Mahlia hugged her tightly. 'I'm sorry. Molly's told me I've behaved very badly.'

Simoney held her at arm's length, shaking her a little as she said in her soft, almost whispery voice, 'Never mind, Mahlia. Our feelings were hurt, but we'll get over that. At least, Molly and I will. Martha's making a major thing out of all this. I think it's menopause with her, she's so irritable lately.'

'I didn't know witches had menopause!' Mahlia was astonished.

'What did you think they'd have,' asked Molly, 'renewable ovaries?'

'I guess I hadn't thought about it,' Mahlia gasped, trying not to laugh. 'I'm sorry she isn't here. But I'm glad you are, Simoney. I suppose Molly told you what has happened.'

'A good deal that shouldn't have happened, that's for sure.' Simoney had changed in the year since Mahlia had seen her. Her tremulous youth was giving way to something sturdier, though no less graceful.

'She's been twitting me,' Molly said, 'claiming I've forgotten my protections and covenants.' Molly smoothed her apron, looking offended.

'I only suggested—'

'Suggested I review the manual. Not very respectful, Simoney, I must say. I think what got in is something my covenants and protections simply didn't work against. There was nothing wrong with them when I laid them.' She snorted, shaking her head and compressing her lips in a familiar grimace of annoyance.

Robby had been looking from face to face, mystified. 'Does anybody care if I eat something before I go out?' he asked at last in his sweetest possible voice.

'Diplomatic child,' Mahlia said. 'Reminding me that he is starving.'

When Robby had been fed and had gone out to play, they sat in the living room. Mahlia built a small fire even though the day was warm, just for the cheerful look of it, and brewed a pot of the tea she knew both Molly and Simoney liked. Simoney asked questions; Molly or Mahlia answered; an hour fled by as they tried to make sense out of the essentially senseless happenings of the past few days.

'Bracelet, bone, hidden room, *vèvè*, one death, and one forcible entry,' tallied Simoney.

'And one possible ghost,' added Molly. 'Captain Bone.'

Robby appeared at the door, demanding cookies for himself and Cynthia.

'When did she get here?' asked Mahlia.

'She's been here, waiting for me. She got away from the little pigs, and she's down in the orchard by the swing.'

As Mahlia doled out the cookies, wondering whether she should say something about Cindy's choice of language, Simoney asked, 'Little pigs?'

'I think Cindy means her brothers,' Mahlia whispered. 'Not without some justification.'

'Rotten kids, hmmm?'

'Not really rotten, just sort of infant-boar-ish, very destructive and loud and generally heedless. I can see why Cindy would prefer to play with Robby. He's better behaved, which means a better playmate. Also, he's verbal, which Cindy's brothers certainly aren't. I'd rather have him playing with her than with her brothers, though I suppose he's going to have to confront the masculine world sometime. I hope it isn't as traumatic for him as it was for Badger.'

'I've been reading the recent articles on male minds and female minds.' Simoney shook her head. 'The male

131

writers, most of them, are condescending about male-female differences; the female writers are angry. What it all seems to boil down to is that more males than females kill themselves doing stupid things; more females than males use argument instead of fists; more males than females perceive the intricacy and wonder of mathematics; more females than males perceive the intricacy and wonder of human beings.' Simoney sighed.

'Nothing new in that,' snorted Molly. 'Been that way as long as I can remember. Mother says nothing's changed since she was a girl, except what we say about it in public.'

'Well, all in all, I'd rather have Robby playing with Cindy than with Bill. He's less likely to get his neck broken.' She stood at the door, watching him trudge sturdily through the grasses toward the swing, hidden behind two gnarled apple trees. It would be lovely not to be either sex, she thought, just to be 'person.' She had a quick image of herself and Badger in bed together as 'persons' and dismissed the image quickly as she revised the idea. It would, however, be nice if children could be persons.

'I've been glancing through Captain Bone's book,' Molly said, 'while you've been fueling up the child.' The book lay near her hand and she picked it up to stroke the stained cover, letting it fall open on her lap. 'You should hear a couple of things out of it.'

The first few pages were full of self-justification, 'testimony,' Mahlia supposed one might call it. All about the religious conversion of Nathaniel Bone and his repudiation of his former career. Not very interesting, really, unless one were a psychologist. Or perhaps an evangelist. The most interesting thing was the way Molly read it. Her voice held not a trace of the countrified accent she normally adopted; instead, it was almost scholarly sounding.

'"Jn. Byers, being in his middle years and full intellect,"' Molly read, ' "was offered that Temptation, the which had been offered me in years past and refused with great pain of care as to the eternal fate of my soul. All that was required of him, as it would have been for me, also, was to cease his depredations upon the tribe of that folk called the Fon in the lands in which we both had gathered slaves, the which he agreed to do. Given then the Password by the people of that place, he went to a certain island of the Caribs and was awarded a woman to give him what he sought together with three handmaidens to do his bidding, these women being descendants of the blacks with whom he had treated, among them a royal daughter bound by filial duty to the will of the Fon Chieftain. And he, from long work in the vile trade we had shared, had stored up a considerable fortune, sufficient to come to the vicinity of Chester and purchase land there enough for his purposes." '

'This land,' said Simoney. 'This very land is what he bought with money from selling slaves.' She gestured, including all of it, meadow and forest, pond and orchard, house and barn, shivering a little.

'The land wasn't created by the slave trade,' Mahlia objected. 'He bought it, yes, but he didn't create it. The land was clean. Only the money that bought it was dirty.' Still, she shivered as Molly went on reading.

' "So it was Jn. Byers sold his soul to the heathen gods of that people, those they call the *loa*; to the god of the crossroad and the god of the graveyard who, it is said in the port of the Caribbean Islands, demand blood sacrifice of their evil sect." '

Mahlia shuddered as Molly put the book down. She had no sense of disbelief. Her own experience had taught her how believable such things were. She had no doubt that Captain Bone had believed it all as well. Still, she did not want to read more of it just now.

'It could explain a lot,' mused Simoney.

'How do you mean?'

'It could explain why Molly's covenants didn't work. If they were just the ordinary kinds of wards and protections, they might not work against – *loa*. I don't know. We've never run into *loa* before.'

'Don't the covenants guard against anything supernatural?'

'No. Not all things,' Molly admitted. 'Just most things.

For some things, you have to know what they are before you can protect against them. You have to see them, or hear them, or know their names. At this point, I haven't the remotest idea what we're up against here.' She furrowed her brow, thinking.

Robby came trudging back from the orchard, possibly on a quest for more cookies. Mahlia went to the door to meet him.

'What are you after, young man?' she asked, trying to lighten her own mood. 'More cookies?'

'Nope. I hafta go. Then I hafta find some rope.'

'What do you have to find some rope for?'

'Cynthia wants to swing, but I hafta tie her in. She can't hold on enough with only one arm.'

'When did Cindy hurt her arm?' Mahlia asked. 'I hadn't heard about that.'

'Not Cindy!' he said scathingly in the tone that indicted adults of never listening to anything one said. 'Cynthia! Cynthia only has one arm. They cut her other one off when they tried to make her a little pig.' Then he set off up the stairs, leaving Mahlia clinging to the door, aware suddenly of a cold wind that came down those stairs from the white, clean little room that was empty – of anything she could see.

'Cynthia?' asked Molly on a rising note of disbelief. 'Cynthia? Not Cindy Robinson.'

'Cynthia,' Mahlia said in a strangled, almost hysterical tone. 'A little girl with one arm. A little girl whose arm was cut off! Oh, Molly, Simoney, I've no doubt at all she wore a bracelet decorated with a wreath of rowan and oak leaves and little blue flowers!'

There was a moment's silence. 'Bone, bracelet, hidden room, _vèvè_, one death, one forcible entry,' tallied Molly, rising to stare out into the orchard. 'And two ghosts.'

CHAPTER SEVENTEEN

Charlotte Grafton had walked farther into the woods than she had intended, right into the center of the narrow neck of forest that reached from the hills along the stream onto the Grafton farm. She kept hearing the child crying, 'Mama, mama.' Twice she had started to turn back to get help in this search rather than try to find the child with her old, nearsighted eyes, and each time the pitiful crying had kept her on the trail. Now she was right in the foothills, well away from any house, feeling like a fool because she'd lost the child entirely and might well have lost herself into the bargain.

'Well, Joseph,' she said. 'You told me to sit still and I wouldn't.'

Carefully she turned herself around, looking up to get some idea of direction from the sun. No shadows here under the trees. Not time for sunset yet, but still the sun was so low she couldn't see it above her anywhere. One way out would be to find a brook, any brook. They all flowed east out of the hills along here, and any way east would take her out onto farmland. Only problem was, she didn't hear any water. Just that kind of rustling she'd been hearing all along, that dry rubbing. Couldn't figure out what that was. No wind to speak of. Could be dried twigs rubbing together. Kind of scything sound, like a sickle through grass.

Well, another way to find her way home would be to go downhill. She headed toward the lowest place she could see, only to find the ground sloping up in every direction. Wearily, she climbed at random to get out of the hollow, went downhill again, this time on a long slope, in and out

135

of the trees, with that sound right behind her the whole way. She was beginning to think it was inside her head, not outside. It was getting darker, too, which made it difficult to walk.

She speeded up a little, reaching out toward what she thought was the pale trunk of a birch, only to draw her hand back with an exclamation of dismay. Something had bitten her – no, cut her. A long flap of skin hung from her arm, attached at the elbow, flayed away as though by a skinner's knife all the way to her wrist. Where it had been, the raw flesh oozed blood. Lord, that was a nasty sight. She smoothed the skin back over the flayed flesh, crying out at the pain it caused her. Blood oozed to the edges of the cut. She fumbled a clean handkerchief out of her pocket and wrapped it around her wrist, holding the flap of skin in place, trying not to panic, trying desperately to convince herself she had been cut in such a fashion by thorns, only thorns. When she raised her head, the paleness she had thought was a birch tree wasn't there anymore.

Something pallid cowered under the black bulk of a bush, though. Was it the child? 'Honey?' she said, quavering, really afraid for the first time. 'Honey, are you lost?' Perhaps the child, frantic with fear, had a knife.

Something ripped at her legs. She turned, not quickly enough to see anything, only quickly enough to get an impression of something papery, flimsy, moving as quickly as the wind. Then she looked down at her legs. Long flaps of skin hung down from her knees, still attached at the ankles, and the blood ran freely. 'Oh, God,' she said, 'God, please,' remembering what Paul had told her about Seepy Paggott: 'Flayed. All the skin off his head – eyelids, all. And then his heart must just have stopped. Or maybe even before they did it. I hope so. God, Aunt Charlotte, who could have done that? . . .'

Who? Who could have done that? Who could be doing that? 'Why?' she screamed. 'Why are you doing this?'

'Mama,' said a tittering voice. 'Mama.'

'Mama,' said another voice from the darkness of the

136

shadow, someone tall, someone bulky, dark, with a voice like silky iron. 'Oh, Mama, this is your time, you see. Time. Got to feed my piggies. Chil'ren got to eat.'

Then they were all around her with their knifelike little nails. Her heart was good, too good, and she couldn't even faint when they cut her face away though she prayed to do so. She stopped seeing anything then, her eyes so full of blood she could not have seen even if she had had eyelids left to blink it away. Then they were cutting her clothes away and beginning on her body. All she could do was pray, a child's prayer. It didn't even hurt yet, though it began to when she fell and her flayed flesh rolled on the ground.

At the very end she stopped screaming and said, 'Joseph,' once, very softly in her throat, as though he were close to her.

CHAPTER EIGHTEEN

Mahlia was in the kitchen with Simoney, fixing supper while
Molly fed Elaine. Robby was upstairs taking his bath. There
had been no one in the orchard when they had gone with
him to the swing. No one. No little girl in a high-necked
dress with ruffly pantaloons showing at the hem, which was
how Robby described her. No little girl in high-buttoned
shoes. No little girl with one arm. Nothing. Only an empty
orchard with the swing moving gently back and forth in the
wind and the three of them standing there, staring into one
another's faces with a new and horrible surmise.

'She left,' said Robby, disappointed. 'Maybe she had to go
hide. She doesn't want the little pigs to get her again. Captain
Bone says she's been hiding since 1880, and that's a long time.'

They agreed, wordlessly, to let it go. Just for the moment,
let it go. Mahlia wondered if the others felt, as she did, that
something heavy loomed enormously above her, palpably
threatening. She staggered as they returned to the house,
and Molly watched her with concern.

As if by mutual consent, they occupied themselves with
homely, ordinary tasks, not talking. There were children
to care for, food to prepare. Now Mahlia turned from the
refrigerator to the sink, holding a head of lettuce, hand and
wrist sprinkled with moisture shaken from the wet leaves.

Which in the instant became drops of blood.

She was holding someone's head in her hand.

The kitchen was gone, vanished. A forest full of prancing
dark loomed around her. Charlotte's voice said, 'Joseph,'
in a whisper so full of pain that Mahlia cried out with it,
feeling it. She was in the forest, burning, burning. The

138

blood was all around her in a cloud, like a river of molten iron, and she was burning in it.

'Charlotte,' she screamed, not hearing Molly or Simoney's exclamations or the answering scream from the frightened baby.

She dropped what was in her hands, looked down to see Charlotte Grafton in a red mist of blood amid a battering of pale shapes, light as leaves, powerful as storm. 'Charlotte,' she cried to the form on the forest floor, not Charlotte at all but a hideous, blood-caked shape that quivered and thrashed. 'Charlotte.'

It was gone in an explosion of pain.

'What is it?' Molly was kneeling on the floor beside her, shaking her. 'Mahlia, what is it?'

Molly's hands on her were only impediments, and she shook them away as she struggled up and ran to the phone, dialing as if by instinct, without needing to look up Charlotte's number. No answer. Again and again. No answer. Cursing herself through tears, shaking off their questions, their hands, she dialed the police.

'Is Paul Goode there? . . . Paul? This is Mahlia Ettison. Listen, I was over at your Aunt Charlotte's this afternoon, and something about the way she looked disturbed me. As though she might not be well.' Somehow her voice sounded fairly calm. Somehow she kept the monstrous knowledge confined. 'I just called her and got no answer. It occurred to me you might . . . Right. Thank you, Paul. That would relieve my mind.

'It won't relieve my mind! I'm a liar,' she howled at them as she hung up the phone, her face wet and sodden, an agony beneath her ribs on one side that made her gasp. 'They've killed her.'

They calmed her as she cried, soothed her as she struggled against them, and gradually her mind began to focus on reality again.

'Charlotte,' she wept at last in the circle of their arms. 'Whatever killed Seepy has killed her, too. Something evil. And it wants me, Molly, I can feel it. It keeps looking closer and closer to me.'

CHAPTER NINETEEN

Paul Goode called late in the evening, well after dark. 'Mahlia, did she say anything about going anywhere? The house is wide open. Her crocheting is lying on the floor of the porch. Her car is out back, and we've covered all the woods close to the house, but we can't find her!'

Mahlia, rigid, cold, trying to keep from crying or screaming or upsetting the children further, already knew what she had to say. 'Charlotte said something about taking a walk, Paul. Can you get tracking dogs? She may have fallen back in the woods somewhere.'

And of course they could get dogs. Dogs that would follow Charlotte's trail, find her. Dogs that would not find anything else. Mahlia was sure of that. They would not find anything else. No more than the searchers had found anything else up in Byers' Fault. No more than Paul had found anyone in her house. No more than Molly and Simoney could find anything, though they had been searching ceaselessly since noon. No, the dogs would find someone dead, horribly dead, and nothing else at all.

CHAPTER TWENTY

Steve Ware was parked under a towering purple beech about a quarter mile down the Chester turnoff with the radio playing, angry at having been ordered to appear, but unwilling to risk Marcy's retaliation if he didn't show up. Marcy had him right where she liked him, running when she said run and coming when she said come. There was no statute of limitation on what Marcy liked to call murder, even though Steve knew it hadn't been murder; the girl had just died, that's all. Steve and the others had just been having a few drinks, a little fun. It was the girl's own fault for provoking them like that, and who could have known that Marcy was where she could see the whole thing? Now, all she had to do was open her mouth, which she showed some inclination to do when he didn't do what she wanted quite fast enough to suit her. He turned up the radio, distracting himself. He didn't like to think about Marcy opening her mouth. He didn't like to think about Marcy, period.

He didn't realize she was there until she jerked open the right-hand door of his car and turned off the music.

'I really didn't want everybody in Millingham to know we were here, Ware. You couldn't draw much more attention to yourself if you tried.' She spoke in a heavily ironic tone, like a forbearing headmistress, knowing it annoyed him.

'Who's going to hear me, the frogs? There's nobody within a mile of here, Marce, and you damn well know it.'

'Somebody might be walking by, some kids, looking for a place to make out. Never mind. What did you find?'

'I found just what I told you I'd find. Zilch. Zippo.'

She considered this thoughtfully. It was a long way to have

141

driven for nothing. 'Honestly? No papers, even?'

'Papers about what? There's an office with shelves of books floor to ceiling and three or four filing cabinets full up. As far as I could tell, they all belong to him. The husband.'

'The mystery man.'

'No mystery. Everything was right there, contracts and correspondence. One file was locked, but it was only old stuff when I got into it. A lot of foreign addresses. So, he's gone a lot. Hell, my father was gone a lot – it doesn't mean there's a mystery. My dad was no mystery.'

'Listen, Stevie-boy. When somebody's tortured to death, what does that mean? Hmm? It could mean the person had an enemy, but nobody cared enough about Seepy Paggott to hate him. So it had to mean he knew something, right? Or at least someone thought he did. And when somebody breaks into a house looking for something, it's because there's something worth looking for, right? And when both those things happen at about the same time in about the same place, and when Seepy was shown through the house the day before he got killed, what do you think it means?'

'I think it means there's a nut loose, to tell you the truth. Look, I spent the whole day there. The mystery room was wide open. Ossie Jeremy was fixing the door. I looked all through it – tapped the walls, measured the sides. I pretended it was police business and even got Ossie to help me. He said there weren't any hidden panels, anything like that. I went through everything in the house, every drawer, every cupboard. There's nothing there, babe. Nothing. No "ancient artifacts," no maps, no treasure trove, no nothing. Somebody made a mistake, that's all.'

She shook her head, lips compressed to a thin, hard line. 'Wrong, Steve. Nobody made a mistake. Seepy died too quick, maybe, but nobody made a mistake. Somebody knows something.'

'Died too quick,' he mimicked her. 'You've really got compassion there, Marce. Poor bastard you were going to marry, tortured to death, and all you say is he died too quick.'

'Poor bastard is right,' she sneered. 'Seepy Paggott was a nerd – like some boy scout, always ready to take an old lady across the street or pat a kid on the head. I had no intention of marrying him, and you know it. He had a chance at that Chester dig to put his name on the cover of any journal in our field, and what did he do?'

The question had been rhetorical, but he answered it anyhow. 'He gave it to you, Marce. Because he thought he owed you.' Because she'd screwed it out of him, Steve thought. Poor Paggott! So dumb and so grateful for the use of her body that he'd actually convinced himself she loved him and then gone on to believe they would get married, because that's what people in love did. And while Paggott beamed, introducing Marcy as his fiancée, people sniggered behind his back, Marcy included.

'He was a wimp. He gave it to me because he was too lazy to make anything out of it.' Generosity wasn't one of the qualities Marcy respected. 'And don't kid yourself. He knew something.'

'So, what's it to you?' The words were only reflex. He knew what it was to Marcy: something to advance her ambition, something to make people look at her, something to put her name in books. That's all Marcy wanted, really, to be famous. With what her folks had left her, she was already rich. 'Come on, Marce!'

She gave him a quick, cold smile. 'Come on yourself, Ware. There's something there. Up to you to find it sweetums – or the word might get out.'

He got out of the car, unable to sit still under her imperious, ironic gaze, unable to do anything about it, wanting to hit her, maybe kill her. She would drive him to it eventually, he told himself, wondering why he hadn't done it already, unaware that she read him like a gauge and understood precisely how much violence he was capable of at any given time. Now she lit a cigarette and simply stared at him through the smoke. There was a heaviness in the air, a dull, metallic quality, as though a storm were brewing. Suddenly, off in the woods, he heard a series of screams, identifying the sound after only a moment.

Marcy Talent started and leaped from the car to stand peering into the depths of the woods. 'What was that?'

'Peacock,' he said laconically, a little gratified at her obvious tension. It wasn't often he got to see Marcy anything but totally in command of the situation.

'What do you mean, peacock? Don't be stupid!'

'I mean peacock, for God's sake. Mrs Racebill thinks the damn things are pretty, so she's got a dozen or so roaming around the farm.'

'Racebill. Isn't that north of the Byers place?'

'Right.'

'We're half a mile from there.'

'So – so the peacocks wander around. Anyhow, that's what that noise had to be. Couldn't be anything else. They always sound like somebody's being killed. Come on, Marce, settle down.'

'It's you who need to settle down, Stevie-boy. Save yourself some trouble and find out what I want. Otherwise . . .' She let her voice trail into a threatening silence.

'You'd be in it up to your neck,' he said without conviction.

'I'm Teflon, sweetie. It wouldn't stick.'

And he knew it wouldn't. She had been a witness only. And he should get rid of her, he really should get rid of her, except it would be easier to do if he was drunk, and she was never around then. With a silent curse he composed himself to receive her instructions as he had a dozen times before. At least she didn't seem to be in the mood for bed, for which he was damned grateful. At one time he'd come on pretty well to Marcy Talent. It was getting more difficult all the time to pretend he still did, and her so-called engagement to Seepy Paggott hadn't slowed her down any in that department.

CHAPTER TWENTY-ONE

Early in the morning, Mahlia went to Millingham to retrieve the carving, the *vèvè*, partly at Molly's insistence, partly out of her own need to know if anyone had found Charlotte. At the police station, Steve Ware was disinclined to let Mahlia have the thing, but Paul Goode, who providentially showed up in the midst of her exasperated remonstrances, let her into the locked cell and told her to take what was hers.

'You want any of the rest of this stuff, Mahlia? Marcy Talent was here yesterday. She said she'd be back today to pick it up.'

'I suppose those newspapers are mine, but I gave them to Seepy Paggott.'

'The old *Monitors*? I know for a fact that the library has a complete file of old copies.'

'Then there's no reason for me to keep them.'

She vacillated, wanting to ask the question even though she already knew the answer. 'Is there any sign of Charlotte at all?'

'Nothing, no. My mother's fit to be tied. Whole family's out there in the woods messing up the trail. I'm waiting on the dogs. Should be here around ten or ten-thirty. Guy I know over in East Boone has two really good hounds . . .' His oice trailed off and Mahlia stood, hating herself. She could tell him. She could tell him what? No, she couldn't tell him anything. He wouldn't understand and it would do no good.

'Call me,' she said. 'When you find her.'

When she arrived back at the house, Georgina was there, looking distraught, picking things up and putting them down without any sense of what she was doing.

'Go home, Georgina.'

'Grandma would shoot me if I didn't do my job, Mahlia. She really would. It's just we're all so worried . . .'

'Go home, please, Georgina. I've guests here who can help out, and we'll manage nicely. Go on home. Stay with your mother.'

Simoney came to stand beside Mahlia as they watched Georgina's little car move out onto the road.

'You're absolutely sure her grandmother's dead?'

Mahlia nodded. 'I'm sure. Yes. I don't know how, though, or where. Just somewhere, back in there.' She gestured toward the northwest, toward the woods, innocent and green-gleaming in the moist morning light.

Simoney riffled the leaves of the book she was carrying, Charlotte's book. It made a rustling, sighing noise. 'Molly and I have read most of this. Interesting. I looked up the date Robby mentioned, 1880. There's an account of several children disappearing. One of the little girls was named Cynthia Flintknap. There's even a description of the bracelet, given to her by her grandmother, Felicity Flintknap. From the description, I think the grandmother was one of us. You knew the bracelet was a kind of protection?'

Mahlia shook her head. 'I could feel that it was intended as protection. But it didn't protect her, did it?'

'It may have, to some extent. You brought the carved thing?'

Mahlia nodded, digging it out of her capacious canvas carryall. The dark wood shone in her hand with an oily, much-rubbed gleam. On it the incised lines made a slightly deeper darkness. One had to turn the wood towards the light to see the design; Simoney did this now, shivering as she ran her tapering fingers across the curls and twists.

'Something?' Mahlia asked. Molly came into the room behind them to stand silently, watching Simoney's face.

'Yes. Something. I don't know what. Molly?'

In Molly's hands the piece of carved wood looked small, innocent, like some knickknack. Still, when she peered at the design, running her hands over it, she too shivered, as

146

though at some chill wind. 'Right. Something, but nothing I know anything at all about. Do you know what this *vèvè* is, Mahlia?'

'I know the name, that's all. There's an anthropologist at the university named Jens – no, Lars, Lars Sigurdson. He evidently is quite familiar with the Caribbean area. He told – let's see, who did he tell? Seepy? No, Seepy called him, but Marcy talked to him about it. He told Marcy Talent this thing was a record of a ritual design. Probably Haitian, something to do with their gods.'

'*Loa*,' said Simoney. 'If it's Caribbean, they're called *loa*. Molly, we need to talk to Mother.'

Mahlia shook her head in confusion. They had spoken often of their mother in Miami – who could not be the mother of both since they were not sisters, except in a collegial sense, which could be what was meant – but why they would need 'Mother' now was not at all clear.

'Mother knows people,' said Molly. 'She knows people in New Orleans and in Barbados and in Jamaica. Haiti, too, I shouldn't wonder. We have to get some information here, Mahlia.'

'I thought . . . somehow I thought you'd know all about it.'

'How very flattering,' Simoney said, her face compressed into an exasperated look. 'Sorry to disappoint, Mahlia, love, but we are in all respects Homo sapiens – a misnomer, I have long felt – which means we're no smarter than the bare minimum necessary to whap somebody on the head with a thigh bone. No, we don't know about this thing.'

Molly shook her head, turned to stare out at the forest. 'There's some things we know pretty well. It isn't fair to say we don't know anything. Some things are as common as scrambled eggs – opening gates, for example. You've seen us do that, Mahlia. Laying protections, too. Any hedge witch can lay protections, though just now there's something bustin' through ours as though they didn't exist. There's other things, though, things that belong to Indian people or black people. Oh, what would you call 'em, Simoney?'

147

'There are beings,' lectured Simoney in her rarely used pedantic manner, 'that are specific to certain locations or certain peoples. I guess one could say "ethnic deities," or "gods of place." People of African descent have access to certain beings Molly or I would be unaware of. People of Indian or Asian descent would have access to still others. If it were merely a matter of opening a gate or laying a protection, our spells should work equally well for them since the rules are pretty much the same for all beings, but for anything more than that . . .'

'For anything more than that, we need a practitioner who has access,' said Molly.

'I don't understand. Before, that other time, you could do protections and summons with the . . . the demons. And neither of them were anything you'd ever seen before.'

'The difference is that we did *see* them,' said Molly. 'We saw the demon Matuku, and that professor friend of yours *identified* him for us. Then, later, we just summoned up the second one blindly, hoping she'd get into it with Matuku and not bother us, but we'd had her described to us, too. Because we'd seen the one and had the other described, we *could* do it. It still wasn't a smart thing to do, however, and we damn near got killed, if you'll remember. I'm the one who likes to learn from experience, if you don't mind. In future I want to know what I'm dealing with, and here, we haven't seen anything and nobody's identified anything for us. No, if we don't want to risk all our lives again, we need to find out what it is, and that means getting access.'

'To these *loa*?' Mahlia was still confused. 'But how do we know they have anything to do with what's happening?'

'Oh, child, child, put it all together.'

'Yes,' urged Simoney, 'put it all together, Mahlia. Start with John Byers. He made a deal with some tribe in Africa, and part of the deal was that he should obtain a particular woman on some Caribbean island as a wife. Three other women as well – concubines, perhaps; priestesses, perhaps. What is it they call them down there, Molly?'

'*Mambos*,' said Molly. 'The male priests are called *houngans*, and the women are called *mambos*.'

'It would be a relief to think that what John Byers was offered was merely sexual in nature, but I don't believe that. It must have been more than that. At any rate, he came back here with the four women and started not just a family but a whole community. And that community had an evil reputation.'

Mahlia stirred uncomfortably. It was true. Byers' Fault had an evil reputation – then, and now.

Simoney went on in her sweet, high voice, as though reciting a recipe. 'Then the people of a neighboring village called Chester rose up and massacred the inhabitants. We should be clear here that they were the Christian inhabitants of a neighboring village. They did it out of fear for their souls, I should imagine, or fear for their lives, or both. At any rate, the evil, whatever it was, was in Byers' Fault. And the mothers or grandmothers of all the inhabitants of Byers' Fault were the women John Byers brought from the Caribbean. Women who were undoubtedly skilled in the practice of certain religious rituals.'

'Seepy Paggott was killed over some religious ritual?'

'I don't know.' Molly shook her head slowly. 'It's possible. Or more likely because someone thought he knew something or had something valuable. Or had found out something about someone – that's most likely, given who the two victims were. Diggers, both of them, Paggott with his shovel, Charlotte with her pen. It's amazing the amount of information she and her foremothers wrote in that book. I wonder how many people knew about the book. That could be important.'

'Seepy knew. Somehow, I don't think he had told anyone else. Marcia, perhaps, though I doubt it. He was the kind of man who would have respected a confidence. If he told Charlotte he just wanted material about Byers' Fault, that's all he would have read. So, it's likely no one knew about the book. But lots of people knew about this carving. Do you really think he was killed for this?' She picked up the plaque and stared at it, trying to wrest meaning from the enigmatic lines. 'You really think someone wanted it badly enough to break in here too, looking for it? But that doesn't explain Charlotte's death.'

'Perhaps she had seen something, Mahlia. Maybe something she didn't even know she had seen.'

'And all the ghostiness, the visions — all that is merely ancillary?' Mahlia was offended by this notion, though she could not immediately have said why.

'No, child, no. Things like that aren't simply "ancillary." If spirits gather, there's always a reason. If Captain Bone and this little girl with the one arm are nearby, you may be sure it's for a reason.'

'Can't you find out?'

'Of course we could,' said Simoney. 'But we have no idea what we'd be getting into! It's like going out for a walk in a bog. One can do that, very nicely, if one knows the way. If one doesn't know the way, one can end up drowned. Of course we could take a step or two, one step to Captain Bone. One step to the little girl, what's her name? Cynthia. One step to the bracelet, perhaps. And then what? Suppose those three steps lose us in the bog? If Captain Bone and the little girl and the bracelet have something to do with this carving, and if all that has something to do with these Caribbean religious practices, who knows what *else* might come up in answer to our summons? Then we'd be lost, just like that. Sucked down. Probably dead.'

'I see.' Mahlia bowed her head, chastened.

'So, I think the first thing we'll do is call Mother. Let's see. It's Friday. Her hairdresser appointment is Friday morning, but she should be home by now. She knows people who know people down there. There's bound to be some sister with access, someone who can help.'

There were many phone calls to and from that morning. There was one from Paul Goode at noon.

After which Mahlia went to her room and spent several hours alone, too horrified and grief-stricken to be with anyone. Paul had been so shocked he had been unable to keep the details decently quiet. Charlotte Grafton had died from shock and blood loss, but not for some time. Her valiant old heart had gone on beating long enough that she had still been alive when the last of her skin had been ripped away – and taken away. There was no skin where they had found her. They had identified her from the scraps of clothing lying about. Formal identification would have to be made by the coroner, from her dental records. Nothing else about the body even looked human. Paul used those words, shocked, horrified, nothing in his training or experience having equipped him for this. 'Some crazy person, or people,' he rasped. 'Some lunatic . . .'

Paul Goode and his colleagues were now firmly committed to the lunatic-at-large idea. In their minds there could be no other explanation.

Molly and Simoney, burning the phone wires in repeated conferences with Miami, were quite certain no lunatic – at least not under the usual meaning of that term – was responsible for what had happened.

CHAPTER TWENTY-TWO

'Whatever it is, I think we're going to find it at Byers' Fault.' Marcia Talent propped herself against the head-board, pulling the spread beneath her naked breasts and lighting another cigarette to add to the eye-burning haze already floating in the room. From the window, thrown wide to let some of the smoke escape, Steve Ware looked at her covertly, thinking how he hated that little full-hipped form with its short legs and demanding little breasts. It sat there, completely unaware of him now that it had made use of him, eyes half closed against the fog of smoke.

'What makes you think that?' He didn't need to ask. She would tell him anyhow, when she needed him to do something.

'Well, it stands to reason, doesn't it? That's where Seepy was killed. He went there looking for something. Somebody thought the thing – whatever it was – was in the Ettison woman's house, but it wasn't. Which means it's still where Seepy was looking for it. That old woman – what was her name?'

'Grafton,' he mumbled. 'Charlotte Grafton.'

'Well, they found her miles from her house, almost at Byers' Fault.'

'She wasn't really that close.' Every time Steve Ware thought about it, he shuddered. The screams he and Marcy had heard, off there in the woods the night before – they might have come from the place in which the old woman's body had been found. Oh, it could have been the peacocks, but he wasn't sure any longer. Steve had been right behind the dogs when they found the body, and he hadn't been able to forget it. 'She was quite a ways north of Byers' Fault.'

'Yeah, but that's where she was going. It's obvious. She and Seepy were thick as thieves. He was always on about her stories, "oral traditions," as he said. Last summer when we were digging at Chester, he spent hours with her over at her place. I'll bet when he was killed, it made her think of something she'd told him, and she decided to go looking.'

Steve said nothing. There was no point in arguing with Marcy when she was in this mood. She got these ideas, and no amount of discussion could dissuade her. Charlotte Grafton wouldn't have gone looking for anything without her glasses. The old woman's eyesight was a town joke. And the glasses had been right there on the kitchen drainboard, where she'd left them. No, Charlotte Grafton might have been taken to the place she'd died, but she hadn't been looking for anything. Let Marcy think what she wanted to – she would anyhow.

'Which means,' she said brightly, 'that we've got to go up there and get a dig started.'

'You're going to get a bunch of kids involved?' He turned to give her an amazed stare. 'With some maniac running around loose, you're going to go up into those woods with a bunch of college kids?'

'Safety in numbers.' She shrugged. 'Come on, Ware. Nobody's going to attack a dozen students with a knife. It's one way of finding out what's going on.'

'You're crazy, you know that?'

She stared at him indolently, letting the smoke pour from her nose. 'What's the matter, baby? Scared?'

'You're damn right. You weren't there, babe. You didn't see the body. I did.'

'Some old dame without her skin. I can imagine.'

'You can't. You think you can, but you can't.' He turned back to the window, sickened. God, but he wanted to get away from her. Why couldn't the nut with the knives have gotten her instead of Paggott? It could just as well have been her up there, spooking around in the woods.

He closed his eyes in concentration. There had been the tiny seed of an idea there. 'When do you want to start?'

'Sooner the better. Today's Friday. We can't do anything over the weekend. How about Monday? Seepy had the housing all arranged.'

'Yeah, but with him dead, the university isn't going to pay the expenses. You have to have a professor in charge, don't you? You can't run it.'

She hummed between her teeth, a rasping buzz like a dental drill. 'Seepy'd already drawn the advance money for housing and food. It was in his car, and I took it before I left the car at the police station. Nobody's thought yet to ask where it went, and nobody's thought to cancel. The diggers won't know the difference. I can toss the jargon around just as well as Seepy could, and any idiot can set up a grid, assign digging areas, and get the logs going. We can put in a week or two before the money runs out or somebody catches up with us.'

'And when they do, you'll say it's what Seepy would have wanted.'

'Sure.' She stubbed out the cigarette and got out of bed, leaning over gracelessly to pick up her scattered clothes. He shuddered, not letting her see it. 'He was all enthusiastic about the place. It's our memorial to him, continuing with his work.' She slipped her jeans on and turned to confront him, her breasts peering at him like another pair of hungry eyes. 'And I'll want that thing Seepy got from the Ettison woman, that carving.'

'You're out of luck,' he said in a dull voice, knowing what would come next. 'She came into the station and picked it up.'

'You stupid ass. I suppose you just handed it to her.'

'I did not. I pretty well had her convinced she couldn't have it, and then Goodie Two Shoes came in and gave it to her. Nothing I could do about it.'

'Nothing except put it away where it couldn't be found before she ever showed up. God, if you didn't have me to do your thinking, what would you do?'

'Live,' he told himself silently. 'Live, lady.' The idea that had been so fleeting returned. He played with it, enjoying it. Maybe the maniac with the knife was still around, within listening distance.

Maybe.

CHAPTER TWENTY-THREE

'Paggott's girl friend thinks she knows why he was killed,' he remarked to the waitress on Friday evening. He knew her only casually, but well enough to talk to, well enough to share stories with.

'You mean it wasn't a nut?' She refilled his coffee cup, breathless, leaning forward in order not to miss a word.

'She thinks he'd found something up at Byers' Fault, and she knows what it is. She's going up there Sunday with a bunch of diggers to look for it herself.' Across the room, faces turned in his direction. His voice had carried, as he had intended.

'Marcia Talent knows why Paggott was killed,' he told a friend on the street.

'He'd found something up at Byers' Fault,' he explained to Joe Demmis, knowing that Joe would tell his folks before the day was out. 'Marcy Talent thinks she knows what it is.'

'Marcy Talent,' he said at the gas station, raising his voice to carry over the sounds of the traffic. 'That's what she told me.'

* * *

'Irresponsible,' growled Paul Goode. 'What's this story about Marcy Talent knowing something? Way I hear it, you've been tellin' it all over town.'

'I was just talking about what she told me.'

'Well, don't talk about it. Keep your mouth shut. When did you and Marcy Talent get so friendly anyhow? I thought she was going to marry Paggott.'

'Well, sure. We just got to talking, Paul, that's all. I didn't mean any harm by it.'

'You never mean any harm by anything, Ware, but you always seem to end up causing it anyhow. Just shut up about it, you hear me?' Paul Goode wasn't really paying attention. If he thought about Steve's story at all, he considered it unlikely. Just Marcy, dramatizing herself, as she usually did. Being a pain in the butt. Still, it wasn't the kind of talk that helped solve a case like this. Paul didn't want anything interfering with the search for the lunatic. He didn't want any nonsense from Steve Ware and Marcy Talent.

CHAPTER TWENTY-FOUR

On Sunday morning Molly put down the phone and stared at the copious notes she had written on four pages of a lined yellow tablet. 'There's no one Mother knows of in Miami. There are people she trusts in New Orleans, but none of them are around right now. Which means we have to try Haiti. Her one really good source is in Haiti.' She made a weary shrug at Simoney and Mahlia and dropped heavily into a large chair, making it scream in protest.

They were silent for a time, each lost in her own thoughts. Elaine crawled toward Molly with sounds of busy self-congratulation. Outside on the lawn, Robby sat beneath a tree, as silent as they, lost in the wondrous contemplation of a whole cat family. Georgina had showed up early that morning with mama cat and five babies in a box. 'Can you keep them for me, Mahlia? Please. The family is so upset, nothing's getting done. I know Grandma expected you to take some of the kittens anyhow. I'll come back for them when things settle down.'

So far as Robby was concerned, he would keep them forever. Mahlia, grateful to have him occupied, had said yes. Now she watched his intent little face bent over the box, which concealed everything except the tip of a furry tail twitching to and fro.

'They speak French in Haiti,' said Mahlia. 'At least some of them do. Most of the blacks – the *noirs* – speak Creole, if I remember rightly.'

'You speak French,' Simoney murmured.

'I don't speak Creole.'

'You could probably get by in French.'

158

They fell silent again. On the mantel the clock seemed to tick-tock in a constant crescendo, louder than Mahlia remembered having heard it before. 'I suppose I could,' she said finally.

'If you tied your hair up in a kerchief, you would look almost like a native. I suppose there are some lighter-colored people there.'

Mahlia tried to remember what she had read about Haiti. 'At one time the upper class in Haiti was all light-colored, *mulatre*, and French-speaking,' she said. 'There was a lot of class conflict. When Duvalier – the first one – came in as president, I think the *mulatre* aristocracy was regarded with disfavor and relegated to a subordinate role. Duvalier was very dark, of course. I don't remember whether his son is dark or light, not that it matters since he's fled the country. I really don't look that dark.'

'Darker than Simoney and me,' said Molly. 'Maybe you could pass for someone with Haitian parents who was raised in France.'

'I can't just walk away and leave the children,' she snapped. 'You may be right and Badger may be wrong about all this, but Robby is Badger's son, and I love them both. I can't just pretend they don't exist.'

Molly regarded her with a stern look, not much moved by this argument. 'Robby's stayed with us before. Elaine's weaned. I've had enough babies not to regard Elaine as much of a challenge.' Molly picked up Elaine and bounced her, evoking a peal of giggles.

'Thank you very much.'

'She meant it as a compliment,' soothed Simoney. 'Or at least as an assurance. Will you go, Mahlia?'

'If anyone goes, I suppose it should be me. Who is the person your mother wants us to get in touch with?'

Molly said, 'Her name is Mambo Livone. I'll tell you what Mother suggests. She knows this Livone woman, and she knows some others in Haiti who will help you get to her. You can fly from Montreal, because it's better if no one thinks you're an American.'

159

'My passport will help,' Mahlia said. 'It still lists me as a French citizen. Marie Chalfont.' Actually, she thought, her passport didn't even show her birthplace as Tahiti, thanks to bigoted Aunt Irene, who had bribed someone to hide her niece's exotic – and therefore unacceptable – origins.

'All the better. So, you fly to Port-au-Prince from Montreal, preferably by way of Santo Domingo or San Juan if you can't get there direct. Get a plane in Port-au-Prince, charter one if you need to, to take you west over the mountains of Les Cayes, on the southwest shore of the island. In Les Cayes there's a café called the Speckled Cock – ah, *Le Coq Grivele* – which is owned by a madame Rondice and her son, Jean. Jean would be about nineteen now, according to Mother. The Rondices can direct you to this woman Mother used to know, Mambo Livone. When Mother saw her last, ten years ago she says, she was about seventy, tall, walks rather stiffly, like a heron, white-haired, has a habit of putting the palm of her left hand on the top of her head. Remember that – it's important. She's a *mambo*, which is their word for priestess. You'll probably find her in her *houmfort* – which is a kind of cross between a temple and a dance hall; it's definitely a place of worship, so be careful what you do and say.

'We want to ask her about that *vèvè* thing. As a matter of fact, Mother suggests we tell her the whole story and see if she can tell us anything helpful at all. Find out if she can come back with you. Mother doubts she would, but you could ask.'

'It would be a good idea to look as much like the natives as possible,' Simoney suggested again. 'A kerchief turban around your head should help.'

'Why the act, the subterfuge? Is someone supposed to be watching what I do?'

Molly made an equivocal gesture. 'How would anyone know? There's something inimical at work. If I were conducting a campaign against someone, I'd try to shut down any sources of help. On the other hand, who could guess that you might have a source like this? You've been playing it very straight here in Millingham. How would anyone suspect that you know people in our line of work? I don't know, Mahlia. We've found it usually pays to be careful.'

Mahlia shuddered, remembering a previous occasion when being careful had made the difference between life and death. 'All right. When I've found Mambo Livone and told her the story, then what?'

'Then you find out what she knows, that's all. A clue to what's going on here, instructions on how to handle the thing. It really would be easier if she would come back with you. Do you have enough money available to arrange that?'

'Bribes, you mean?'

'Travel expenses, whatever.'

Mahlia nodded. Money would be the least of her problems, thanks to Badger's 'house account.' 'You'd know better what questions to ask than I will, Molly.'

'But you'll get there and back less conspicuously than I would, Mahlia. If we had an exact location, Simoney and I could fly there quickly enough. But we couldn't talk to her. No, you'll do it best. Two or three days, that's all.'

'It feels very – unsettling,' Mahlia said. 'Not merely adventurous, but somehow dangerous.'

Simoney nodded. 'I'd go for you, if I could, Mahlia. We could set a spell on my appearance, but no amount of witchery can teach me a language I don't know. Language is one of the things that lies outside the realm.'

'Where did my Haitian parents supposedly come from? I'll be asked.' She could not shake the conviction of danger.

'Ah, let's see. If they came from somewhere near where you're going, you'd have a legitimate reason to travel there. Possible relatives? You'll have to play it by ear.'

'And you really think this is necessary?' Now that she had committed herself to going, she found the idea extremely unpleasant. Planes, boats, being alone. Times and places when one was vulnerable, when disaster could strike.

Molly heaved herself erect and walked to the window where she stood staring out at Robby, still intent upon the kittens. 'I don't know. You could take Robby to New York, him and the baby. Maybe whatever is here is just here and would not follow them or you. I'd say there's a good chance that's true. On the other hand, he's seen the little girl and the Captain. He dreamed about Paggott's death. He's been touched, which means there's a kind of . . . circuit open between him and whatever is going on. And between you and whatever's going on, of course. But still, you've had that before. You could go back, if you liked. You could try that.'

'You're not telling me anything, Molly!' she protested. 'You're not giving me any answers.'

The older woman shrugged her heavy shoulders, ran quick fingers under the shoulder of her shirt to adjust a strap, unself-consciously shifting her large breasts into a more comfortable position. 'I can't. I can't tell you, honey. I just can't.'

'Then I'll have to go.' Mahlia sighed, looked out at Robby, who was now hugging the ginger tom kitten. 'You take good care of them, Molly.'

And she thought as she said it that perhaps Molly couldn't take good care of Robby, couldn't protect him. Something huge and uncontrollable was loose. Something that even the three of them together might not be able to do anything at all about.

CHAPTER TWENTY-FIVE

Mahlia had never cared for airline terminals. The Montreal terminal on a Monday morning was no better and no worse than any other. All except the very smallest of them echoed. All of them promised to swallow her into a cavernous machine that would herd her down narrow corridors, crush her into a seat too close to others, daze her with a hammering vibration of engines, then spit her out at some distant place, disoriented and aching. She always dressed for this attack by making herself as inconspicuous and neutral as possible.

Today, in compliance with her rule, she wore dark glasses that hid half her face, concealing the rest of herself under a loose tan coat and a wide-brimmed hat. Beneath the coat was a simple white shift. Her feet were bare inside low-heeled sandals, and inside her large, canvas carryall was a makeup kit, a change of clothes, and a white cotton scarf that she had practiced knotting about her head, Haitian fashion, under Simoney's scrupulous gaze. One small bag had been checked; she could get by without it if she had to. Most of her money was in a belt beneath her dress. If all went as planned, she could step into the lavatory shortly before arriving in Port-au-Prince and emerge a few moments later looking almost like a native.

Waiting for the plane to be ready for boarding, she tried her role on mentally, thinking her way into it. Be ready for dusty feet, she told herself, for walking a lot. Little or no public transportation. A dearth of good roads. Lots of drums. Dancing as a big part of life in religion. Belief in possession by the spirits – *loas*, she corrected herself; belief in possession by the *loas*. Sacrifice of animals. Tropical greenery; white beaches; steep mountain valleys plunging toward the sea. Not unlike Tahiti. Different customs, but not unlike Tahiti. She attempted to convince herself of this, without much success.

'Jessie's pretty pissed about your taking off this week.'

The woman's voice was almost at her ear, so close that she started, almost dropping the French magazine in her lap, thinking someone was speaking to her. Then as she turned realized it came from behind the movable partition she was sitting against. There was something familiar about the voice.

'So I need a holiday, Lois. Some amusement. You should be able to understand that.'

John Duplessis's voice. Talking to his sister. Mahlia closed the magazine and sat very quietly. This trip was supposed to be a secret. She was not supposed to encounter anyone she knew.

'I understand it,' Lois Duplessis responded. 'But all Jessie understands is that you have a habit of missing family reunions. It makes things a bit . . . touchy.'

'I missed *one* family reunion – hardly enough to be called a habit. It wasn't convenient for me to get back in '80, that's all.'

'Well, after all the trouble she's taken to make up for it, you'd better plan to be back on time for Thursday's event. Otherwise you won't get the present you've picked out for yourself.'

He laughed, a sound of enormous self-satisfaction. 'Oh, but I particularly want that present, Lois. Very tasty, that one.'

'You're sure? You only got to look it over once.'

'Twice, actually. My other efforts were stymied, but twice was enough.'

There was the sound of a lighter being flicked, the smell of smoke. Mahlia remembered that she had seen him smoking, in which case he would be in the smoking section of the plane – unless he was in first class.

As though in answer to this thought, the woman's voice behind her asked, 'Where are you sitting?'

'Not among the common herd, my dear. I don't like cattle runs. I'll wait until they're all on before boarding. That way one can miss most of that unpleasantly intimate shoving.'

Without even thinking about it, Mahlia found herself on her feet, moving toward the small crowd at the gate. There was the usual pre-boarding milling about, and she lost herself in it, keeping her back to the seating area. With any luck at all, she could be on the plane and seated in her window seat before he got on. When they landed, she would wait until he had gone. The crowd moved forward, pushing her along with it, and she became a mere particle flowing down the ramp to the plane.

Across the aisle from her seat a harried mother with a baby in her arms tried to cope with four mutinous children, all under the age of six, who were disinclined to sit down and fasten their seat belts.

'Could I hold the baby for you?' Mahlia offered, thinking mostly of the disguise potential the baby provided. It was a very dark, dimpled, and delightful baby. Once on her lap it – he or she – settled down with a little murmur of pleasure and began to pat at the window with sticky hands. Mahlia kept her attention focused on the child. If John did look back into this end of the plane, he would see only the baby and the top of Mahlia's head.

During the early part of the trip she hid behind magazines, behind lunch, behind the baby again while its mother took the other children to the lavatory in relays. When her legs were so cramped she could scarcely move, she risked the trip to the lavatory herself.

In the cramped little cubicle she washed her face and hands, splashed cologne down the neck of her dress, brushed her hair, and spilled the contents of the bag on the counter looking for her lip gloss. Her passport flipped open and her own face stared up at her, as it had been two – almost three – years ago. Marie Chalfont. Marie Chalfont had been a different woman, she assured herself. A schoolgirl, insecure, a bit of human flotsam, really, washed this way and that by whatever wave came along. A girl who saw true visions of the future and the past and was scared to death of both. She looked at her own face in the mirror, forcing her eyes to see what was there: the soft brown of her oval face, the dark troubled depths of her eyes. Perhaps Marie Chalfont had not been that different, she thought. She felt a little like flotsam now, pushed one way by Molly, another by Badger. 'Nonsense,' she told herself. 'You are doing only what you decided to do yourself.'

What was it Molly had said? 'Don't let other people decide your life for you, Mahlia. Not even Badger. Don't let other people *use* your life for you. Use it yourself, for what purposes you think are important.'

Well, so. Robby was important. Elaine was important. And there was a threat to them both – to say nothing of a threat to Mahlia herself. If Badger couldn't buy that, to hell with him.

In this overtly rebellious mood, she tucked her passport back into the little zippered bag and returned to her seat to turn her face to the window, nestle her head into a pillow, and close her eyes. It had been late last night before she had fallen asleep. And up at the crack of dawn this morning to make it to the airport on time.

She found herself thinking of John. She could have enlisted his help for this expedition, would have done so if not for Molly's insistence upon secrecy. But, no, John would have been a distraction. He was simply too good-looking by far, improbably good-looking. He broadcast a kind of fatal fascination. Like Count Dracula. The kind of man who eats women for breakfast – and lunch and dinner. A carnivore. A what? Femivore? The thought was only momentarily amusing. If faded and she was really asleep.

She woke to the sound of the pilot's voice on the loud-speakers, fuzz-edged words that seemed to obscure their own meaning. Landing, obviously. Then the flight attendant, a girlish, treble voice in English and then in French, with sloppy enunciation and a fit of the giggles in both languages. Seat belts fastened. Tray tables in their upright position. Extinguish all smoking materials. Stupid. Since pipes and cigars weren't allowed anyway, why not just say 'put out all cigarettes'? 'Smoking materials' made one think of hookahs and hashish.

Through the window she saw John Duplessis striding off across the tarmac. Still she did not move, not until there were only a dozen slow-moving passengers left shuffling off the plane. The children across the aisle had gone, leaving a shambles of crumpled candy wrappers and torn comic books behind. A man in green coveralls stood looking at the mess with annoyance, trash bag at the ready. Mahlia slipped out of her seat, off the plane, and into the nearest ladies' room.

With the hat and coat off she looked much less citified. Her hair took a bit of doing. She was not accustomed to wearing it up, and it kept slipping out of its high-fastened coils. Braiding it would be better, but that would take too much time. She took out her white kerchief, smoothed it, and tied it around her head, putting off the next step. Putting off the adventure. She didn't feel adventurous.

Under the French magazines in her carryall was a flat, brown-paper-wrapped package – the *vèvè*, hidden. And she was Mahlia Ettison, also hidden, going on a mission. As she put the magazines back into the carryall, she noticed that two of them were subscription copies, addressed to Mahlia Ettison at the city apartment address and forwarded by Vivian. She tore the labels away, angry at herself for having overlooked them. So. Now she was Marie Chalfont.

First item of business was to exchange some of her Canadian money into gourdes – so named for the calabashes that had served as the first Haitian currency. She listened to the local patois, letting it filter into her own voice, blurring and softening her words so they did not sound so crisply foreign. 'Marie Chalfont,' she kept reminding herself. 'I am just Marie Chalfont.'

She waited at the tourist information desk while two fat American women struggled with the language and a stack of brightly colored paintings. The shop had promised that the paintings would be wrapped and boxed; they had been

167

delivered to the hotel, not wrapped or boxed. Now the plane was to leave in moments and there were too many to carry. The young woman behind the desk did not care, it was obvious, and the tourists were growing angry.

'Is there a plane I can charter to Les Cayes today?' Mahlia interrupted.

'No need, ma'm'selle. There is a flight already going, in an hour, perhaps. Does ma'm'selle require any other assistance? A hotel, perhaps?'

'Thank you, no. I have relatives living near Les Cayes.'

'What are we going to do with these?' one of the American women wailed in a voice like a lost soul. 'They're all paid for!'

The paintings, stacked against her ankle, chose that moment to collapse, brilliantly colored primitives sliding across the floor in a slippery cataract. Wide-eyed gods and beasts stared up at her from the floor, accusingly. Accusing herself of being a traitor, Mahlia strolled away from them. She might have been able to help, but not without speaking English. She couldn't speak English. Marie Chalfont spoke very little English. Marie Chalfont wanted only to take the flight that left in an hour or so. She fetched her small bag from the baggage area and merely sat, waiting almost fatalistically for what would happen next.

An hour later she was trailing along behind a straggle of passengers for Les Cayes, getting into a plane in which one could not stand upright, stowing her small suitcase in a bin just behind the cockpit, struggling down the aisle into the first available seat – only one seat to a side – hearing the propellers whanging away as though there was something broken in one of the engines. There were six passengers. The pilot mounted the stairs behind her and paused beside her seat. He looked the passengers over carefully, his eyes finally coming to rest on her, at first seriously, then with a lighter expression.

'It's nothing,' he said, grinning at her, seeing her apprehension. 'It will stop when we fly.'

It wasn't really French, but she got the gist of it. 'That

would be nice,' she replied, trying to return his smile. 'It's very noisy.'

'Where are you from?'

'France,' she said, nodding, smiling. 'I'm from France.'

'Ah? Are you really! We don't get many tourists from France.' He pushed through the little curtain that separated the cabin from the cockpit and seated himself, shouting something unintelligible at his copilot, who leaned between the curtain flaps to stare at her, eyes brilliantly white in his black face. Then they became very busy with the lurching, leaping machinery that carried them bouncing into the air and upward, circling, away to the southwest.

It was quieter in the air, though not by much. Below them valleys reached southward into the mountains, into the long spine of the southern peninsula, the Massif de la Hotte. The mountains looked furry, like some tumbled blanket of heavy green kneed up from beneath by a drowsy giant. The forest was dotted with little buildings like a child's blocks, some roofed with metal, some with thatch. White trails, as narrow as goat tracks, wound through the trees, showing up at a certain angle, then disappearing beneath the burgeoning green. Silver glints of streams ran north from the summits. Then, suddenly, they rose above the mountaintops and the whole peninsula was beneath them with the sea rimming it. The metallic glimmer of streams marked both sides, north and south, and the ridge ran ahead of them to the west, a giant backbone.

Around all lay the level line of ocean horizon; closer, a white line of surf and beaches. There was a roar of static as the pilot announced their descent at Jacme. For a moment she panicked, afraid she had taken the wrong plane, but the pilot's face emerged from the curtain once more to shout at her. 'A brief stop only, ma'm'selle. Then to Les Cayes.'

Some passengers got off. Others got on. One or two looked at her curiously, one or two admiringly. Mahlia stared out the window and ignored them. The plane shuddered its way into the sky once more.

Now outside the right-hand window were deeply plunging

valleys, an endless series of corrugations, silver-centered, green-sided, narrow and deep at the top, wider at the sea end where huddled buildings clustered beneath spiky palms.

'Bainet,' called the pilot, grinning at her through the curtain slit, pointing down. Below them tiny ports fled beneath the wings, boats like toys moored at docks no longer than her finger. He pointed again. 'Cotes de Fer.'

And then they were descending once more.

'Les Cayes,' called the pilot, nodding. She nodded in response, suddenly fearful. What if she couldn't find the Rondice woman? What if the Speckled Cock had gone out of business? The plane dropped like a seabird, down like a fishing pelican between the mountains and the sea.

When she left the plane, she stood on the tarmac for a moment, dazed, looking through the small terminal building toward the setting sun. There were shouts from behind a stretch of fence. Other passengers moved in that direction, calling out. Someone called to her and she turned. It was the pilot, holding out her small suitcase. She had forgotten to get it when she left the plane.

'We would be honored to offer ma'm'selle a ride into Les Cayes.' The pilot was beside her, his colleague at his side, both jacketless now, the sleeves of their white shirts rolled halfway to their shoulders.

'An imposition,' she murmured. 'Surely there is a taxi . . .'

'One,' he admitted, with the ever-present grin, 'which you must share with us, ma'm'selle. Where is such a pretty woman going on such a lovely night?'

It was, truthfully, a lovely night. The sun was setting in a self-congratulatory frenzy of amber and rose. Palms danced gently in a light, salt-laden wind. Voices called. Somewhere people were singing. It could have been a movie setting. She relaxed a little.

'Do you know a café called *Le Coq Grivele*?' she asked them.

They exchanged glances as they laughed. 'We are going there. For our *'ti mange*, our little supper. Later we will return to Port au Prince. So – we take you with us.'

The matter seemed foreordained. The taxi was waiting, and the driver greeted the other men familiarly. There was much laughter among them whenever she spoke. It was hard to tell whether they were teasing her or simply trying to understand her. Between the condition of the road and that of the vehicle, there was little opportunity to speak except in shouts, imprecations, bellows of laughter. They gave her no time to become concerned, no time to worry about where they were going. Lights bloomed around them in the darkness, lanterns, the glimmer of buildings along a street. They turned away from the light, however, into a twisting way along which trees bulked black against the purple, star-pricked sky. A long, low building emerged from the dusk, white walls looming along the road, its forecourt haphazardly occupied by two or three cars and a number of bicycles and scooters. Through a break in the surrounding trees she could see a line of silvered surf.

'*Le Coq Grivele,*' called the driver, pulling up with a great flurry of gravel and turning off his engine. He obviously intended to come in with them.

They tugged her out of the car, and drew her along with them through the door into a candlelit interior where a dozen men and women sat in unmatched chairs at scattered, bare tables, most with glasses or mugs in front of them, one or two with plates of food.

'You're hungry,' the pilot said to her, allowing no disagreement. 'I know what's best!' He shouted an order to someone in another room, reacted to a responding shout with delight. To Mahlia it sounded as though he had ordered four pigs with garnish, but what was set before them seemed to be fish. She prodded it with her fork, doubtfully took a bite, then realized how hungry she was.

'Delicious,' she murmured, smiling her thanks. 'Really good.'

'Just caught,' he responded, pouring something into her glass. She took a swallow and choked, and her companions roared with mirth. '*Clairin,*' he said. 'White rum. You don't have to drink it. Now, who are you looking for?' he asked, handing her a paper napkin.

She responded without thinking, without wondering why his French had improved so suddenly. 'Madame Rondice,' she said more loudly than she had intended.

The words fell into a hush, one of those temporary holes of silence that come now and then in every conversation, even in the babbles of a large gathering. 'Madame Rondice.' There was no laughter, no conversation. She became aware that many eyes were fixed on her, glittering in the half-lit room.

'Ah, ma'm'selle, how sad. Madame Rondice is gone. Very suddenly. It is thought she is dead.'

The food stuck in Mahlia's throat. Without any warning at all, shadows swam into the room and a vision created itself, against her will. A woman stood in the door to the kitchen, her arm flung across her face as though to protect if from a blow. Bulky forms surrounded her in a light of leaping flames. There was a knife. Ears and fangs, like animals. The woman screamed, silently. Through the vision, Mahlia could see the wall of the room, the open door into the kitchen, the two people working there at a wooden table, laughing. The knife at the vision-woman's throat might have been one of the knives in her hands. The blood that streamed from that throat might have been the red from the large fish they were gutting there.

'She is gone,' the pilot said again, his eyes intent upon her face. 'What a pity.'

Mahlia kept her face carefully expressionless. Inside she was shivering with a fear as inexplicable as it was sudden. Why had she come here with these men? What had possessed her?

'We have never introduced ourselves,' the pilot said now. 'I am Phillipe Designe. My friends, Renee Duchamp, Yves Mentor.' Yves was the taxi driver.

Mahlia said, 'Maria Chalfont,' pleased to hear her own voice sounding calm, unruffled.

'Well, Marie Chalfont. You intended to visit Madame Rondice? You are related, perhaps?'

The room was far too quiet, as though waiting to hear her answer. 'No. I came to Haiti to see if any of my father's relatives are still here. It is my understanding that Madame Rondice knew my great-aunt or my cousins and would know if any still live around Cotes de Fer.' It was the place she and Molly had agreed upon, a town no great distance from where she sat. Phillipe was still too quiet, his eyes boring into her over the smiling lips. What the hell was going on here? 'Since my parents died, I have been interested in locating their families. I came on an impulse. My father spoke occasionally of Madame Rondice. A friend of his people's I think.' She was inventing now.

'Ah.' Phillipe nodded, seeming to relax. Across the room people began talking with one another once more. Yves the taxi driver touched her arm in seeming sympathy as Phillipe went on. 'And your aunt's name?'

She shook her head. 'I don't know whether she married or not. She was born Dechant. Irene Dechant. My father's mother's sister. My grandfather left here when my own father was only a baby . . .'

There was a stir at the table. Someone had come into the circle around her – a light-colored, slender young man in his late teens or early twenties with a tray on one arm and an expressionless face. 'Madame Chalfont? I am Jean Rondice. Isabel Rondice was my mother. She spoke to me of the Dechants. Your great-aunt is dead, but my mother thinks you have a cousin living still near Cotes de Fer.'

Philippe Designe was staring at the new arrival, one corner of his mouth twisted into an uncertain smile. 'How miraculous you should know this.'

'Not at all. Madame Chalfont wrote to say she would come if she could. Some time ago . . .'

Mahlia took the cue from him, licking dry lips. 'Some months ago, yes. At that time I didn't know if I'd really be able to come.'

'Before her . . . death, my mother sent a message to your cousin. She would want me to take you there. We can go now, if you like. I have a boat.' Still he looked at her with

173

that expressionless face, as though only by speaking in that particular tone was he able to speak at all.

Mahlia nodded. ' I would appreciate that.'

The pilot exchanged glances with Yves, shrugged as though to say, 'Who knows?' When he turned to her, the watchfulness in his eyes was still there, but good humor seemed to have replaced the slight hostility he had shown when Madame Rondice was mentioned. 'All works out for the best, ma'm'selle – no, madame. Ah, an evil day that one so beautiful should be already married.'

'Married and with children,' she said quietly. 'I must get my search over and return to my own family quickly.'

'You are going east of here?' He exchanged glances with his companions again, smiling slightly with satisfaction when the boy nodded. 'Ah, good. Perhaps you will return to Les Cayes when you have met your kinfolk. Perhaps we will meet again.'

There was no reason this should sound sinister, but it did. Was it her imagination, or did Jean Rondice nod to her, so slightly it could hardly be seen. 'Yes,' she said, smiling carefully. 'Of course.'

They did not let her leave alone. All three of them accompanied her for the walk to the beach, at first along a line of dark houses and then across the sand to where the boat was drawn up. Jean had a torch. He lit her way into the ugly, clinker-built little vessel. It had a tiny, squat housing over the engine and a cramped cabin in the bow. Uneven letters straggled across the chopped transom, but she could not read the name in the dancing light. Phillipe and his friends pushed them out onto the water. The boat drifted, rocking slightly, while Jean Rondice fiddled with the engine. After a moment it started, making loud, rackety bangs with choking sounds between. Under her the boards of the deck began to vibrate, and a plume of white foam showed briefly at the stern, beyond Jean's crouched form.

They moved out, away from the shore, then turned left along it. Shore lights came slowly out of the night, passed them, dwindled to the rear. After about twenty minutes of this, Jean did something with the engine and it quieted – not precisely to a purr, but to something approaching that. He came toward her in the half-light of the stars, crouched before her in the door of the cabin.

'Now, madame, perhaps you will tell me what you are really looking for!'

Mahlia stared at him. All she could see was the glitter of his eyes. 'Mambo Livone,' she said at last. 'I was told to ask your mother to take me to Mambo Livone.'

'Who told you this?'

'An old lady in Miami. Her . . . her friends call her "Mother".'

'Ah. And are you really Marie Chalfont?'

'That's what my passport says. What was going on back there?'

'Those rotten *bocors*. Phillipe Designe, him and his friends. My mother didn't just die. He was after her and after her, but she wanted nothing to do with him. He did something to her.'

Mahlia tried to swallow, her throat dry. She struggled for the meaning of his words. *Bocor*. Some kind of wizard, she thought. 'I know. She was killed.' The vision had been very clear.

'How did you know that?' His voice was suddenly angry, full of hostility.

She equivocated. 'I could tell. If she had merely died, they wouldn't have acted that way – so watchful. You called them *bocors*. Doesn't that mean – magician? Wizard?'

'It means devil,' he replied. 'One of them did it. Phillipe, or Yves, or maybe Renee.'

'How?'

He was silent once more. 'It would be better not to say what I think. Mama would have laughed at what I think, but Mama laughed at many things. She never laughed at Mambo Livone. Mama used to say that Mambo Livone knows a great deal.'

'You can take me to the town where she lives?'

He laughed mockingly. 'Town! It is a *houmfort*, only. She

lives there, in the *houmfort*, with the *mysteres* and the *loas*. It's going to take us a while. At this speed the boat is quiet, and we want to be quiet. If they follow us, they'll listen for the sound we made at first. So, we don't make that sound.'

'Why would they follow us?'

'Why would they kill Mama? Who knows why these beasts do the things they do? Perhaps Mambo Livone will know.'

Mahlia dozed after a time, woke, dozed again. The mountains moved against the stars. Sometimes Jean Rondice told her what little villages they were passing. Sometimes they saw the masts of fishing boats, briefly silhouetted against the sky.

He was speaking good, simple French, not Creole, and Mahlia commented on this.

'My mother. She was a *mulatre*, you know – light-colored. Educated. Well, so am I a *mulatre*, and so am I educated. She taught me, and she sent me to school. I speak English, too. Not as well as I speak French, but pretty good. She taught me that, too. It is a *mulatre* custom, I suppose, to be educated. Those *mangeurs-mulatres* – the *noirs* – they don't like us much. Used to be we were on top, the aristocracy. Now they are. Except they're so ignorant, so stupid. Mama used to say they had *loas* coming out their ears but not enough sense to build good roads. Ah, she had a mouth, Mama. Maybe that's why . . .'

He fell silent. In the starlight she could see his face dimly outlined. Off to their left the surf surged onto the sand in a pearly line. Out to sea there were lights moving. High above them a plane flew eastward, low over the mountains. Here was only quiet and the muffled chug of the little engine. 'Perhaps it isn't fair for me to blame the *noirs*,' he said. 'They're not educated, that's all. Some few, perhaps. Now that Duvalier and his *tonton macout* are gone, things may be better.'

'Mambo Livone? Is she . . . *mulatre*?'

He shook his head. 'A *noir*. Black as night. But she's a different thing, a great *mambo*. She knows the *loas* by their

176

nicknames, so Mama says.' After a moment he added, 'Would have said. Mambo Livone, she knows all the *mysteres*.'

On the shore infrequent lights showed among the trees, some few high upon the mountain. He pointed up toward the summit. 'The *houmfort* is up there. Watch for the river coming down.'

She watched. Her eyes played tricks on her, glimpsing silver streams where there were none; then all at once there was one. 'There.' She pointed. He followed the line of her finger, then nodded.

'I think that's it. Look for three pillars of rock as we come in to shore.' They turned toward the beach, the engine throttled down to a murmur. As they came near she saw the pillars, rough columns laid up out of chunks of coral. Jean killed the engine, then leaped from the bow to pull the boat close but not up on the sand. 'You'll have to get a little wet,' he urged her. 'It's only up to your knees.'

It was a little higher than that, but the horse-hide sandals she was wearing would not mind a wetting. She hoisted her skirt up around her waist and went over, holding the carryall out of the wet. At the edge of the beach she stood in the surf, letting the wavelets wash the sand from between her feet and the soles of the sandals. 'Where now?'

'As soon as it is light enough, up the trail, there. Right now I have to move the boat down the beach. There's a place there I can hide it. If they come looking for us, we don't want it right out here in the open.'

'And when — when I've finished with my business? Do we have to go back to Les Cayes?'

'Don't be foolish, woman. That's the last place we should go. We'll go across the border. I pray *Bon Dieu Bon* you have enough money with you to give me some. Maybe the only reason they let us go is they think we are coming back.'

'What have they got against me, Jean? I've never seen any of them before.'

He shrugged. 'I don't know. They were looking at you like cats look at a mouse. You're *mulatre*, at least you look more *mulatre* than anything else. That's probably enough.

177

I don't know. Some excitement. Something wicked. Those three, they get all fired up, drinking, laughing, daring each other. Then something happens. Maybe with you it's just – you know. Being a woman.'

'Rape?' she felt remarkably calm. There were things she knew, things Molly had taught her. There were protections against rape.

He shrugged again. 'There. Dawn along the sky. Wait for me here.'

When he returned they went up the path, a well-defined surface among the surrounding greenery, not at all overgrown. It was obviously in frequent use.

There were palms at first, and palmetto. Then there were coffee trees, overgrown with brush and lianas, as though someone had started a plantation and then left it. Higher up, the forest began to have an almost primitive character, with occasional monstrous trees and a quality of age-old wilderness that made her glad of the increasing light.

Several well-used side paths left the main one, branching off to the right, away from the stream. They stayed with the water, guided by its plunging flow. When they had been climbing about an hour, she heard a cock crow and the sound of someone knocking on a pan, as though with a wooden spoon. The sound of chickens led her through the final stretch of woods, and she saw the *houmfort* ahead of her – a much-trodden earth floor around one large tree; an openwork roof above tables littered with gourds and bottles; an iron staff with an iron snake twined about it; and behind this a long, low building, one door opening into it like a throat of darkness. From the clearing, paths led away in all directions.

Mahlia stood regarding this doubtfully. The area before her would be the peristyle, where the dancing took place. The tree was where *Papa Legba* lived, he who opened the way to others of the *loas*. *Damballah* lived on or near the iron post. Since the snake was *Damballah*'s symbol and servitor, there would probably be a sizeable snake around somewhere. The ritual drums would be in the building.

178

Rada drums, she trusted, rather than the evil *Petro* drums. The belief was that the *Rada loas* had come from Africa and were benign, whereas the counterpart *Petro loas* had developed in Haiti and were malign – malign, but more powerful than the others, which explained why they were worshiped. The tables around the clearing were altars to various of the *loas* in both their aspects.

Mahlia had learned that much from her reading before she got on the plane. Not from any local books. Molly and Simoney had disappeared briefly and returned with a couple of books from a library some distance away. Now Mahlia blessed them, glad that they had found something to make this scene seem halfway familiar to her.

Sitting on a low stool in the doorway was a woman, her hair bound up, plucking a chicken. The woman was black, black-haired, crouched. Mahlia shifted from one foot to the other, undecided.

'Come on,' the boy said, starting toward the clearing.

'You stay here.' Mahlia put her finger to her lips, indicating that he should keep silent and moved into the light.

The woman stood up and came toward her, rolling through alternate squares of light and shadow, a huge woman, with fat on her that billowed as she walked. She was not as tall as Mahlia had expected, and she was much younger.

'Who comes to the *houmfort*?' she asked in a deep, rough voice. 'I am Mambo Livone. Who are you?'

The words 'Mahlia Ettison' were on her lips, but she did not say them. 'I am Marie Chalfont,' she said instead. 'My people once lived near here. Would you know them by chance? Anyone named Dechant?'

The woman stared at her, through her. 'How did you get here?' she asked at last, as though she had not heard Mahlia's question.

'Oh, I'm on my way to Cotes de Fer, with a friend. He needed to fix his engine, so he dropped me off on the beach. He'll be back for me later.'

'Dropped you off here? Empty-handed?'

Mahlia fumbled with the folded edge of her kerchief, brought forth some folded bills. 'I carried only enough to recompense those who might give me information, madame. And to buy a meal, if that is necessary. If you have any information about my family, I would be glad to . . .' She held out the money, waiting while the woman regarded it with the same intense scrutiny she had given Mahlia herself.

'I do not know any Dechant,' she said at last, turning away toward the house.

'I do,' said another voice. In the doorway a taller woman stood heronlike, one hand flat on the top of her head. She was as thin as a lath but unbent by her years. Her head was covered with a great bush of woolly white hair. She looked a hundred years old, then twenty, then a hundred again. 'A message came about someone called Chalfont. Whose name is not truly Chalfont, but Mahlia Ettison. Come in *'ti moune*. Tell the boy to come in.'

Jean emerged from the woods. The tall woman strode toward them like a young woman. 'You are careful. That is good. Sometimes it is better if people do not know who Mambo Livone may be. There are those who cast the *ouangas*, curses, as though they were melon seeds. So, they cast in my name but with another person in mind, and the death curses go wide, seeking a fat woman who is Mambo Livone. You see?' She laughed, charmingly, with real amusement, and Mahlia found herself smiling. 'Since she is not Mambo Livone, it does not hurt my friend Cecile. She does not mind.'

The fat woman cast them a resentful glance over one shoulder, and Mahlia thought that she might mind more than Mambo Livone had said.

'So. The message told me you needed help. Come to the *houmfort*, and we will drink something.'

When they were seated over cups of some hot brew that Mahlia did not recognize and was not sure she cared to identify too closely, she took the wrapped package from her carryall and gave it to the woman. 'At home two people have died. They died very strangely, Mambo Livone. My house

180

was broken into in a way that seems impossible. It seems likely that whoever broke in was looking for this thing. My friend said to tell you it may be your gods, your *loas*, who are somehow involved, and we don't know how to summon them or petition them.' Or protect ourselves against them, she thought silently, which might be most important.

Her voice trailed off as the old woman unwrapped the polished plaque of wood and sat staring at it, unspeaking, turning it over and over in her hands.

'Jean Rondice,' she said at last, 'take this and chop it into little pieces with your machete. Then burn every piece until it is ash.'

'We thought we might need it,' Mahlia objected. 'We thought we might need it to call up—'

'Hush. I might call those up, but I would not need this thing to do it. You would not call those up – not ever. Now, tell me everything that has happened.'

Mahlia told the story, everything: Seepy and Charlotte, the break-in at the house, the search of Seepy's belongings, finally the strangeness in Les Cayes.

'Jean says we can't go back,' she concluded, looking out into the peristyle where he crouched over the fire. 'He wants to go to the Dominican Republic and from there to America. He says he knows where to get papers. And my friends would like you to come with me—'

'It would be wise for Jean to go, and wise for you to take him with you, if you can. He is a good cook, Jean. A good, how would you say it, houseman. You need a houseman, a *grand blanc* like you. Oh, you do not fool me with your kerchief, child. You are no *mulatre*. I cannot go with you. I must stay in my own place. There are evil men here who must be put down. *Bocors*, wizards, callers of evil. The *cochons gris*, the gray pigs.'

Mahlia slumped, exhausted. 'But – what am I to do? I was sent to bring you. Bring someone who could tell Molly and Simoney what's going on. I haven't learned anything. Not anything.'

'You will learn. We three, we will all learn. Don't you

181

hear the sound of the drums?' The woman put her hand on her head, flat, as though to help herself hear or press in a certain thought.

'Drums?' Mahlia listened, not sure she heard anything except the comfortable crackle of the little fire. Then she did hear them, far off in the hills. Insistent, but not loud, some of them almost treble.

'Tonight we will go toward the drums,' the old woman said. 'That path beside the water goes on to the top of the mountain, and there it joins a road. We must come there very early, long before the drummers come. Have you any skill, *'ti moune*? Have you been taught?' She made a sign, which Mahlia returned. It had been one of the first things Molly had taught her.

'A little,' she confessed. 'I'm out of practice.'

Mambo Livone nodded, giving her a long, speculative look, as though Mahlia had confirmed something she already suspected. 'In time it comes like breathing,' she said. 'After that, one does not need to practice. Now, I will make a place for you to sleep. Sleep today, and in the afternoon, we will go.'

Mahlia lay down on the cot she was shown. Sleep came all at once. As she dropped into it, she wondered what Mambo Livone might have put in the tea. She wondered that again when she woke with the sun in her eyes, low from the west, to find the old woman packing odds and ends into a sack. 'If you have any money, leave it here,' the *mambo* told her. 'Leave it in your bag. Do not concern yourself. Cecile will keep it safe for you.'

Awkwardly, under the woman's clear gaze, Mahlia divested herself of the money belt, putting it into her carryall and thrusting that under the cot. 'So?' The *mambo* nodded.

Mahlia went out to find Jean curled beside a tree, just rousing from his own sleep. 'She says you're right, Jean – we should not go back to Les Cayes. She, too, called the men there *bocors*, she said they were gray pigs. We're going somewhere now where we can find out what they're up to.'

'Perhaps we can find out what happened to Mama,' he

182

said, brushing himself off. 'It saddens me that we never found her, not even her body.'

Mambo Livone beckoned to them from the far side of the clearing, and they joined her on the upward path. The way was more rugged here, with taller trees. As they moved northward, the stream became smaller.

'It is only about twenty kilometers from the ocean on one side to the ocean on the other,' Jean told her as they puffed their way upward. 'The land here is like a long finger, pointing at Jamaica.'

'I hope we're not walking all the way to the other side,' Mahlia said, looking ruefully at her sandals. They were not exactly climbing shoes.

'Only over the ridge,' said Mambo Livone, striding along like some shore bird, untroubled by the steepness.

Beyond the ridge the land sloped away more shallowly, allowing views of the distant sea. Not far below them a road ran east and west, and they turned east upon it, following Mambo Livone in her seemingly tireless walk. Mahlia estimated that they had walked three or four miles when they came to the bridge.

'You rub your feet with *tobac* here,' the woman said, 'before we go on the bridge. The demons, they smell *tobac*, they won't follow. The ghosts, they smell *tobac*, they won't follow either.' She handed them bits of caked tobacco from her sack and watched while they obediently rubbed it on the soles of their shoes.

'Now, we go over there.' She pointed at the far side of the bridge where a church spire showed above a broken line of trees.

They went over the bridge in single file, so silently that Mahlia wondered what it was they feared. It was obvious from the slant of Mambo Livone's shoulders that she feared something. Jean was as quiet as any small thing that went in terror of its life. Mahlia merely followed, wondering.

At the eastern end of the bridge, another road came up the hill from the north to make a cross-roads. In the northeast corner of this was a ruined settlement, tiny houses half fallen in, doors hanging on one hinge or fallen into the dust. The church was doorless and windowless amid tumbled headstones, and over all the buildings vines and shrubs had grown to make a wilderness, laden with dust.

'You see here,' Mambo Livone said. 'A graveyard. A crossroads. Those who come here need those things. Likely in your own home there is someone using these things also. One of the *loas* must be called from the crossroads; one from the graveyard. Now we go up.' The old woman directed them to her right. 'We must hide ourselves above this place, on the mountainside.'

They climbed once more. Below them a car plowed its way westward along the rutted road, rumbling over the bridge to leave a slowly settling cloud by its wake.

'Come,' the old woman said, working her way to the left along the ridge. 'In order to see, we must come a little lower down.' They crept through the trees, hidden from watchers although there seemed to be no watchers. An outcropping of rock offered a resting place almost above the crossroads. Across it, the ruined town crouched beneath the trees, houses leaning against shore wind and one another, doors gaping into deserted interiors. Curls of metal roofing hung from the steeple and bled rust down the walls. In the graveyard, grasses slanted across the tumbled headstones.

'Now what?' Mahlia breathed.

'Now we wait for the *service* to begin.'

They lay in the dusk. Before the light was quite gone, two additional cars made their rumbling way over the bridge together with one lonely bicyclist, then all traffic stopped. The drums that had been beating in the far hills all afternoon drew closer. Torchlight glittered among the abandoned houses, in the ramshackle church, like the eyes of a wakening dragon, still half asleep. Far down the northern road on one of the long, snakelike loops, more torchlight showed briefly. People were coming up that way.

The old woman pointed off to the left, across the bridge. 'The trail from my *houmfort* joins the road down there. We

184

came early so we should meet no one on the road. People will come from that way soon.'

As they did, black forms that slipped across the bridge like shadows to disappear into the derelict village.

Stars spiked the sky. The drums drew in, closer, fell silent. Along the road came a flurry of bushbeating, muffled shouts. 'They search for spies,' Mambo Livone told them. 'A part of the *ceremonie*. They do not really suspect that anyone observes what they do. If they knew we were here, they would . . . It is better they do not know we are here. You must be silent. No matter what happens!'

Mahlia nodded, not really listening. Jean looked at her oddly, apparently wondering if she had heard. Mambo Livone leaned close to him and whispered urgently in his ear.

The treble drum began again, a wild chatter of sound, like some huge, primitive creature asserting its claim upon the place. Voices rose. Singing and drumming together, more torchlight. A pulse in the night, repetitive, enthralling. Mahlia quivered with it, and the old woman laid a hand on her shoulder until she quieted. 'You do not want to listen to those *Petro* drums. They are not good drums, girl, not the good drums of the *Rada*.'

'Yes,' Mahlia said distractedly. 'Yes.'

Out of the village, from among the trees, a torchlit procession came, capering, dancing. Red robes and white. Animals on their hind legs. Animals with tails, long ears, prancing. People and animals. People dressed as animals. They carried a small coffin, clearly visible beneath a burden of lit candles. Even up on the hill they could smell the burning tallow, an ancient smell that spoke of beast flesh charred over campfires. On her skin, Mahlia felt the old woman's hand, cold. Her own flesh blazed with the dancing.

'Jean. Remember of what I spoke to you. Be ready,' said Mambo Livone.

'But yes, *mambo*. I am ready.'

The forms gathered at the crossroads, leaping and prancing. Some among them were engaged in quieter business,

185

crouching in the road. 'They draw the *vèvè*,' Mambo Livone whispered in her ear. 'They smooth a place on the road and draw the *vèvè* in cornmeal there, to summon the *loa* of the crossroads, *Maite Carrefours*.'

'Is he good or evil,' Mahlia asked, her voice remote and uncaring. 'Evil, or good?'

'He is *Carrefours*. He draws people upon the road, along the road. He is the *loa* of direction. In his name are peopled summoned upon the road.'

'But is he good? Or evil?'

'Must he be one or the other?'

'They are not both the same.'

The old woman stared at her, as though wondering how to explain. 'Look down at the sea,' she said at last. 'See it there, like a mirror, bright in the sunset. Fishes in it to feed us. Water in it to swim in, to carry our boats. Then consider how the great storm comes. Then the waves eat our boats and our bodies. Then the water comes ashore to break down our houses. We drown. Are both oceans the same?' The old woman put her hand flat upon her head, stared with burning eyes deep into Mahlia's.

'You're saying . . .'

'I say if you give yourself to the ocean, ocean may seek you out when storm comes. A wise man gives himself to the ocean on good days and goes inland when the wind comes. If he does not, the ocean may take him.'

Mahlia thought of Molly's comments about rivulets of power, about connections being established. 'Molly, my teacher, would say he had opened a door to the power and may not be able to close it.'

'So. Yes. That is one way to say it. So, when we beat the *Rada* drums, we call the *loas* who smile on us. We call *Maite Carrefours* in his beneficent mood. Those who beat the *Petro* drums, they call him to do terrible things.'

Below them the capering dance went on. The crouched figures had finished their drawing and stood back from it. Even from where they were, well above the road, they could see the design. 'That was my *vèvè*,' Mahlia said.

'Yes. That was one of the patterns,' the old woman said. 'The summons of *Carrefours*.'

Mahlia stood up, abruptly. She had been summoned. She had to go down and get a better look at what was going on. But sudden as her movement was, Jean Rondice was quicker. He had his hand over her mouth before she had a chance to call out. Then both he and the old woman were on top of her, gagging her, tying her. Somewhere deep inside her a little voice thanked them while another, huge voice screamed imprecations at them.

'I thought so,' said the old woman. 'I thought so. One of them set a *drogue* on her, a charm to summon her.'

Inside her bonds, Mahlia struggled to be free. Inside the struggling Mahlia another person sat, watching, remembering, thankful to be tied. Down upon the road a chant took possession of the night, loud and rhythmic. Several of the voices, raised above the rest, seemed almost familiar to her. Several of the forms left the group from time to time to stand at the side of the road, listening, searching in both directions.

'They are searching for you, girl. For you.'

Abruptly one of the shadowy figures straightened with a shout, began strutting about, demanding, commanding.

'*Maite Carrefours*,' Jean whispered. 'He has come.'

'Yes,' said the old woman in a strangled voice. 'He has come. He has found a *choual* among the initiates, a horse. He will ride that one. Now they will summon the other.'

The procession fled into the cemetery and crouched on the ground there, the drums building into a frenzy.

'Now they make summons of *Baron Cimeterre*,' Mambo Livone whispered, 'often called *Baron Samedi* or *Baron Croix*. The *loa* of the dead. That is his *vèvè* they are drawing. They are the *Sect Rouge*, the blood people. They draw his vèvè in yellow cornmeal mixed with blood. The blood is dried, then ground upon the stone together with the meal, double-ground until it is as fine as powder. When the *loa* comes who is so summoned, he comes for blood.'

'It, too, was carved upon that wood you had,' Jean whispered to Mahlia. 'You had them both.'

'So, girl. In that northern place you come from, someone summons these two in the same way? An evil thing, wherever it is done.'

Up the looping road the torches came nearer. In the cemetery, someone shouted in a deep, bass voice. When the forms surged back onto the road, one among them wore a top hat, unmistakable against the flare of the torches.

'The Baron is there,' whispered the old woman. 'He comes riding one of them.'

Now the group danced at the crossroads, blocking the bridge. Toward them along the northern road came the torches of the travelers. Mahlia could see them now, half a dozen men and women with captives – bound captives. A woman carrying a child, several half-grown girls, a young man.

'You are not to do anything, Jean. Do you understand?'

'Yes, *mambo*. I understand.' He was panting, and Mahlia wondered why, remotely, uncaring. Her body bowed with the urgent need to get down to the road, and the hastily tied knots gave way. She slithered out of them as though she had been a snake, pulling the gag from her mouth. She had been summoned. They would not hold her again. Jean Rondice leaped after her, his clutching arms sliding down her body as she eluded him easily, her feet taking her surely down the hillside. Behind her she heard the old woman's voice calling, words she did not hear, could not understand. They did not matter. Nothing mattered except the drum, the voices below.

She came out onto the road in a little slide of rocks and dust, eyes fixed on the drummer. The figures that gathered around her were mere shadows. Only the drummer mattered.

'Marie Chalfont,' someone said, tittering. 'See how she comes to join us, out of the night.' Was that a voice she knew? Somewhere deep inside her, she identified the voice, but that identification did not reach her conscious thought. There was almost no conscious thought.

She was not alone. Several girls were dragged along by the dancers, and a young boy and a woman with a baby.

They crouched together, hemmed in by the dancing bodies, all like Mahlia herself, surrounded.

Someone stood before her. Someone she should know, asking a question in Creole. The question made no sense. She shook her head. No sense. None. They were asking all the captives (captives? were they captives?) – that same question. No sense. No one understood it. Why were the dancers laughing? Because no one understood their question?

'*Mot de passage*,' demanded the dancing figures. '*Mot de passage*!'

Why did they want a password? Mahlia swayed, hummed, swayed. Then the dancers were taking them into the cemetery, forcing them to kneel there, in the dust. The woman with the baby knelt in front of Mahlia. They were tearing her clothes off, gathering around her to place their hands on her head.

'Take the baby,' the woman cried. 'By *le Bon Dieu*, take the baby! Keep the baby safe.'

Someone took the baby, laughing as he did so. 'By *le Bon Dieu*,' the dancers mocked. 'Keep the baby safe. Oh, we will, we will. Safe, '*ti cochon*.'

They had their hands on the woman's head, putting something on her. Pouring something on her.

The woman dropped forward on her hands. There she was, her back to Mahlia, rising on her feet and her hands, her bare buttocks high in the air, then lowering as she crouched, trotting, hands and feet like hooves, trotting round and round, nose in the dust, grunting, grunting, breasts dragging their nipples in the dust.

'*Hou, cochon*,' the dancers sang. '*Hou, cochon*.'

Someone dropped the baby into the dust beside its mother. It butted at her, nuzzled at her, grabbed a dangling teat in its mouth. The woman flung herself sowlike into the dust, arms and legs rigidly stretched, like an animal. The child lay suckling, its own arms and legs folded beneath it.

'*Hou cochon*,' the dancers sang.

Now it was Mahlia's turn. They pressed her down, ripped her clothing away, put their hands on her head. She felt something warm and sticky poured over her head, over her body, felt herself falling forward. Then her nose was in the cool dust, good things there in the dust, root them up, up, trot, trot. Her fingers and toes felt like horn, tappy-tap, she could hear the sound of her hooves in her head.

And the dancers were all around, driving her, driving all of them, deeper among the gravestones, there behind the church where the shadows gathered in drifts under the flaring light of the torches. She looked up to see a familiar face. She grunted at it and it stared in surprise, started back, words spurting from its mouth: 'Who? Where did she come from? You damn fools! . . .'

Then the Mahlia pig lay in the soft dust, obedient, waiting among all the other pigs while one of them was dragged towards the fire. Shadows. Stillness. Soft dirt. Contentment. She could see the leaping fire between two gravestones. They had the woman bent over a gravestone, one of the leaping forms thrusting himself over and over again at her rear while two others held her head. Then there was a knife, the woman's head drawn back. She squealed, an agonized, high-pitched shriek, and then blood spurted all over the stone and the forms around her leaped away, laughing.

The shriek disturbed Mahlia pig, but only for a moment. She rolled over to dig her nose in the dirt once more, to smell the lovely smells.

'*Hou, cochon,*' came a new voice, softly, not from the noisy crowd at the fire but from the dark bushes. '*Hou, cochon.*' A woman's voice. 'Come, *'ti cochon*. Come, little Mahlia pig.'

Mahlia pig turned her head. Someone calling her. She rose unsteadily and moved toward the underbush. '*Hou, cochon,*' came the voice, moving away before her, up the hillside. She trotted after it, obedient, through the tangled brush into a space among the trees.

Someone had their hands on her. Someone was tying her, and she squealed in dismay. From the firelit place below voices were raised, shouts of anger. 'Where is she! You idiots have let her get away!' And then, 'Chalfont, hell. Her name isn't Chalfont. She's the wrong member of the family.'

A voice, nearby, almost in her ear. 'Mahlia Ettison. I summon you, Mahlia Ettison.' Something acrid and biting was in her mouth, her nose. The voice was a bleeding whisper, sharp as knives. She tried to spit away the bitterness and couldn't; someone held her mouth shut on it. 'I summon you,' said the voice once more. Mambo Livone's voice.

'Let me alone,' she answered.

'Mahlia Ettison . . .'

She wept. Naked, tied, she wept. Shamed.

'Jean, there is a dress in the bag, give it to me.'

'Yes, *mambo*. Did you know they would do this?'

'It was very strange, their interest in her. It is always good to be prepared.'

'What did they do?'

'One of them set a spell on her, to summon her. And then an *ouanga-a-bet*, a beast curse. It is probably the same thing they did to your mother, Jean. I wonder when they did it to this one.'

'I watched them at *Le Coq Grivele*. I saw nothing.'

'Sometimes one cannot see it. Come, we must get away from here. They are coming after us.'

Shouts came from below them, a rat-a-tat of furious drumming, answered by others to the west, to the south. Close by on the hill a voice screamed directions, ran past to the east, shouted again as it circled and returned. Mahlia stumbled along among the trees, unable to feel fear, Jean tugging her on one side, Mambo Livone on the other. '*À l'ouest*,' the old woman puffed, 'toward my *houmfort*.'

'Madame, there is a chasm west of us. We will have to go down the road and cross the bridge!'

'*Finissez donc!*' she hushed him. '*À l'ouest*! There is a way across.' They lumbered up the hill on a long diagonal, thrusting the underbrush away from their faces, finding their way only by starlight and that of a dim quarter moon, low in the western sky. Suddenly the forest fell away beneath their feet, a precipitous cliff plunging past treetops to the silver shine of a river, like a ribbon in the night.

'Look along here, up and down. There's an old footbridge here somewhere. Look.' They thrust through the tangled brush at the edge of the chasm, peering into it and across it while the sounds at their back grew louder.

'Up here!' an angry voice shouted from below them. 'At the old bridge.'

Mahlia saw it then, a line, three ropes – perhaps vines? One for the feet, two for the hands, netted together with lianas. '*Allez*,' hissed the *mambo*. 'You first, Jean. Drag her after you.'

She was dragged, only half of her own volition, sideways onto the rope, feet pointed out, hands on a rope at either side, step by step, left foot, right foot. Left hand, right hand. The line beneath them swayed, bounced, swung wildly over the abyss. The *mambo* was behind her, whipping her into motion, all three of them inching over, inching over.

'There's a bridge here somewhere,' someone shouted from above them. 'Up the hill here.'

'*Bon Dieu Bon*,' muttered the old woman. 'They have not found us yet.'

They were at the middle of the chasm. Voices came loudly from down the hill, another group coming along the cliff edge to join those higher up. '*Halloo? Où êtes vous?*'

'*Allez à la bois! Cherchez là!*' An answering shout from above them. The calls from below were replaced by sounds of chopping, brush being cut away.

'*Bon Dieu Bon*,' said the *mambo* again. 'Move along, girl. I have no wish to die here.'

And then they were at the other side.

'Jean, quickly! Cut the lines. They will not know whether we have come this way or not. Likely they will not even see the ropes once they are cut.'

Jean knelt to swing his machete. The foot rope dropped away. He swung twice more. The two hand ropes leaped away into the chasm, to hang invisible among the lianas that grew there. Abruptly the dizzy haze fell away from Mahlia, as though the act of cutting the ropes had also cut some

192

remaining connection to that pig Mahlia she had been. Her mouth filled with bile, and she spit it onto the earth, retching. All of it was clear in her head, everything. The sounds. The face. The familiar face. She drew herself up, aware once more. On the far side of the chasm flickering torches moved in and out among the trees. None of them stopped where the ropes hung into the chasm, lost in the tangle of branches and vines. Below them and to the east the drums went on, endlessly. As the three of them struggled on to the west, the drum sounds increased in volume, pursuing them, a painful pulse in the blood, a throb in the heart. The old woman sighed, stopped to lean breathlessly against a tree, looked closely into Mahlia's face.

'Well, 'ti moune? Well, child?'

Mahlia was pale with shame and embarrassment, shivering with horror. 'I should have protected myself. I do know how, mambo.'

'I'm sure you do, but you did not suspect any of them. Who is he, that sang-mele who had made the engagement between himself and the evil ones?'

'Sang-mele? Mixed blood? It was a man from Millingham, from home. His name is John Duplessis. I saw him in the airport in Montreal.' It was not until she heard her own voice identifying him that she realized it was true. The leering face in the torchlight had been John Duplessis. The man raping the woman when she had been killed was John Duplessis. She blushed, feeling the hot blood flush her from brow to ankle, remembering her own naked body in the dust.

'I saw Phillipe Designe,' said Jean, perceiving her embarrassment, drawing the mambo's attention away. 'Clearly.'

'You saw him down there?'

'Yes. In the torchlight.'

'When was the ouanga, the spell, put upon you?' the mambo demanded of Mahlia.

'I don't know. It must have been at the Speckled Cock. They gave me rum to drink.'

'Ah. You wouldn't know why they set an *ouanga* upon you to come to this place?'

'I've never seen any of them except John before.'

'Coincidence, then? They thought it amusing to eat a pretty woman who came here alone? Or did he tell them to do it?'

'No. He was surprised. Annoyed, I think. He cursed them.'

'Perhaps they intended . . .' Jean blushed. 'Something extra in the *ceremonie*.'

'That is possible. You are very pretty, girl. Sometimes it is easier to be wise when one is old and ugly, like me. Well, we have seen what we have seen, but we must know what *you* have seen. What happened to you, girl?' Mambo Livone set off through the trees, they struggling after her, as the drums drew ever closer over the ridge.

Mahlia shivered, gagged, tried to get the words out and couldn't. 'They made me . . . made me . . .'

'Yes, yes. Tell us. We saw. But what did *you* see? What did you feel?'

'They made me a pig, *mambo*. I was a sow. The other woman, she was a sow. And the children, little pigs. I felt it. I could feel the bristles on my hide. I could feel my hooves.'

'Oh, yes, they had many pigs there tonight. Lucky for you there were so many — some had to wait while they attended to others. Well, does it help you, girl?'

'I don't know. I don't understand what happened there . . .'

'You saw the *Sect Rouge* preparing for a feast. Some accuse them of eating human flesh. They deny this. They say they eat only animal flesh, the flesh of *'ti cochons*, little pigs.'

Mahlia's stomach heaved, and she sagged into the bushes to be violently sick. Jean turned aside and also retched. 'My mama,' he cried. 'Oh, Mama . . .'

'She will be avenged,' the old woman said. 'Be at peace.'

'Is *she* at peace,' he screamed almost soundlessly at her, from a throat so tight it would not give him a voice. 'Is she?'

'I will take care of it,' said Mambo Livone, her words

194

like whips. 'She will be at peace. Come now. They are still after us – hear the drums? They are coming west along the road now. They will come over the ridge. I must be at the *houmfort* when they come down the trail. I must see who all of them are, these *cochons gris*.'

'Why do they do it?' Mahlia whispered, aghast, even as she stumbled after the old woman through the trees. 'Why?'

'It is said that some *bocors* can live forever if their victims are young enough. They prefer to eat children and young women. So long as these *mangeurs* eat the flesh, they believe, they will not die.'

'That can't be true!'

'It is not true for them,' she said, turning to spit behind her in the direction from which they had come. 'They do not know enough. They know only enough to do a part of what is needful. They die, like anyone. They will die, like anyone, I will see to that. But there is another rite, a very old rite, that does give the practitioner endless life. When I was young I heard this from a *houngan, a gros neg, très sage, très dangereux*.'

'What do you mean, "another rite"? What worse thing could they do?'

'Ah, 'ti moune, I did not learn everything. I did not want to ask too much. It depends upon four *mambos* calling up the *loa* the first time, four *mambos* of a certain heritage drawing the *vèvè*, and the *vèvè* must be drawn on a certain crossroads and in a certain graveyard where the four *mambos* have done certain things. Then those same places must be used whenever the rite is done. And those four *mambos* must live all the rest of their lives within sight of those places. If ever they want to leave, they are killed there, within sight of that crossroads, that graveyard. When the four *mambos* are dead, then those two places can be used forever after for the rite. That is all I know. In order to have that *connaissance*, one must sell oneself, become a *choual*, a horse, for the evil *loa*, join the *Sectes Rouges*, like those *mèchants hommes*. It is enough for me to be what I am. I am a good Catholic. I will not risk my soul.'

'Will you come with me to Millingham, *mambo*?'

'No. I must stay here. Tell your teacher this: In your home place is a *bocor*, a wizard. You have seen him. You know his name. It was this *bocor* who used the *vèvè* to call the *loas*. Listen, now: Those who you watched tonight did not need a *vèvè* carved of wood to remind them of the pattern. No, not these devils. They know because they do this thing often, they can remember from one time until the next. But your *bocor*, the one from your place, that one needed an *aide memoire*. So, he had this carved wood you brought with you, to remember with. This means he does not do this thing often. Still, he does do it. You must find out why. You must stop him. If you stop him from eating, he cannot live.'

'But you won't come help us? How are we to learn these things? Molly said she had no . . . no access to your *loa*.'

'Yes, this is true. And our *loa* have no access to her. To you, perhaps, because of the *ouanga*, the curse, but not to her. She will know this is true. It is a protection. Still, you know names. That will be enough for her. Come, save your breath for running. We have no time to talk.'

They were at the *houmfort* well before dawn. 'They will be coming down this trail very soon. You must be in your boat and gone by sunrise,' the *mambo* said. 'Go in wisdom, '*ti moune*. I have enough to do here without worrying over you. Tell your teachers you were a stupid and silly child to let that curse be laid upon you without knowing it or protecting yourself. It will not hurt you to be chastised. Wait now. There is something I must give you from the *caille mystere*.'

She went into the inner sanctum of the *houmfort*, returning in a moment with Mahlia's bag and an earthenware jar. 'This is a *govi*, girl. Spirits live in this jar. I have put other things in here, as well. I used what is in here to call you back when they made a pig of you. So, you will use what is in this jar to call back the pigs in your home, for they are there. I know it. Take Jean with you. He is in danger here. When your matter is taken care of, perhaps he will

196

wish to return.' She turned to the young man, striking him sternly upon the breast with a bony finger. 'Come to me if you return to this place, Jean Rondice.'

'What of Phillipe Designe?' he muttered, eyes on his shoes. 'Yves and Renee? What of them?'

'What of them? They are my business. Go now, before they come and find you here.'

They fled. They fled from the drums that had come over the ridge and were pounding down toward the sea. They found the boat, clambered in, and putted away toward the east, along the forested valleys toward Cabo Beata and the coast of the Dominican Republic. Behind them at last the drums fell silent. But even when they were silent, they seemed to continue, a drumming in the blood, a threat in the heart.

'It will take a day to get to Santo Domingo,' Jean said, 'perhaps a little more.' Mahlia could not believe it had been only three days since she had left Montreal. Years seemed to have passed, eons. The miles of sea ran out behind them. From time to time she shook so hard that the little boat trembled beneath her, but no leering beast dancer reached out toward them from the shore, no drum sounded. She almost wished one would, as proof, perhaps, that it had not gone home before her to wait for her there.

CHAPTER TWENTY-SIX

Campfire embers glowed in Byers' Fault, lighting the dirty faces of a dozen diggers. Some of the crew had chosen to go back to town when evening came, but the hard-core devotees lingered at the site until dark, taking refuge at last in sleeping bags as they heated cans of one thing or another over the fire. No one had thought to bring a washbasin, so washing up had been sketchy. Everyone had remembered to bring beer. In the dark they waxed eloquent and melodic, though not as significantly either as the singers believed.

Slightly away from the group, Marcy Talent lay on her air mattress beside a leaf-crowned mound, a cigarette dangling from one corner of her mouth. The smoke coiled upward, then, as though drawn by an invisible mouth, was sucked down into the mound itself. Marcy didn't notice. She was absorbed in studying the bits and pieces spread at her side on a piece of tattered canvas. Glass and metal, mostly. One bottle with only a tiny chip out of the side. Buckles. A knife handle, the blade long since reduced to rust. And one other thing.

'Hey, Marcy. You goin' to stay here tonight?' This called with a leer from a pimply-faced youth.

'Somebody's got to keep an eye on you dolts,' she replied jeeringly, fingering the piece of rough metal that had been found near the knife. If was covered with a black coating, more like paint than anything else she could think of. Something that had hardened, at any rate. Only at the corner of the piece could one see a gleam of another color. Judging from the size, it must have been a coin, or a ring

198

that had melted. Something about that size. A brooch, perhaps. But gold, definitely gold.

An isolated piece? Or an indication of a hoard someone had stashed away?

She shook her head in irritation. Too early to tell. They had staked out the site on Monday and had been digging ever since, three days. Nothing worth mentioning until today, Wednesday, but today had been interesting. She certainly wasn't going to go back to town and leave these kids in possession. The next time anyone touched a trowel, Marcy was going to be leaning over his shoulder. This might be what the maniac had been looking for. That carved piece of wood the Ettison woman had found might actually have been a map, carved to look like something else. And because Seepy had had it, someone had assumed he knew it was a map. And because the Ettison woman had had it, someone had assumed it was still there. It would explain a lot. Not about the Grafton woman, of course, but maybe there wasn't any explanation for that. Unless she'd seen or heard something she shouldn't have.

Marcy wondered whether she could borrow the carving back from the Ettison woman. Or, if borrowing didn't work, Steve could probably get into the house on some pretext or other. Steve owed her one anyhow, for being so stupid as to let the thing get away in the first place. She leaned forward to cover the glow of her pocket flashlight as she shone it on her watch. Ten o'clock. Steve Ware was supposed to have been here by now. They had agreed that if she didn't come back to town by nine, he was to come out here. Where the hell was he?

She lit another cigarette, lying back against the mound. Strange. She thought she'd put her mattress and sleeping bag much nearer the others, over by that large beech, as a matter of fact. Maybe one of the kids had moved it, wanting her a little farther away. Hell, did they think she was some kind of chaperone? She didn't care what they did under the blankets. She snorted, her eyes flicking upward to watch the smoke curl, pinky white in the firelight. Up and back and down. The kids had settled, finally, tired from the day's digging. The smoke rose up, curved back and down. For a time it didn't register, but then it did, all at once. The smoke was being drawn down! Into a hole? Into some passageway? A tunnel? She rose slowly, not wanting to attract the attention of the group by the fire, leaned toward the trail of smoke until she found where it dropped from the cigarette end directly into the earth.

Under the drift of leaves, packed into layers almost like wet cardboard by seasons of snow, her probing fingers encountered an open space. A hollow. The leaf layers tore, coming away in paperlike sheets that she piled silently to one side. They came so easily, almost as though they had been recently disturbed. She looked over her shoulder, seeing only the embers of the campfire and the bulky shapes of the sleepers. No one moved. Where was Ware when she needed him!

Except, she told herself with a quirk of her lips, it might be better not to have anyone along. Better to explore on her own.

When she had pulled the leaves away together with the half-rotted twigs that had supported them, she slipped her pocket flashlight into the hole and turned it on. A shaft, wider than her shoulders, stone-lined and fairly dry. Perhaps a chimney? Whatever it was had plenty of air at the bottom end. The smoke from her cigarette flowed strongly downward, into the dark tunnel.

Tunnel. Not quite, Crawlway, perhaps. The slope would be easy to get down. There was plenty of room to carry the flashlight to illuminate the way. Briefly she debated waiting for Steve before exploring, but the lure of the possible treasure trove was irresistible. She gave one final glance at the huddled shapes around the smoking campfire, then slid on her stomach to the opening. It was wide enough to be fairly comfortable, certainly wide enough that she needn't worry about getting wedged in, and not so steep that she couldn't wriggle out backward if need be.

A few yards down the shaft her light caught a glitter among

the stones. She fumbled it out, feeling the unmistakable weight of it, the unmistakable shape of it. Gold. An old coin. And another one at the limit of the light. Almost as though someone had put them there for her to find.

Behind her, by the fire, one of the students shook another by the shoulders and there were whispered giggles. '. . . up to something. Come on. Wake Thompson up. Somebody tell Beastly Ben.' Whispers, more subdued laughter. 'Old Marcy pulling a fast one, as usual. Remember that pile of stuff Joe Lerner found in Chester last year? Marcy had it in her basket before the poor guy could even photograph it.'

The young people moved toward the shaft into which Marcy Talent had descended, hung over it, listening. After long, impatient moments of waiting, they slipped into the hole after her, one by one, with muffled curses and laughter.

When the last of them had disappeared below, a shadowy form detached itself from the surrounding forest. Steve Ware stood looking down at the hole, a puzzled expression on his face, lit by the glow of his own cigarette. This wasn't what he had thought would happen at all. Trust old Marce to find something – probably something valuable – right under his nose, when he wasn't even around to share it. After a moment, he muttered a curse, threw away the cigarette, and went down into the hole after the others.

The last of the fire fell apart into gray ash and one wisp of ascending smoke. Silent hands restored the twig and leaf covering that Marcy had removed and moved her sleeping bag some distance away from the newly hidden shaft. A leafy branch wiped away footprints. The embers of the fire stopped smoking. The sleeping bags lay empty. A dark figure stood peering down through the forest at the lights of Byers' Farm, something very like a snarl on its face for a moment before it darted away through the trees, leaving the abandoned camp behind it.

CHAPTER TWENTY-SEVEN

Mahlia and Jean arrived at Byers' Farm late Thursday afternoon. Mahlia drove from the airport in Montreal, a distance that seemed endless, even in comparison to all the miles between Cotes de Fer and Santo Domingo. Those, too, had been endless and fear-ridden. The situation had not improved in Santo Domingo, where Jean's contact for 'papers' had proved illusive. Where Mahlia had been almost at the point of throwing Jean on the mercy of the American embassy, a fidgety little man had turned up to demand an outrageous price for what Jean called a very simple forgery.

Mahlia paid it. She would have paid it six times over if they could have left any sooner. As it was, there was still a long, idle hour in the airport when her imagination took full rein and rode her as she had been pig-ridden high on the Massif de la Hotte.

Now they were home. The headlights of the car picked out the graveyard at the corner of the property, sending shadows fleeing as though there had been people crouched there, engaged in some secret rite. Then the turning into the driveway, then Molly peering through the window at them, unlocking the door to let them in. She took one look at Jean's exhausted face and led him upstairs to find him a place to sleep while Mahlia tearfully hugged Robby.

'What's that?' Robby asked, pointing to the jar she still carried, the jar she had not let out of her hands for an instant since Mambo Livone gave it to her.

'A remedy,' Mahlia giggled, half hysterically. 'Something to put an end to little pigs.' She put the jar on the hall table and burst into tears. Simoney came into the hall, arms

202

outstretched, and Robby glared at her as though she had been responsible for Mahlia's outburst, then shouldered his sword with an air that said more clearly than language that he didn't want to be involved in all this adult emotion.

'Now, Mahlia,' Simoney said. 'Now, now. Come in by the fire. Martha! Mahlia's back.'

'Is Martha here?' Mahlia asked, disbelieving, bursting into tears again when the huge figure appeared in the kitchen doorway, buttonholes straining over her mighty bosom. 'When did Martha get here?'

'In the middle of the night,' the woman snapped, 'trying to come quietly and running smack-dab into twelve layers of protection, instead. Damn near broke my neck.'

She turned and stomped back toward the kitchen, where they shortly heard the sound of the teakettle singing. By the time she returned with teapot and cups, most of the tears were dried and Molly had come back from upstairs.

'Pleasant young man,' she remarked. 'Asleep before his head hit the pillow. I put him in the cot in the nursery, Mahlia. There's a fire there, and he looked cold. No place else for him. Martha, Simoney, and I have the place pretty well filled up. Now, suppose you tell us what happened?'

Mahlia told, as consecutively as possible, as tearlessly as possible. 'I feel such a fool,' she said at last. 'Robby could have done better than I did.'

'Not necessarily,' Molly said, head on one side like a chicken examining a worm. 'You had no reason to suspect that someone in Haiti was going to set a — what did the *mambo* call it? a *drogue?* — to set a curse on you. Likely it was done at that café.'

'How? By whom?'

'By the pilot, probably. No doubt he picked you out the minute he saw you,' Martha snorted, glaring at them all.

Simoney nodded. 'It doesn't matter. What does matter is that you're back and we have some idea now what we're up against. A lot of things make sense now that didn't make sense before.'

'I don't know what does,' Mahlia cried. 'What happened

203

in Haiti was nothing like what's happening here.'

'Well, now,' said Molly, 'there are points of connection, Mahlia. Settle down. First point is that business about the little pigs.'

' *'Ti cochons,*' murmured Mahlia, 'So?'

'That child Robby spoke with, or, I should say, that child's ghost. Cynthia. She said she got away from the little pigs.'

'Second point,' said Simoney, 'the designs carved on that piece of wood were the same designs to call up the *loas* when you, Mahlia, were also made into a little pig.'

'Third point,' said Martha, 'which is something you'd have thought of if you'd ever lived on a sensible farm, is it's customary to skin a pig. 'Specially if you want the skin for something, like gloves, or a jacket. Or something.'

'Oh, Mother of God,' said Mahlia from the depths of her convent-educated years. 'Seepy? Charlotte? They weren't eaten. They weren't – oh, it's too horrible to talk about.'

'*It can't be too horrible to talk about,*' Martha corrected her, eyes blazing. 'My Lord, woman, have you gone completely soft? Are you going to be one of those dolls who cowers in the corner murmuring, "Oh, don't, don't, oh, please, don't," while the vampire bites you or the demon sucks you dry? For heaven's sake, Mahlia, what's got into you!'

'Sorry,' she mumbled. 'Honestly, Martha, I'm sorry. I just keep thinking about Charlotte—'

'We're sorry for her, too,' said Martha, firmly, 'sorry for anyone who's the victim of something like that, but this is no time to give in to our feelings.'

Molly said, 'Martha's right. Things haven't exactly let up since you've been gone. Today we've had a dozen college kids disappear, the ones who were digging up at Byers' Fault. Paul Goode was here this morning, wondering if we'd seen any of them. When their friends got out to the dig this morning, the ones who'd stayed at the site were missing. Them and that Talent girl. Oh, and Steve Ware, too, though from what I hear, he may just be tomcattin' somewhere.' She thought for a moment. 'Now, first thing, it seems to me, is to call up the ghost of that little girl. She's the one who knows about the little pigs, so that's the place to start.'

'Where should we do it?' Simoney asked. 'Out in the orchard by the swing? It's a bit public out there.'

'I think not,' Molly opined, looking up the stairs. 'What did you say you found in that little room up there, Mahlia? Comic books, I remember that. Kids' clothes, mattresses, a chamber pot. Like that was a place some children had been kept, maybe? Locked in for a while?'

'Oh, God,' Mahlia said again. 'Straps. With buckles. And knives.'

'Skinning knives. That's what Charlotte Grafton called them, wasn't it?'

Mahlia could not answer. One of her visions had overtaken her, flooded in upon her so that she stood half in reality and half in dream. There were children on the stairs, five of them. Being led upstairs by – by someone. She couldn't see who it was, not even whether it was male or female. It was only a dark shape against the light wall, and the children ran up the stairs after it, as though it had been the piper of Hamlin. What had it told them? What had it promised them?

Then there were straps, buckles, gags, small struggling forms, knives. Knives.

Martha was shaking her. 'Come on, Mahlia. Upstairs. There's no time to waste, so we're going to do it right now.' They were halfway up the stairs before she could protest. They were seated on the floor of the little white room before she could think of a good reason to protest, and by then it was too late.

Martha had the tiny brazier going. She must have had it nearby, ready for this, bringing coals from the living room fire, though Mahlia had not seen her do it. Molly was tossing pinches of stuff onto the glowing embers to make clouds of pungent smoke, dizzying and yet calming, too. Simoney had her tambour in her lap, tapping it as she mumbled to herself, outlining a spell.

'I think not a direct call, Molly. The child is shy. Perhaps something general that will sweep her in with others?'

'Up to you Simoney. You're the expert.'

'I'll try to focus on this general area. The people and creatures who might be found around here . . .'

Molly nodded, dropping a pinch of amber crystals into the brazier. 'Whatever. Better get on with it, Simoney, while I've got myrrh left.'

The younger woman tapped the tambour reflectively, staring at the featureless wall. 'I summon all guides,' she sang at last. 'All guides, come to my call . . .

> 'I summon all guides,
> all things that will direct me,
> needles northpointing in compasses,
> trails, roads, rivers, and watercourses,
> maps, charts, instruction, and direction,
> named roads and titled places,
> locations named for things that happened there.'

'I swear she gets more long-winded every time she does a new spellsong,' growled Martha. 'Might as well read a dictionary into the casting.' She puffed on the brazier as Molly dropped another crystal into it.

'Shhh, She's good at it, Martha! She's not so impatient – like some I know – that she forgets parts that'll come in handy later. Now, hush. Concentrate!'

> 'I summon all guides,
> all people who will direct me,
> scouts who can track the wily fugitive,
> torch-bearing mobs who have the monster in sight,
> lantern-lifting grandfathers who lit the path,
> grannies who remember the way,
> children who have found a shortcut,
> men and women of the coyote's persuasion,
> travelers who share the otter's nature,
> sniffers-out of the wide earth's hidden places.'

The little room began to fill with fog. Forms swirled in that fog, images that emerged and then fled away once more, buckskin-clad men, women with lanterns, pale forms leaning over parchment with quill pens. Among them wandered a child, never still, always moving behind another form, away from them. 'Cynthia,' breathed Mahlia. 'Is that her? She only has one arm.'

'I summon all guides,
all creatures who have found the place,
the shrieking hawk from the high gyre,
honking geese in southflying lines,
the lead dog after the fox,
the sounding hound at the bear tree.
I call all guides.
I seek a place
where the evil one crouches,
he who eats,
in the place of the little pigs.'

The fog began to swirl, roil, twist in on itself. Images vanished, fled away into distance, leaving only two behind. One of these stood in a corner, almost invisible. The other circled at the center of the room, a wisp.

'Oh, she's a wary one,' sighed Molly. 'I see her, but she's not coming clear.'

There was a haze in the corner of the room, circling slowly, a mere wisp of fog, tentative as spring.

'Try anger,' Martha whispered. 'If it had been me, I'd have been mad as a wet hen.'

Simoney sighed, nodded, hummed for a moment, tightening the thongs of the tambour to make it throb with a high, tight voice.

'He who did evil walks free in the sun,
child, child,
laughing for no one knows what he has done,
child, child.

We are no friend to him,
help make an end to him,
Come to us calling ones,
child, child.'

A whisper, faint as dawn wind. A child's voice, full of
anxiety. 'Give me my bracelet.'

'We don't know where it is,' Simoney whispered. 'We
would give it to you if we could.'

'Give me back my bracelet. If you give me my bracelet,
I'll help you. I'll show you where the little pigs are, where
they are.'

Molly sighed. 'Let her go, Simoney. We'll have to try
to locate the bracelet, first. Captain Bone should know.'

Mahlia put her hands to her forehead, conscious of a
sudden pressure there, something coming toward her, like
a wave, a towering wave.

'We'll find your bracelet,
child, child.
Come, when we call you,
child.'

Simoney put down the little drum, rubbed her forehead
ruefully. 'Poor little thing. She's afraid to trust us.'

'We thought she might be. Come now, Simoney. Let's
do the Captain. Sure as anything, he'll know where the
bracelet is.'

Mahlia lurched to her feet, the room swimming before
her eyes, the center of a vortex of swirling images. 'I know
where it is,' she gulped. She swayed, certain of this the
way she was sometimes certain of things, without knowing
how or why. 'You don't need to call the Captain, he's
here — or he was a few minutes ago. And the bracelet is
back in the drawer downstairs. Where I left it. Robby put
it there.'

'When, Mahlia?'

'I — I don't know. Just now. Recently. He thought we

might need it . . . he and the Captain . . .' Her certainty gave way to a flood of suspicion, and the suspicion came out in a strangled shout of fear.

'Where is Robby?'

All of them ran for the stairs. There was no need to search. The drawer was slightly open, the dirt-stained tissue that wrapped the bracelet peeking from it.

Something hovered just out of her reach. Mahlia rubbed her head. Something.

'Where's the jar I put here?' she asked. 'Martha? Simoney? Did you take it?'

'What jar?'

'I forgot to tell you. Mambo Livone gave me a jar, a *govi*. Spirits live in it, she said. I know there are herbs in it, some kind of mixture. She said it would call back the little pigs. I put it right here, on the table. Robby was standing right next to it. *Where is he?*' Now there was panic in her voice.

'Did you lock this door when Mahlia came in?' Martha demanded of Molly.

'I certainly did.'

'It isn't locked now.'

They stared at one another, only for a moment, not in surmise but in hideous conviction. Mahlia did not need a vision to tell here where he had gone – where he had taken the jar and what he intended to do with it. 'Cynthia must already have told him where the little pigs are,' she said, terrified. 'Her, or Captain Bone.'

'Back upstairs,' ordered Simoney, pulling the tissue-wrapped packet from the drawer. 'Quickly.'

Molly left them at the door of the little room, went toward the phone.

The brazier was still alight, but the herbs that Martha now dropped into it were not sweet-smelling but harsh, urgent. Simoney unwrapped the tissue packet and laid the golden circlet upon the floor. Martha exclaimed, took it up to look at it briefly.

'By all that's holy, whoever made this knew what she was doing. Rowan and speedwell and the flowers of periwinkle, set with skystones. No wonder the wizard cut it off of her . . .'

The drum in Simoney's hands was a summons nothing could resist.

> 'Your friend goes to danger
> at hands of a stranger
> who'll take him and bind him
> unless we can find him,
> come, Cynthia, lead us,
> or Robby will die.'

A whirling mist in the corner, a sound. Was it a sob, a cry?

> 'Come to us calling ones,
> child, child.
> Come to us, lead us,
> or Robby will die.'

Mahlia could hear Molly out in the hall, talking on the phone. 'Mr Goode? I'm calling for Mahlia Ettison. We've found out who killed your aunt. You'll find it hard to credit, but it was John Duplessis. Yes, we have evidence.'

A whirling mist, a child's voice, as if from very far away: 'Is that my bracelet?'

'Take it,' chanted Simoney. 'The gold your granny gave you. Take it.'

On the floor the bracelet moved slightly. Beside the brazier the mist thickened, resolved itself into the figure of a pinafored little girl. A ghostly left hand reached down toward the bracelet, stopped, frustrated. She had no right hand to hold it, no way to put it on.

Mahlia leaned forward and lifted the bracelet, held it in the air, saw the single smoky hand slip through it, saw that hand solidify, become real.

Molly's voice from the hall. 'We think he has Mahlia's son, Robby . . .'

Simoney, singing:

'Lead us, Cynthia,
child, child . . .'

'The place is under Byers' Fault,' whispered the child's voice, softly musical, terribly weary. 'It starts in a cave. I'll show you.' Her misty form seemed to leave them, seemed to melt, flow, move like smoke away from them, out of the room, down the stairs.

'Up at Byers' Fault, we think. We're on our way there, now. Get whoever you can to help us look.' Molly dropped the phone and ran into the nursery. As Mahlia fled down the stairs, she heard Molly shouting, 'Jean! We're going up to the forest to look for Robby. That way! Look after the baby. We'll be back as soon as we can!' Then Molly was plunging after them into the night.

To Mahlia, close behind the child-ghost, it seemed that the child now had two arms. It seemed that the child was larger, gowing larger as they went.

'The bracelet,' panted Martha. 'I was right. Power in it, mighty power. And she's drawing on it now.'

'Don't go so fast,' Molly grunted, heaving up beside them, her breasts jouncing up and down with each stride. 'Why are we running?'

'Simoney isn't.' They looked ahead to where Simoney's form floated weightlessly after the darting ghost. 'Sorry, Mahlia. Come as quickly as you can.' And the two of them were flying, leaving her.

Anger filled her, quick and hot. It didn't matter what she had promised Badger. Her mind found the words, the connections, and her feet left the ground in one smooth, silken motion. She arrowed after the others, mouth set grimly.

Ahead of them Cynthia fled, lengthening, flattening, becoming a white spear of mist. It pointed westward, upward, into the gloomy forests below Byers' Fault. It seemed to Mahlia that the spear became solider, harder as it went. Wind filled the sky. High on the horizon the Duplessis house blazed with light, its windows peering down at the valley like glittering, hungry eyes.

'Do they know, his family? Do you think they know about him?' Mahlia was trying to remember something she had heard, where? Something important. 'His mother? His sisters and brothers?'

'I don't know,' Martha grunted. 'Possibly.'

'If they do . . .' The white spear had resolved itself into a little girl again, just before them, and Mahlia's thought was lost. The child's form pointed, with both hands, pointed into a darkness between two towering pines. On the shadowy wrist the bracelet burned like a star with a chill, unwavering radiance.

'There,' it whispered. 'There's where they keep the little pigs.'

'Where are you going?' Molly asked it. 'Where, Cynthia?'

'I'm going for help,' the ghost said, as simply as any child would say it. 'For help . . .' It dwindled into some direction their eyes could not follow.

'No time to wait.' Simoney thrust her way through the brush and between the trees, disappearing into the dark throat that gaped there. Mahlia thought distractedly that the place was probably invisible in the daytime. The lights of her own house were close in the valley, directly to the east; she could have walked past this place a dozen times.

Blackness filled the cavern. Simoney and Molly held up their hands, fingers flickering upward, witchfire burning on the tips. In that greeny glow Martha bent forward to scan the ground. Clear in the damp, sandy soil were small boot prints and a single wavering line, like a dragged tail. 'His sword,' said Mahlia. 'He was carrying his sword.' The opening was almost a tunnel, narrow but high enough to walk in, sloping upward toward Byers' Fault.

They walked, too slowly, following the line of tracks – tracks that did not hesitate or stray. 'How could he see in here?' Mahlia whispered. 'How could he?'

'We'll have to assume someone had a light,' said Molly. 'Someone – or something.'

The tunnel widened. Their light fell on a rock pillar to the left, laid up out of mortared stone. 'Built,' hissed

Simoney. 'Built long ago – when Byers' Fault was built.'

'This is probably where John and William Byers hid out,' Martha said. 'When Byers' Fault was burned, back in 1760, that's how they survived.'

The boot tracks went on. Though the tunnel branched now, both to left and right, the trail they followed continued upward. From time to time air stirred around their faces, and the witchfire rose into stone-lined chimneys that stretched upward into the night. 'It took a lot of people to build this,' Molly said. 'The whole town. If they'd been warned, the whole town could have escaped down here. I'll bet there was an entrance to these tunnels in every house.'

'Meant to be,' said Mahlia, knowing it was true. 'There was meant to be an entrance in each house, eventually, but they hadn't been dug yet. The people from Chester came too soon. Only John and William had warning, because they were down there, at the farm. The noise wakened them. They were – oh, all that blood! They had decided that the women might try to leave, the women from Haiti. They killed them in their beds that night so that they died in sight of the crossroads and the graveyard. And when the people from Chester came, John and William were awake. There were torches. Torches, fire, blood. Terrible.' She wiped cold sweat from her brow, the vision swirling around her, a long time gone.

'So they escaped down here and got away,' said Molly. 'Then, twenty years later, William came back.'

'And John,' whispered Mahlia. 'Captain Bone wrote that he saw him . . .'

'Saw his ghost. He'd have been a hundred years old.'

Mahlia shook her head stubbornly. 'Saw him, I think. He came back when his son did.'

'He'd have been very old, but perhaps he did. This may be why none of the family are buried in Millingham. Perhaps they were buried down here.' Simoney turned restlessly, the witchfire on her fingers burning hotly. 'How far do these tunnels go?'

Martha looked back the way they had come, counted

under her breath. 'We've come the better part of a mile. That should have brought us almost under the old town, according to the map in Mahlia's library. He can't be far ahead of us.'

'Shhh! What's that?'

They were all silent, holding their breaths. From one of the side tunnels had come a soft susurrus, a rustling.

'Wind,' said Martha, 'coming down those chimneys.' She raised her hand to light the side way. Carved over the arched entrance was a date: 1730.

'They built that one when they built the town,' said Martha. 'The rest is all uphill from that. Maybe it came later.' Her own uplifted hand lit the next tunnel mouth: 1780. 'Fifty years apart.' From this tunnel came the same rustling sound, disquieting. 'Must be a storm blowing up out there.' She bent over the little tracks. 'Let's catch up with that boy of yours, Mahlia.'

They passed another tunnel, 1830, leading off to their right, and at the next one, leading left, the little boot prints turned aside. The date carved above it was 1880.

'Got him,' murmured Martha. She stepped through the opening, only to stop short as a voice echoed in the darkness ahead of her.

'You stay away from me!'

Robby. Mahlia thrust between the others to run blindly toward that voice.

'I'm telling you. You'd better stay away.' Robby's voice was more angry than frightened.

They rounded a corner to see the little boy silhouetted against a pale glow of ghostlight. Against the rock wall of the cave stood a tall, cadaverous form, eyes burning from a bony, ascetic face with a great prow of a nose over wide, mobile lips. The figure was dressed all in black, with a small white ruffle at its neck and a curved sword in its belt. It lifted a pale lantern and turned toward them, staring with ghostlit eyes from a face pale as chalk. The women halted, arms out, watching as the figure lifted the lantern still higher and cried in a wraith's voice, 'Devils they are, lad, devils!

214

Cast 'em out. I've tried with the Word of God, but they're proof against that.'

'We'll get 'em, Captain Bone.' Robby, brandishing his sword, stooped to set something on the ground.

Six small skeletons hung upon the wall, skulls locked in the eternal grin of death. They did not move. Something else moved. Pale. Rustling. Like leaves circling in a vagrant wind they circled the boy; like moths they battered toward him, hands outstretched . . .

'Skins!' breathed Simoney. The pale things turned toward her at the sound of her word, drifting away from the boy. The skins of the children. Whole, their bellies striped with a vertical line of stitchery from jaw to groin, their hands and feet like gloves, gloves filled with terrible wind. Around the dreadful faces the hair fell in tangles. In the empty eyeholes little flames burned, violet and horrid.

One of them darted at Mahlia, struck at her, moved back, and she looked foolishly at her hand to see a strip of skin dangling there, blood oozing from beneath it.

Robby had taken the lid from Mambo Livone's jar and set it on the ground, then stuck his sword into it to stir the contents round as he always stirred everything. But when he saw the pale form approaching Mahlia, he left the jar and darted up to strike them from behind.

'You let my Mahlia alone, you pigs! You let her alone. You let Cynthia alone, too.'

From the skins arose a wailing, a high keening that shivered the rock. Dust sifted across them in an ominous cloud. From the main tunnel came an answering howl, treble ghost voices in a shrieking wail and the sound of rustling like leaves in a storm.

Molly shouted, 'Martha, help the boy. One of those devils is hit.' It was true. A skin had been struck by the lath sword, and it spun on its toes like a top, dwindling, blackening, screaming. Robby hit it again, shouting, his face red and angry.

'He stuck his sword in Mambo Livone's jar!' Mahlia screamed. 'Use whatever's in it.'

Against the wall the ghostly old man held his lamp high, alight, burning with an increased fury. They had no time to wonder at it as a cloud of other skins poured through the tunnel entrance, dozens of them. Mahlia dipped her hands into the jar and turned to face them, her hands dripping with an oily, pungent substance that made her flesh burn. One of the creatures struck at her with nails as sharp as knives, touched her, screeched, and fell away. Martha and Molly were to either side of her, their hands dripping. Behind them in the cavern Robby was still flailing away and Simoney was rubbing some of the stuff onto her tambour.

Throb. The tambour sounded. Throb. A heartbeat. The skins shrieked, beat at them in a circling fury.

Strike. Martha cried out as one of them nicked her wrist. Blood dripped. She rubbed her hands up both arms in one swift motion and moved purposefully toward them. 'Put it on your arms, your face.' She obeyed her own words by rubbing the back of one hand over her cheeks and forehead and was rewarded with a screaming howl as one of the skins touched her above the eye. Simoney began to sing.

> 'Got no bones, little pigs,
> got no bones to hold you up.
> Got no guts to feed you.
> Got no eyes to see with.
> Got no mouth to speak.
> Got no heart to beat, little pigs.
> Lie down, lie down, lie down.'

The whirling figures jerked at each throb of the drum, darkening, their pale surfaces aging like winter leaves.

> 'Got no brain, little pigs.
> Nothing inside but wind and fire.
> Nothing inside but hunger and hate.
> Fire goes out. Wind dies down.

Hunger and hate are over, little pigs.
Lie down, lie down, lie down.'

The chant faltered, halted as Simoney cried out. One of the skins had crept along the floor to her legs and was tearing at them through the tough trousers she wore. Molly turned, slapped at the thing with both hands, smeared the pungent stuff on it, did not stay to watch it shrivel. Half the creatures had fallen under their herb-smeared hands. The others slowed, their keening fading under the renewed throb of the drum. Now the three moved purposefully, picking their targets. Behind them on the sandy floor Robby did a war dance, whooping. Mahlia did not spare him a glance. He was obviously fine. Perhaps in the morning he would think it had been a dream; perhaps in the morning so would she. They stood panting. The drum fell silent. Around them were only flakes, small heaps of blackened leather, with no shape to them. On the wall the tiny skeletons grinned, endlessly. Six of them.

'Look over here,' said Molly. 'Behind this stone.' A seventh skeleton lay there, crumpled, one arm missing. 'This is Cynthia. Evidently he couldn't use her. He couldn't get at her with the bracelet on, and after he cut her arm off – he must have done that back at the farm, that's why the arm was in the pond – the spell wouldn't work. So the bracelet did protect her, not her life, perhaps, but something else. Perhaps the animation spell will only work on whole skins.'

Abruptly the light went out. Molly cursed, lit a wavering flicker from one thumb. 'God, I'm exhausted.' The figure of the tall old man had vanished. Robby plopped onto the sand, tears streaming down his face.

'Did we get them? Captain Bone said we had to get them all. Where did Captain Bone go? He told me he'd hold the lantern. Where did he go?'

'I don't know where he went, but I think we got them all, honey. We sure did.' Molly lifted him into her arms.

'Let's get Robby back to the house.' Mahlia wasn't

217

thinking; she was only reacting to her own weariness, her own hysteria. She wanted to howl. She couldn't howl in front of the boy.

'Can't,' Martha grunted. 'We don't *know* if this is all.'

'Oh surely—'

'Surely, nothing, Mahlia. We have to check.'

They went back to the tunnel marked 1730 to find many children's skeletons hung on the walls, grinning rows of them. In the tunnel marked 1780 there were only two. Martha rubbed her head fretfully at this. 'Why only two?' she asked Simoney.

'I don't know. Perhaps that's all there were available. It was after the massacre, and most of the people had moved away. Let's see how many in 1830.'

There were five in the tunnel marked 1830.

'And six in the place we fought the skins,' said Martha, '1880.'

'1930,' murmured Molly. 'How many in 1930?'

Six.

And in the tunnel marked 1980, no skeletons, not yet. The blackened, twisted forms that hung there were not bones but flesh. Dried and hard as jerky, still on the bone. Knives lay ready upon a stone. Charcoal littered the floor. 'A smokehouse,' breathed Simoney. 'Oh Molly, how could he?'

'Oh, my God,' said Martha. 'Something's been eating them.'

The five little bodies hung there, flayed, dried, dark meat with random strips of flesh cut away so the bones showed through. A sixth hook in the wall was empty. 'There were supposed to be six,' Simoney whispered. 'Why are there only five?'

Mahlia leaned forward to pick up a pair of children's shorts. Blue, with red gingham ducks. Matching the little shirt Charlotte had so carefully folded in the upstairs room at the farm. 'Five children disappeared on Bent's Mountain,' she whispered, 'while their parents were fishing.'

'Captain Bone says the devils are eating them,' Robby

218

declaimed in a high, shrill, almost hysterical voice. 'Eating them up a little at a time.'

'A devil, yes,' said Simoney. 'A devil.'

'Devils,' he repeated stubbornly. 'That's what Captain Bone says. He says he'll give me his real sword to fight them.'

'Shhh,' said Mahlia, patting him. 'Shhh.' She picked him up, and cradled him on her shoulder, where he gave a great, wrenching sigh and fell into an exhausted passivity.

'Is that jar empty? ' Molly asked.

Martha shook her head. 'Half-full, still. What do you want it for?'

'On these bodies. What was it the *mambo* said to you, Mahlia? If they can't eat, they don't live. I doubt the devil can eat the stuff in this jar. If we cut off his supply—'

'If we cut off his supply, he'll kill more children,' she cried, clutching the child at her bosom. 'We have to do more than that!'

'Of course. But this will be a start.' Molly smeared the pungent stuff on the corpses, watching without surprise as they shriveled, as the flesh dropped away, as the bones showed through.

Mahlia's head throbbed, pressed, demanded. 'Why are there five of them?' she said. 'Why only five?'

'What do you mean, only five?' Simoney asked.

'There were only five in 1830. But since then there have been six. Six. Every fifty years, six. Until 1980 . . . My God. Simoney. John Duplessis wasn't here in 1980.'

'Wasn't here?'

'In the airport – his sister was talking to him. What did she say? Jessica Casternaught Duplessis was angry at him, because he hadn't attended the "family reunion" in 1980. And he said that to Jeannie Horan, too. He'd been away. What else in 1980? Oh, that's the year the neighbors complained about the noise at Byers' Farm – the Primacks said it sounded like a pig killing.' She gagged, retched.

Molly was shaking her. 'What else, Mahlia? There's something else! Think, girl. Think!'

'She said – she said he had to be back by Thursday, or he wouldn't get the present he'd picked out for himself. And in Haiti, when he saw me, he said it was the – he said it was the wrong member of the family.'

'Robby?'

'Robby's here with us.'

'Duplessis couldn't have known that. Normally Robby would be in the house. And someone got into the house before. Something did. I guess we know what did, now.'

'Oh, my God,' breathed Simoney. 'Let's get out of here.'

'Yes,' Molly assented. 'Let's find Paul Goode and show him what's in this tunnel. He's probably out there by now.'

They straggled down the sandy corridor, sickened, longing for the open air. 'Those things, those skins. They came through the window in the little room.' Mahlia mumbled. 'That's what got in before. They burst the door.'

'That's what he would have sent for Robby,' Martha agreed grimly.

They emerged from the tunnel mouth and stood taking deep gasps of the clean air. Above them on the slope flashlights flickered. Someone was yelling, someone else answering. Another voice yelled, from down the slope, 'Mahlia! Mahlia!'

It was Jean Rondice's voice.

'What's he yelling about? Jean! Up here!' Molly bellowed.

He came thrashing toward them out of the underbrush, shouting hoarsely, 'Mahlia! Mahlia! The beasts. They took the little baby . . .'

He staggered into the circle of their witchfire, shreds of skin hanging from his hands and face, wild-eyed. 'I fought them, but there were too many. They took her . . .'

'Elaine?' Mahlia gasped, unbelieving. 'They've taken Elaine?'

'Go, Simoney,' breathed Molly. 'You're the fastest of us. Go!'

'Elaine!' Mahlia cried, stumbling in her anxiety, turning to run toward the house.

'Wait!' Molly and Martha held her and Molly said, 'If

the baby is at the farm, we'll go there. But she won't be there. Simoney won't find her there, because they took her away. We've got to find out where they took her! Where would they? *Where*, Mahlia?'

'They?' Stupidly.

'They,' said Martha. 'The Duplessis family. Six of them, girl. Use your head. You just said it yourself. It isn't just John Duplessis, it's the whole family. Many children disappeared in 1730 because there were many in the Byers family. Then came the massacre. Only two children disappeared in 1780 because there were only two Byerses alive, John and William. Five in 1830 because there were five Byerses. One more was born after that, and then there were six. There have always been six in the family since then.'

'They must purposely have kept the family small,' said Molly, 'kept the numbers down. I guess they only had children when one of them was killed. Who was the one Charlotte wrote about, the one who wanted to have children and couldn't? An outsider. Her husband wouldn't have allowed it. After the massacre, they kept the numbers small—'

'No,' exclaimed Mahlia. 'That isn't it at all.' She pressed her hands to either side of her head, visions streaming across her eyes like a film run at high speed. 'First there was John Byers. Then William Byers. Then Harriet, William's daughter, and her son and daughter, Jerome and Eloise. And last Eloise's daughter, Jessalee, born after 1830. Six of them . . .

'*There never were any others*! It's always been those six! Those six knew what Mambo Livone called the "full rite." They didn't die. That's what Charlotte saw down in Millingham! That's why they killed her, so she couldn't tell. They didn't just look the same, they *were* the same! None of them ever died. They never will die!'

She began to shake, uncontrollably. Molly took Robby from her as Martha fumbled in the bag at her belt. There was a flame and the sharp stench of something cleanly resinous. Mahlia took a deep breath and stopped shivering.

'How old would he be?' Martha growled. 'He was about fifty when he came to Byers' Fault in 1730. Lord. That means he's more than 300 years old . . .'

A voice approached, calling. Simoney soared into the witchfire glow, her hair disheveled, her face angry. 'The baby's gone. They were in a terrible hurry or Jean would be dead. This means we didn't get them all. There are more skins around – more. I don't know if we can—'

'We must,' said Molly. 'We have to try.'

'Where?'

'Where else? That house at the top of the hill. The tunnel runs up. Why did they build it there except to connect to these tunnels?'

'They need to be close to their larder,' Martha spat. 'One child corpse for each of them every fifty years. But none for John Duplessis this last time. He missed the ceremony. Probably he's been sharing theirs. So they're giving him one of his own tonight.'

'Why did they take Elaine?' Mahlia cried. 'She's so little. Smaller than any of the other—'

'Expedience. They'd planned on Robby. He wasn't available, but the arrangements were all made. Whatever those are. Lord, girl, get a move on. We haven't time to stand about.' She turned to Jean and told him to find the searchers on the hill above. 'Send them down here,' she said. 'Fast!'

Then they stumbled upward, into the tunnel once more. 'How?' Molly asked in a conversational tone. 'Anybody got any ideas?'

'I'm fresh out,' said Martha angrily. 'I wish that woman had come back from Haiti with you, Mahlia. I don't even know what these things are we're facing – zombies? What's that other thing they have down there? Dupies?'

'The Duplessises aren't zombies or dupies,' Molly said with a snarl. 'Not animated bodies or ghosts. Oh, no, the Duplessis family is really alive. They eat and drink and bleed just like you and me, Martha. They're human.'

'Human,' Mahlia said with a sob, laboring along a little

222

behind them. 'Yes. But if you keep them from eating what was down there, they'll die. Mambo Livone said so.'

'Keep them from eating it for how long? A day? An hour? A week?'

'I don't know. I don't think Mambo Livone knew. Somehow, though. Somehow.'

'Where's that light coming from?' They stopped, peering ahead to where a round, greenish glow hung in the darkness.

'Captain Bone?' asked Robby. 'Is that you, Captain?'

The glow moved up and down, up and down, a lantern signaling.

'Something there he wants you to see,' Robby said drowsily. 'Something there.'

They moved onward. The lantern glow faded as they arrived to discover a stone cell in the side of the tunnel, a deep pocket of rock, lined with old stones, huge stones, set without mortar, closed off by a heavy grated gate on rusting hinges. Molly pulled at the gate and it swung toward her, protesting.

'Put the devils in there,' Robby suggested sleepily. 'The Captain says it would be po . . . poetic justice.'

There were tiny manacles within. The room was an earlier version of the one at the Byers' Farm. Less convenient in location, therefore superseded by the other? Martha growled deep in her throat as they stared at one another.

'If we could get them in there,' Molly whispered, 'all of them. But there's no lock on the gate.'

'The hasp is solid,' said Martha. 'Any solid bar would fasten it – a bolt, even a stout stick of wood.' She pulled the gate ajar, partially blocking the tunnel. 'Anyone running down here in the dark would end up in there,' she said, pointing into the cell.

'Elaine!' Mahlia hissed. 'You're standing here talking while they're—'

'No, they aren't,' grated Martha. 'Not yet. Use your senses, girl. You know they aren't. They've got her, yes, but they haven't hurt her yet. You'd feel it if they had.'

Trembling, Mahlia reached out, trying to see. Nothing. No horror, no blood, no pain. Threat, an ominous heaviness of spirit, but nothing worse than that. 'Then let's go while there's time. Come on.'

They began to climb, up a steeply slanted floor at first, then long shallow steps that ended in a spiraling metal staircase. Above them were sounds, music, drums.

'We're under the house.'

'Obviously. Now what?'

'We go up.' Molly eased around the curves of the stair, spiraling upward. A door stood ajar at the top of the flight. 'Now. Mouse-still, all of you. Those drums are nearby.'

They peered through the door to see only vertical folds of heavy curtain, slipped through the door to stand behind it. Molly found the joining, parted it with a fingertip. They saw shadowy dark just beyond the curtain, a puddle of torchlight at the center of a circular paved floor. They were in the vast, vaulted cellar of the Duplessis house. Stone stairs curved upward into darkness. An altar was centered in the huge firelight. Drums. Mahlia realized hysterically that the sound came from a recording. All six of the Duplessises were before her, gathered around the altar.

Molly clamped fingers over her mouth just in time to prevent her crying out. Elaine.

The baby lay sleepily in her blanket on the altar, staring at the torchlight, her hands waving before her face. 'Shhhh. They're not doing anything to her yet,' Molly breathed in her ear. 'They haven't even gotten around to drawing those designs yet. Settle down, girl. You did better than this last time we had a crisis.'

Mahlia subsided. Molly was right. She had behaved far better the last time. But she hadn't been Badger's wife then – or the mother of his child.

They drew back onto the spiral stairs, easing the door shut behind them. 'What do you think, Simoney?'

'I've been wondering about Cynthia. She left us outside the tunnel, said she was going to get help. What would that have meant?'

'She went to get the others,' Robby answered, His head alertly poised, suddenly awake. 'The other children. The ones they made pigs of.'

'I don't suppose you'd know where Captain Bone is?'

'He went to get the others, too. From Chester. That's the town he lived in. He said they hadn't finished the job last time. Now they will.' He wriggled and Molly set him down.

'I see,' said Simoney, kneeling before him. 'Robby, does the Captain want us to do anything?'

'He wants us to . . . lure them away. Down there. Where he showed you. Mahlia and me have to do that. And you have to get old Elaine.'

'I see.'

'We're not in control here,' grumbled Martha.

'We haven't been in control here since we arrived,' said Molly snappishly, 'which I find just as annoying as you do, Martha.'

Voices rose in the room behind them. A chant. The hair on Mahlia's neck rose. 'Molly, they won't call the *loas* from here! They've already done that! They did it at the old Byers' crossroad, at the old Chester Cemetery, where the four *mambos* did it originally. I saw shadowy figures there when Jean and I drove up tonight, and I didn't even realize it. The full rite – it has to be done on the ground originally consecrated. Mambo Livone said so. Here, near Byers' Fault! And it's already begun—'

Loud voices echoed from the vaulted room, speaking Creole, threatening, demanding.

'The *loas* are already here!' Mahlia whispered.

'*Mot de passage!*' cried a man's voice from a woman's throat. '*Mot de passage!*'

'They're asking the baby for the password,' Mahlia screamed in a thin whisper. 'They do that just before they turn the victims into pigs. I've got to distract them—'

'Lure 'em away,' quoted Robby, as though acknowledging an order. He slipped between their legs, through the curtain and into the stone room. 'Hai, you devils.

225

You leave my sister alone!' It could have been the Captain speaking.

'Quick, behind the curtain,' Molly commanded them. 'Mahlia, see if you can get them to follow you down into the tunnel. We'll be right behind you.'

Then Mahlia was parting the curtain to stand there, her head thudding as though it would leap from her chest, her voice as calm as ice.

'John Duplessis. Give me my child.'

They turned on her, the six of them. Tight, black hoods they wore, eared like beasts. Beast paws they wore, with terrible claws. Their eyes were violet flames, like those in the empty skins, burning terribly. Robby stood before her brandishing his sword. It seemed to glint in the torchlight. The drums kept on beating, chattering, clamoring.

John Duplessis showed fangs in a beast's snarl. 'So, you got away from my friends in Haiti, did you, Mahlia Ettison? I was sure they would get you when you returned to Les Cayes, you and that Rondice boy. They said you were coming back there.'

Lois Duplessis growled, 'I told you it was foolish to leave her there. No time for talk, John. Kill her.'

He moved toward her, his beast's claws outstretched, ignoring the child in his path. Robby swung the sword in a great, two-handed swirl, and the man screamed with pain, blood dripping from one paw. Mahlia grabbed Robby from behind and darted back between the curtains. It was a real sword he was holding, slightly curved, a saber, dripping blood. 'Where did you get that?' she gasped.

'Captain Bone gave it to me just before he went away. He dipped it in that stuff you had.'

Shouts of rage came from the room behind them. Mahlia snatched up the boy and ran for the stairs, almost falling down them in her haste to get away. Feet pounded across the floor behind her – more than one pair of feet. She could not tell if all of them were coming, because the drums were too loud. She fled downward, lost in the darkness of the place, seeing without seeing in a dim,

226

fluorescent glow of ghostlight. 'The Captain?' she breathed.

'He's here. Somewhere.'

The ghostlight brightened. She reached the foot of the stairs and stumbled away down the tunnel as feet thundered on the iron steps behind her. More than one of them, she told herself. More than one. However many followed her made it that much easier for Molly and the others. She ran, not seeing the ghostlight go dim behind her to leave her pursuers in the dark.

'Captain says go around the gate,' said Robby, both arms tight around her neck. 'Then put me down.'

'We should hide—'

'No. Just go around. They'll hide us. Cynthia is bringing them all, and they'll hide us.'

The gate blocked almost the entire way. She edged around it, took refuge in a shallow niche, put Robby down. He peeked out past her legs, watching the way they had come.

Pounding feet, panting. Human sounds. Angry voices muttering. Women, one man's voice, then another. The tunnel was barely lit, filling with mist.

'Where did this fog come from?' Jessica Casternaught Duplessis, her voice boiling with fury. 'I can't see.'

'Shut up, Jessica. None of us can see.'

'Hurry up, you idiots.' One of the men, his voice imperative. 'We've got to get her before she gets out!'

'She can't see any better than we can! Someone go back and get a torch.' Jessica.

'We don't have time. Come on.'

Mahlia felt the gate shudder. Someone had touched it. 'To your left, here. I don't remember this bend.'

Robby tugged at her legs, moved out into the tunnel, pushing the gate before him. It shrieked on its hinges. Mahlia threw her weight behind it, felt it crash into place – remembered only then that she had no way to fasten it, no way at all. Faces turned toward her in the mist. Beast-human faces. Lois. Jessica. Bill. Jerome. Harriet. Five of them. Only five of them, turned toward her, snarling, ready to thrust the gate open and—

227

A snick, a sound like a snapped twig in the tunnel. And then silence.

She backed away. The sword was thrust through the hasp, and Robby stood staring at it, eyes glazed. She caught him as he dropped.

All around them the children stood, rows of them, knickered and pinafored, freckle-faced and clear-skinned, boys, girls, solidified out of the fog, moving now toward the iron-grated cell. Some in smocks, some in homespun, and first among them a girl with a golden bracelet.

'Mahlia,' came a seductive voice from the cell. 'Mahlia. There's been some misunderstanding. Let's talk this over. You don't want to lock us in here. Come, now.'

'When were you born?' Mahlia asked through a dry throat. 'What year, Jessalee? Wasn't it 1855?'

The children moved closer to the cage.

'What a silly question? I'm only seventy-five. Not young, I'll admit, but—'

'Jessie. The fog is coming back,' one of the women said, her voice tight. 'That damn fog is coming back.'

'Mahlia,' said Molly. 'I think we'd better get out of here.'

Malia turned as in a dream. Molly was there with Elaine in her arms, flanked by Martha and Simoney. She put Robby down and took the baby, turned back to the cage. She could hardly see it now, there were so many children. Above them, throbbing through the rock, the drums still pounded.

'Come, Mahlia,' said Simoney and tugged her away.

'I want to see what the children are going to do,' said Robby as Molly took him by the hand.

'No, you don't, dear. Really you don't.'

They went down the tunnel, their feet crunching on the sandy soil. 'John Duplessis isn't there,' Mahlia said. 'He wasn't with them.'

'I know. Robby cut him with that saber, and he screamed something about needing *'ti mange*. What does that mean?'

'A little meal. Something to eat. Why would he say that?'

'Because he was wounded. Maybe they have to have — you know — in order to heal.'

'Where would he get any?'

'Where we're going, Mahlia. He took another route, that's all. To the larder, where the children's bodies were.'

'But we destroyed them.'

'He doesn't know that.'

They stopped, suddenly aware of a sound in the tunnel ahead of them, another at their backs. Behind them came a thin, eerie wailing, a gurgling, an agonized whisper. Before them was the shuffle of feet. More than one pair.

'People from Millingham?' Molly whispered.

'People from Millingham would be making some noise,' said Martha, her face anxious. 'Shouting, looking for us.'

'Where are they?'

She pointed upward at the tunnel entrance they stood beside, 1880. 'This is where we fought the skins. They're below us, coming this way.'

They waited, holding their breaths. Robby stirred restively in Molly's arms. Elaine whimpered. An evil light bloomed at the curve of the tunnel. The shuffling came nearer.

And they came.

A dozen of them. Half-skinned. Half-scalped. Lidless eyes wide. Lipless mouths gaped. Skinless bodies stumbling in a parody of motion. Unseeing. Moved by someone else, something else. Unbreathing. All that remained of Marcy Talent and her crew and the luckless Steven Ware. Behind them, in the shadows, the skins rustled.

Mahlia screamed, a tiny rabbit sound from empty lungs, unheard over the sound of shuffling feet.

'Stop!' John Duplessis's voice thundered. 'Stop there.' He stood behind the flayed figures, gazing between them at the women where they stood, his hand twitching as it dripped blood. 'Back off, old women,' he snarled.

They stepped back. Back again. The bodies of the flayed ones shuffled forward. 'Lois!' he bellowed. 'Jerome? Jessie?'

Mahlia trembled, stepping back again, past open tunnel mouths, involuntarily. Around her the others retreated, too, holding their breaths, shivering, as the zombie crew shuffled forward.

He shouted again, snarled as he waited in vain for an answer, then pressed forward to step into the 1980 side tunnel.

As though by mutual agreement, Mahlia and the others retreated, putting space between themselves and that tunnel entrance.

The howl, when it came, was shattering. They bent, hands over their ears as his voice battered at them. 'I need . . . damn you . . . filth . . . I need . . .'

And he was out into the main tunnel once more, eyes blazing with a mad light, coming toward them, the dead bodies around him pressing forward, their hands raised to clutch, moving forward, blood from his hand dripping on the sand in a steady stream.

'Simoney,' gargled Molly. 'Simoney?'

'Just a minute, Molly. I've got to think. Lord, I have to think—'

'Martha?'

The big woman trembled. 'I'm working on it, Molly. Give me a minute.'

The three murmured, hummed to a rapid tapping of Simoney's drum, taking one step back as the maddened beast that was John Duplessis came toward them, then another. Another step, then another. Behind them the eerie whispering. Before them the slow pace of the dead, their bodies clotted red and black, eyeballs rolling in open sockets, teeth showing through maimed cheeks, and John Duplessis moving at their center, his beast's face contorted in rage.

He slowed, stopped. He was staring over their shoulders.

They stopped as well, glancing quickly back.

Cynthia stood there. Her long, pale hair hung down her back, neatly combed. Her gingham dress was buttoned high at her neck, and white pantaloons showed at the hem. Her

230

face was set like ice, hard and cold, and her lips were bloody. The bracelet on her wrist burned like a star. Captain Bone was behind her, holding up his lantern, his mouth open in a snarl of rage. Around them was a host of ghostly children, a host of the people of Chester . . .

'Get back against the wall!' Molly said. 'Get out of the way.'

John Duplessis – John Byers – howled again, his head thrown back in a wolf's cry, the cords of his neck standing out like cables, then turned and fled. After him rushed the children, teeth already stained with blood, and after them the Captain, the light fading as he passed.

The flayed ones dropped, remaining where they fell. Behind them the skins scattered like leaves into dusty fragments.

'Let's get out of here,' Martha sobbed. 'I've never felt so stupidly helpless in my life.'

They ran, leaping over the flayed bodies, stumbling, hard on one another's heels, feeling the fresh breeze of autumn as they burst out of the tunnel into the night. On the slope around them torches bloomed, flames and flashlights both; people were calling; shouts and flares occupied the night. They leaned against one another, panting. Jean came toward then, trembling. 'What was it? The thing that went past? It looked like an animal, Mahlia . . .'

'You go,' said Molly at last. 'You, Mahlia. Go with Simoney, take the children. Martha and I will handle the people here. They'll need proof. We want them to see those bodies. Before anything more happens . . .' She stumbled toward the nearest torches, calling out as she went, while Martha, trembling, stood guard at the tunnel entrance.

Mahlia trudged down the hill, Robby at her heels, Elaine upon her shoulder.

'I don't want to go back to that house,' Mahlia said. 'Not ever again. I don't want to see that room.'

'Your furniture,' Simoney said. 'All your clothes.'

'I don't care. I don't want to go back.'

'It's insured, isn't it?'

Mahlia didn't answer. She couldn't answer. She could only feel the weight of the child on her shoulder. When she looked up again, Simoney was gone. She trudged on, down through the trees, a long, slow way. She was tired. They were all tired. She stopped to rest at the edge of the forest.

Below her, beyond the meadow, fire bloomed in the windows of Byers' Farm. As she watched, the flames leaped higher. Silhouetted before them were two figures. Jean, she told herself, and Simoney. Watching the house burn. The Millingham fire department didn't come out this far, only the volunteer fire fighters. It would take them ages.

Almost placidly, with a sense of deep relief, she sat down at the top of the meadow with her children and watched her house burn down.

CHAPTER TWENTY-EIGHT

'I think you told me once that all your sagas begin with a change of place,' said Fred Smarles, leaning companionably on the fence beside Mahlia. Out in the meadow, Molly and Simoney were playing with Robby, while Jean amused a chortling Elaine. Behind them the wood and stone of a long, low house stretched above bright gardens, glittering through a wall of glass. 'Does this start a new saga?'

'It's a very nice house, Fred. I know we'll be very happy here. And the fact that the Wilsons sold it already furnished is perfect for me.'

'Not much history to it, I'm afraid. Only built in '79.'

'That's old enough. To tell you the truth, I'm a little weary of . . . history.'

'I can certainly see why.' He didn't push the point. Everyone in Millingham had sense enough to know why. Lucky for that Duplessis fellow he'd been dead as a doornail when they found him, or Millingham would have lynched him! 'Exsanguinated,' the medical examiner had said. 'Bled to death,' translated Fred and his cronies. And a good thing, too. The man was crazy as a grizzly bear. Skinned old Charlotte Grafton and that archaeologist fellow. Killed his own mother, his sisters and brothers, skinned all those kids from the university. And Steve Ware! Though what Steve had been doing up there, no one could say. Duplessis had been a walking nightmare.

And those bones! Skeletons of children! Think of his killing all those children! Though the medical examiner had said some of the remains were centuries old, and Duplessis might have had a kind of Byers family madness.

233

'Good thing your house burned down,' he blurted, not really meaning to say it aloud.

She gave him a sideways glance, wondering briefly what he would say if he knew about the skins as well. 'Duplessis must have knocked over the fire screen in the nursery when he kidnapped Elaine,' she said mildly. 'If you mean it was fortunate for me in an insurance sense, yes, it was. I don't imagine we could ever have sold the place, even if I'd wanted to. Not that close to Byers' Fault.'

'There's talk of timbering out that whole stretch up in there, running great big 'dozers through it, and making it some kind of park. Tell you something for sure, that Duplessis house isn't going to sell.'

Mahlia nodded. Privately she thought it wouldn't be long before something happened to the Duplessis house. Vandals, probably. Kids fooling around. It was less than a month to Halloween. That might be a good time for it to burn, for it to collapse into those great cellars so that bulldozers could cover it up forever. Martha and Molly and she had already taken care of the crossroads and the old graveyard. No evil *loa* could ever be summoned from those places again, no matter how many *mambos* had died within sight of them.

'Hear your husband's coming back,' Fred said.

'Day after tomorrow. I got a call from him last week.'

The call had been forwarded from the previous number to the one she had now. Badger had been so startled and apprehensive at hearing she had moved that he'd been quiet about the other matter.

'Molly, Martha, and Simoney are here for a few days,' she had said to him doggedly, knowing she sounded rehearsed. Hell, she had rehearsed. 'And I don't want to hear anything about it, Badger. You were wrong to insist I give up my friendship with them or attempt to ignore my own skills. That insistence has had very dangerous consequences. I won't interfere in your business, but from now on, you must not interfere with mine.'

There had been only silence at the other end of the line

for a very long time. When he spoke at last, it had been in a gentle, almost tentative voice. 'Mahlia, something must have happened. If you think it's best—'

'It has, and I do,' she had said firmly, thinking it was only the first salvo in what might be a long battle. He might press the matter again when he got home, but he'd have Molly and Simoney to deal with when he did.

Fred waved good-bye as he pulled out into the drive, and she went into the meadow to join the antic Frisbee game Simoney and Robby had inflicted on Molly. Mama cat had joined in as well, and the kittens. Their box had been in the barn, untouched by the fire. In fact, considering everything, the fire had done very little damage. Of course, there was nothing at all left of Byers' Farm, not even the original chimney. Old tumbled stones and charred wood and lonely lilies, still blooming in autumn's chill.

Molly came toward her, wiping her forehead. 'Too energetic for me. Time Simoney and me got home, Mahlia. I called Ron. He tells me he hasn't had a decent meal since I left. And he's out of cookies. Ron's a placid sort of man, but he doesn't like being left without cookies.'

'Thank you, Molly.'

'For what? We came close to all of us getting done in. Think we're so smart, then something like this comes along and we haven't any idea what to do about it. Here's the family, living right here in New York state; two, three hundred years old, most of 'em, killin' kids and eatin' 'em like kippers, and we're as green as corn. Martha can fuss all she likes about Simoney bein' long-winded, but when Simoney does a spell, she really does one. You remember in that guide spell she did, there was a line about "torch-bearing mobs with the monster in sight," and something about all kinds of hunters? That's what brought the ghosts out for vengeance. Trust Simoney. She always does it right, even when she doesn't know what she's doin'. Instinct, I guess.'

Mahlia agreed that Simoney was very talented.

'Tell you one thing, though,' Molly went on. 'Some of us are going down to spend some time with Mambo Livone.

235

There's things she knows we need to know. Like how to make that stuff in the jar. And how to make zombies lie down dead. If John Byers hadn't run when he did, we'd sure have needed to know that!'

Mahlia shook her head. 'I can't figure out that Haiti business. John Duplessis – John Byers – didn't need that!' She flushed angrily, remembering it.

'Well, he just *wanted* it. After three hundred years, he'd gotten bored with the family rites. They were routine, always the same. They'd kidnap the victims and hold them somewhere, in that cell up in the tunnel or in that room in the house. Then they'd call up the *loas* there at the crossroads and the cemetery, using that piece of carved wood as the pattern. When the *loas* came, they'd do the ritual and turn 'em into little pigs, skin 'em and hang 'em and smoke 'em. After that, they'd eat a little every now and then to keep themselves alive. It could have gone on forever, I suppose, if we hadn't come along.'

She saw Mahlia shudder and patted her, 'I know, girl, but that's what they did. Only it wasn't enough for John. He was the one who made those horrors out of the skins – for amusement, mostly. He used to take them out hunting. He was the one who killed Seepy, of course, and Charlotte Grafton. He liked a little spice, liked to sex things up a bit, so he went down to Haiti and learned some things, how to make bodies walk, things like that. It was there he learned to sew up the skins and animate them. What you might call a zombie variation.'

Mahlia frowned, remembering a recent conversation. 'Jeannie Horan told me she'd had an affair with him – with what he seemed to be – years ago, a time when she and Lanson were separated and she was half-nuts and very lonely. She thought she was pregnant, and John Duplessis went crazy when she told him. She said he acted like a madman. It turned out to be a false alarm. She told me that if it hadn't been, she truly believes he would have killed her.'

'I guess the six of 'em agreed there weren't to be any more

236

Byers children — not another Byers' Fault. There were just the six and they'd decided that's all there would ever be. They thought they could live safely that way. Kids disappear all the time. Who's going to make a fuss over six more disappearing every fifty years? That's all they needed in order to keep them alive, one body every fifty years for each of them. If they hadn't had to stay here, near the crossroads and the cemetery, they might never have been caught.'

'You think their condition was . . . hereditary?'

'Well, we'll never know, really, will we? Jessica Casternaught Duplessis and the other four in the cell were bled dry and the bodies have been cremated. Same with John.'

'We were lucky. If the ghosts hadn't shown up when they did . . .'

'Well, like I said, that wasn't luck. The ghosts of Cynthia and Captain Bone may have gone for help, but they didn't have far to go. Simoney had already summoned those hunters, and they sure disposed of the Duplessis family.'

'And the family won't come back? Even as ghosts?'

'Might try, I suppose. Got a hunch Captain Bone's probably got the matter under control, wherever he is.'

They stood looking at the children. 'Robby doesn't seem to be any the worse for it.'

'He's half forgotten it already. By the time he's grown, he won't even remember it.'

'He doesn't talk about Cynthia anymore.'

'Well, he sort of does, you know. "Cynthia" — that's what he's named the tortoiseshell kitten.'

'He doesn't talk about the Captain, either.'

'That's the ginger tom's name. You're goin' to have them and their descendants around for some time, Mahlia. Robby's way of memorializin' the occasion.' She grinned at the expression on Mahlia's face. 'Well, the Captain did what he meant to do all along. I guess he's moved on.'

They thought about this for a time, leaning on the fence. Simoney was leading Robby up the hill to the house. Jean, holding the baby, waved from the terrace, Martha looming in the doorway behind him. Lunchtime.

'I thought I'd take some flowers to Charlotte's grave up at Mount Olive Cemetery this afternoon, Molly. Want to go along?'

'Mmmm.' A little wind tossed yellow leaves into their faces. 'Strange place to be buried. When we went to her funeral, there was only that one tended grave there. All the rest were grown over.'

'I know. Well, now there'll be two graves tended. Charlotte's family will see to that.'

'Funny. Most times in graveyards, I get this feeling there's something hanging around. Spirits, something. A kind of *waiting* feeling. At Charlotte's funeral, I didn't get the feeling there was anything hanging around Mount Olive at all. Nothing at all. As though it's all gone on somewhere.' Molly mused over this.

Mahlia, remembering something Robby had said many days before, only smiled. 'Probably there isn't anything there,' she said. 'Except what doesn't matter anymore.'

THE END

BLOOD HERITAGE BY SHERI S. TEPPER

Badger Ettison does not believe in demons. Until a shrieking, freezing horror escapes its ancient prison. A soulless hunger. Hunger that turns a beautiful woman into a shrivelled husk before she has time to scream. Hunger that has no form, no substance – but fangs and claws and eyes to seek its prey.

Badger Ettison does not believe in magic. But the old blood-rituals are the only way to stop the voracious evil that pursues his wife and son. And they demand that Badger must sacrifice one of the two he loves to save the other.

Badger Ettison does not believe in terror. Now he is living it.

0 552 13193 3

A SELECTED LIST OF HORROR TITLES
AVAILABLE FROM CORGI AND
BANTAM BOOKS

THE PRICES SHOWN BELOW WERE CORRECT AT THE TIME OF
GOING TO PRESS. HOWEVER TRANSWORLD PUBLISHERS RESERVE
THE RIGHT TO SHOW NEW RETAIL PRICES ON COVERS WHICH MAY
DIFFER FROM THOSE PREVIOUSLY ADVERTISED IN THE TEXT OR
ELSEWHERE.